SIX WEEKS THIS SUMMER

SIX WEEKS THIS SUMMER

A.J. JONES

TensionBooks.com

For two wonderful men whom I loved and miss dearly.

Casey Motter, my frequent lunch partner, was the public address announcer of the Atlanta Braves for nearly 20 years. We frequently appeared on television together. Casey loved his Braves, his family, and Jesus Christ. Not a week went by that Casey didn't phone to tell me that he loved me.
Casey, I will see you again.

Tony Jones, my father. He was simply the greatest man I have ever known. I never heard anyone say a negative word about my father. He was dedicated to his family, his job, and his Lord and Savior, Jesus Christ. He's been in heaven for almost four years now, and I deeply hope he's had fellowship with his heroes, Mickey Mantle and Jimmy Stewart.
My father always put others first. I am attempting and often failing to do the same. I no longer watch "Field of Dreams," or if I do, I stop it before the end of the movie.
If you had an awesome role model like I had, one who always spent time with my sister and me, one that never turned down a game of catch. If he's left this earth, you understand why I stop the film. There is a void in my family that can't be replaced. But because the only sinless person to walk this earth suffered an excruciating death, his selfless act guarantees my family will be reunited with my father.

"Success is not final; failure is not fatal. It is the courage to continue that counts."

Winston Churchill

CHAPTER ONE

"All it takes is one person who is committed, focused, and on a mission to spark an entire team into believing in themselves."

Bruce Brown

August 10, 2024

August 10 was a Saturday, the 32nd Saturday of 2024, the 223rd day of the year. Six weeks remained in the summer, and seven weeks remained in the Major League Baseball regular season.

The New York Yankees, the most successful franchise in sports history, were ten games out of first place in the American League East and eight games out of the final Wild Card. Their franchise player was done for the year. Things were not ideal.

The Yankees' dwindling hopes of reaching the playoffs had taken another hit only one night before. The best player in baseball, Aaron Judge, suffered a season-ending injury in a 4–0 loss to the Kansas City Royals.

The trade deadline had come and gone. New York needed immediate help. The Yankees needed an outfielder, someone to provide a divine spark, a player who could help save what appeared to be a lost season. New York desperately wanted to avoid missing the postseason for consecutive seasons.

New York general manager Jason Giambi got on the phone. Scranton, the New York AAA affiliate, was the destination of the call, with a man known as Coach Al of the RailRiders on the other end.

CHAPTER TWO

"Winning is like shaving – you do it every day, or you wind up looking like a bum."

Jack Kemp

How many kids do you know who played youth baseball? Take a few minutes to think about that. The number is substantial. The Little League World Series in Williamsport, Pennsylvania, represents only a small fraction. Now, how many of those kids eventually made it to the big league, MLB? No, not him. The One you are thinking of only made AA, potentially AAA. The answer is none! Well, perhaps one. The One!

Who was that One? Was he destined to be The One? No one who watched the classically handsome Stanford University centerfielder, Miles Fuller, for four years would have selected the athletic six-foot-six-inch Cardinal as The One. One reason was that, although blessed with height, Fuller played for four years for a high-standard academic institution. Major League prospects generally don't play four years of college ball. If they go the college route, they become professional players after three years, once draft-eligible.

Fuller was a gifted centerfielder with powerful legs but average upper body strength. The 245-pounder with light brown hair had wheels and elite instincts. He was vastly intelligent, borderline brilliant, graduating summa cum laude from one of America's most progressive and demanding universities. Qualifying for the Scripps National Spelling Bee Finals twice and finishing each year in the top five, his vocabulary was stellar. However, a national television audience watched him come up short both years, failing to correctly spell 'shtetl' in the first year and then 'ranunculaceous' as a twelve-year-old.

Fuller was a star-studded defender. Following his senior season at Stanford, his intelligence, coupled with his defensive skills, including an above-average right arm, was good enough to convince the Milwaukee Brewers to select him in the tenth round of the 2017 MLB Draft. The selection came as a shock to some. One Stanford baseball season ticket holder recalled saying in the spring of 2016, "I don't believe he will be drafted. He can't hit home runs." That season ticket holder was almost correct. Fuller hit only five homers in four seasons. All five were on the road. In four seasons, three as a starter, Fuller never launched a ball out of his home park, Klein Field, at Sunken Diamond.

This drove Cardinal hitting coach Brad Carey crazy. "With your height, your size, and your weight, you should be able to hit mistakes and leave the park with your eyes closed. I would think you could at least homer a few times by accident."

Fuller had perspicacity. He possessed leadoff foot speed. He swiped forty-nine bases during his senior season in Palo Alto. He didn't chase bad pitches, and his discipline at the plate allowed him to work the count, turning walks into extra bases.

When he was down in the count, he used his strike zone discipline and his fast hands with fewer moving parts, shortening his swing while utilizing more loft in his swing.

Fuller was an ideal doubles hitter. His keen eye allowed him to understand when the opposing pitcher was most vulnerable to yield a swiped bag. Sixteen of the forty-nine steals were of the third base bag. Cardinal assistant Matt Meyer told him, "You may not be the fastest, but, fortunately, you are quick." Fuller had no idea what that meant, but he viewed it as favorable.

While in college, his lack of power was baffling, aluminum bats and all. But Fuller still hit for average, going to both fields, finishing in the top ten in doubles in his final two seasons in the Pac-12. His hitting improved each year:

Freshman Season (2014) .288

Sophomore Season (2015) .291

Junior Season (2016) .326

Senior Season (2017) .336

The right-handed, clean-shaven Fuller had his seminal moment for Stanford in his junior season, playing at Berkley against hated rival, the University of California. Wearing the eye-catching gray uniform, with 'Stanford' written across the chest in classic, cursive, cardinal red, Fuller came to the plate at the top of the ninth, with two on and two out, and Cal holding a precarious 2-1 advantage.

The game was clearly on the shoulders of No.14, and since Cal had already beaten Stanford 8-3 and 11-2 in the series, Fuller felt a sense of urgency to extend the game and avoid a sweep. Fuller faced a 1-2 count, but a wild pitch from California closer Charlie Hudson moved both runners into scoring position.

Two foul balls later, with Hudson showing frustration, the count remained 1-2. Hudson got the sign, but his curveball hung over the plate, and Fuller, with his hands choked up on the bat, guided the ball, gently and softly, safely to right centerfield. Both runners scored easily, and Stanford ace Tristan Beck delivered a

1-2-3 bottom of the ninth, securing the Cardinal road victory over its rival.

On the bus ride home, Carey, often a critic of Fuller, told the junior centerfielder, "Your jersey says No.14. But today, Miles, you are number one! Congratulations, kid!"

CHAPTER THREE

People in the South live for September, fall within reach, thinking, 'Alright, summer…it is September, and it is time for you to go. Go on now…git'.

Anonymous Southerners

Growing up in Newnan, Georgia, Miles Fuller had access to the Atlanta Braves. The Braves played at Turner Field and later at their current stadium, Truist Park, only about forty-five minutes from his home. All the Braves games were on television, though the channel was not always convenient to locate, especially when one considers how easy they were to find back in the day on WTBS.

The classmates Miles grew up with were mostly all Braves fans. The Braves were a powerhouse. The days of the once popular bumper sticker, "Go Braves! And take the Falcons with you!" were long gone. Now, you were cool if you were a Braves fan. Everyone loves a winner. The only kids who weren't Braves fans were those who had moved with their parents from major cities, such as St. Louis or Chicago, but those were few and far between.

All his extended family located throughout the South were backers of the Braves, so Miles easily found himself a Braves fan as well. He was the only child of Greg and Celeste, who met while students at Auburn University. Greg was an officer while a member of the Lambda Chi Alpha fraternity and completed an internship at Delta Air Lines. At six feet two inches tall, he was an ideal height for a pilot. While in school, Celeste served as a Student Recruiter and gave tours to prospective students. An English literature major, Celeste was a voracious reader and a gifted writer. With sandy brown hair and piercing green eyes, she was often seen at Auburn's tennis courts and competed on an intramural team. This particular passion carried on to her adult life in Newnan as she was a fixture on the courts at Newnan Country Club.

Miles was a better student than a ball player. In the early days, he had more success on the basketball and tennis courts. But a chance meeting in seventh grade with Newnan High School baseball coach Kenny Morris changed the path of his life, and it eventually served to facilitate a career on the diamond.

In the grocery store, grabbing paper towels for his mother, the then twelve-year-old was in front of Morris at the checkout line, lane number fourteen to be exact. Three years later, thinking back to the day at the grocery store, Morris issued Miles the No.14 Newnan High jersey.

Miles would proudly wear that white jersey with blue names and the No.14 for three varsity seasons. After an average beginning to his high school playing days on the junior varsity roster, Miles thrived under the tutelage of Morris, an old-school true baseball man in his mid-50s.

Morris believed in pitching and strong defense when his

boys were in the field. At the plate, he was a "get them on, get them over, get them in" kind of coach. It was Morris who taught Miles the significance of working the count, and Morris marveled at the ability of his young pupil to understand the strike zone on offense and read the ball coming off the bat while patrolling centerfield at Joe Pope Field.

It was that conversation at the grocery store that left a lasting impression on Morris. Knowing nothing of his athletic ability, Morris was quick to pick up on Miles' intelligence and knowledge of the game. Morris told his assistant coach, "Our program will always need a smart catcher and a smart centerfielder. Defense up the middle is imperative."

Miles did not play baseball all year round. No travel ball for him. Nor did he want to play all year. His father, Greg, all but demanded he get a job and be a productive citizen. Miles stopped playing other sports when he reached high school. Although he didn't desire to play travel ball, he knew his love was baseball.

His sophomore year was sensational for Miles, Morris, and the Newnan High School Cougars. The fifteen-year-old hit .355 batting second, setting up the upperclassmen, the run producers, in the middle of the lineup. However, those veteran varsity players weren't initially welcoming to the tenth grader. It was believed at the beginning of the season that Cougar left-handed lead-off man and speedster Cooper Allen would be the every-game centerfielder. But Allen, who also pitched, aggravated his left shoulder in a relief appearance, and it sidelined the senior for almost a month. By the time Allen had healed, Miles had secured the starting spot in center. Newnan made a deep run in the state playoffs, and Fuller celebrated his sixteenth birthday with a walk-off single to send the Cougars to the semifinals.

The postseason run ended there in a painful fashion. The Cougars were denied a berth in the state finals and swept out of the tournament, 3-1 and 9-4, by arch-rival East Coweta, located in nearby Sharpsburg.

It was about this time that Miles started noticing an attractive, long-haired blonde who was around five feet seven inches tall. Her name was Brooke Yarbrough. She was a freshman, having moved recently to Newnan from Virginia.

Miles had no car and was reluctant to get his driver's license. He did make good on getting a job, landing a fun position inside the pro shop at Orchard Hills Golf Club, a Scottish links course, just off Interstate 85 in Newnan. It was easy work, and he admired the two professionals who ran it, assistant Dano Korytoski and head pro Wyatt Detmer. Miles spent downtime at the pro shop, perusing newspapers and reading classic novels. Rainy days were a welcome sight, providing more time for reading and watching classical movies from The Golden Age of Cinema on Turner Classic Movies (TCM), headquartered just up I-85 north in Atlanta.

After two months of either finding rides from friends or his parents, on July 22, Miles passed his driving exam. He spent the rest of the summer working at Orchard Hills and researching potential college destinations. He was already a little over six feet tall, seemingly growing daily. Two short years later, as he walked across the stage inside Drake Stadium to be handed his high school diploma, he was nearly six feet four inches.

Miles continued to work at the pro shop during his junior and senior years in high school. He would continue to be tempted by Brooke, although as his junior prom neared, he still had never asked her out. The soon-to-be Division I college baseball talent was afraid of being rejected.

Brooke had no boyfriend, but Miles felt like there was something or *someone* back in Virginia. His friends and many of his teammates were starting to date, with some in serious relationships. However, Miles was focused on baseball and had yet to enter the dating pool.

While the results were not good for the Cougars on the diamond at Joe Pope Field, they were much better for Miles. Now batting at the top of the order, Miles roared out of the block his junior season. He hit almost .500 over the first two months of his junior campaign.

Although the power was lacking, his ability to make contact, steal bases, defend centerfield, and twice climb the wall to bring back bombs didn't go unnoticed. College coaches and professional scouts were often in the stands. The results were impressive for a guy who was scared to ask out a seemingly sweet and harmless girl a year younger than him. The more college coaches who packed the seats, the better Miles performed. By the end of his junior year, the defensive stalwart, still growing at six feet three inches, had offers from over forty college programs.

Unfortunately, the Cougars were eliminated in the first round of the playoffs. Miles now had more time to visit schools and find a home for his academic desires and major while pairing that with a place to play baseball.

Every Southeastern Conference (SEC) school was in on the centerfielder. Auburn University was most desirable concerning proximity. Most of his teachers and friends had him pointed to the in-state University of Georgia (UGA). Louisiana State University and Mississippi State University interested him from a baseball tradition standpoint. Vanderbilt University was now a national power, but Miles wasn't comfortable with the university colors, and despite its academic advantages, he despised the liberal direction of the school and the city of Nashville itself.

He planned to commit before the beginning of his senior year, maybe as early as his seventeenth birthday, which was May 15. After visits to Arizona State University, the University of Texas, the University of Tennessee, the University of Arkansas, Auburn, and Georgia, it was UGA that maintained the lead.

The draw for Auburn was appealing. It was closest to

Newnan, but that convenience was equaled by the proximity of the baseball program itself. All aspects of the Auburn program were located together. Hitchcock Field at Plainsman Park, the freshman dorm, and the dining halls were all a short walk from each other. Auburn even brought out a chef to speak directly about nutrition. No other school had done that. Auburn was a second choice, close behind Georgia.

Miles loved Athens. It's called "The Classic City" for a reason. The pull of playing in-state was appealing, with Miles' classmates enrolled in huge numbers. He was a Braves fan, proud to be from Newnan, and would be honored to represent the red and black.

Stanford was his dream school. It had all the academic advantages, an amazing baseball program, and The Hoover Institution, a well-respected conservative think tank that included his idol, Victor Davis Hanson. But, outside of a lone letter, Miles had no other communication with the California school. Perhaps his fate would change if he could only get a korero with Stanford's legendary coach, Mark Marquess.

Now seventeen, nothing had changed for Miles at the close of August.

Then everything changed in early September. The Fuller home phone—not many of those landlines remained—rang, and on the other end was legendary Stanford coach Mark Marquess. The Cardinal leader requested to speak with Greg and asked if he could come to visit tomorrow. Marquess said, "I know tomorrow is Labor Day, but I am in Atlanta and would welcome a chance to talk with all three of you about the possibility of Miles getting the greatest education possible while helping our program to another national title."

Greg hung up with Coach Marquess and then asked Miles, "What do you have tomorrow at 3:00? Someone is coming to the house, and I don't believe you'll want to miss him."

Miles responded, "Who?"

Greg, trying to remain calm, responded, "Mark Marquess, 'Nine' himself."

Miles was initially stunned, almost placid, saying, "Talk about a liberal university. THE liberal university, but that's my first choice." He quickly collected himself and excitedly exclaimed, "I can be here!"

CHAPTER FOUR

"When you receive your first love at first sight, consider it as a vaccination that would save you from the disease of a second one."

Anonymous

September 3, 2012

The following day, Monday, September 3, Labor Day, Marquess arrived sharply at 3:00 p.m. ET. The Hall of Famer, who led Stanford to national titles in 1987 and 1988, entered the two-story upper-middle-class home of the Fuller family and greeted them all with handshakes.

He wore a Stanford polo with that beautiful "S" on it, impossible not to catch sight of. Marquess, who began his era at Stanford in 1977 and eventually stayed at the helm for forty years, covered all the bases, admitting that he respected the SEC schools but saying that Stanford offered unlimited opportunities.

Greg was the first Fuller to speak, "There's no doubt he wants to play baseball for you, but I would be remiss if I didn't ask and if we didn't point out that you are a little late compared to the others."

"I realize that. We had some unforeseen circumstances. But we have been doing our homework on Miles. I've seen the video. I've looked at over one hundred pages of notes. We like what we see. And if he hasn't committed, and he hasn't, I'm going to make a push to get him in white and cardinal red," Marquess responded.

Miles didn't hear anything else for the next five minutes. He couldn't get his mind off playing center while gazing down at that gorgeous white uniform with "Stanford" displayed prominently in cardinal red. A couple of minutes later, he asked, "Can you excuse me for five minutes?" His parents were caught off guard and sort of laughed it off in an attempt to cover their embarrassment. While Marquess reviewed the high academic requirements, Miles ran upstairs to his room. He grabbed his cell phone and thought this was his day, his time, his fifteen minutes of fame; he, a player not known to hit the long ball, was about to knock this moment out of the park.

Miles put his fear of rejection behind him, and for the first time, he phoned Brooke.

She answered, and speaking way too fast, he stated, "Brooke, this is Miles. Let's not play any games. I like you, I always have, and you know you like me. Let's go on a date tonight."

For a split second, not knowing the number, she thought, *"Who is this?"* But she kept that to herself. Instead, she responded, "Last week, I went golfing with my dad. You were at work. You didn't even acknowledge me. Now you are asking me out?"

"Yes," he said.

"I do not understand boys," she returned.

"Hey, I have to go. I will pick you up at seven," Miles concluded.

Just as she was asking what they were going to do, he hung up. Brooke went downstairs and made sure it was okay if she went out since school was back in session the next day.

When her father asked who she would be seeing, Brooke said, "I just got asked out on a date, I think, with that guy I showed you at the golf course last week."

Her father, reading *The Newnan Times-Herald,* responded, "The star high school baseball player? Well, okay. We just need to meet him. But it doesn't surprise me. You sure seem to enjoy playing golf there and only there."

Miles returned to the ongoing conversation downstairs. Seeming to forgive his mysterious disappearance, the Stanford coach asked, "Miles, how would you like to come out and visit our campus and our facilities just to get a feel for the Stanford experience?"

Miles responded, "When?"

"Quickly. This Saturday. Five days from now."

Miles had one additional request, "On one condition, Coach."

Marquess wasn't expecting that. "Can you get me a tour of the Hoover Institution?" asked the rising senior.

This request alarmed his parents. They weren't positive they knew exactly what The Hoover Institution was.

Miles explained, "It's a conservative think tank that stands for liberty and less government and other things I believe in. Condoleezza Rice is a faculty member, and Victor Davis Hanson works there, and I'm an enormous fan of both. It's located right there on campus."

Celeste asked, "How do you know all of this?"

"Well, I don't want to get into a whole rigamarole on this on such a momentous day. But we've been watching a great deal of Fox News lately at the golf course," Miles answered.

Miles arrived at the Yarbrough house at 7:00 p.m. Brooke came to the door and let him in. Not sure where the two were going, she wore a shirt with nautical stripes, True Religion jeans, and booties. Miles held a small white gift bag in his left hand, and a single red rose in his right hand. Brooke walked him through the hallway to the living room. Miles walked over to Mrs. Yarbrough and handed her the rose. "Thank you for allowing me to come in and say hello," he said. "Please sit down," she said as she thanked him for the rose and found a small bud vase.

Mr. Yarbrough then walked in from being on the back porch where he was watching the Sweet 16 round of the US Open Tennis Championships.

"Miles, so very good to see you and meet you. We enjoy reading about your success with baseball."

Miles responded, "We are excited about our upcoming year. This is my final opportunity at a state title."

The baseball stalwart almost forgot about the gift bag but then looked at the ground to his right, grabbed it, and handed it to Mr. Yarbrough. It was a dozen Titleist Pro V1 golf balls. Mr. Yarbrough was pleased, "You have permission to date my daughter."

Everyone laughed. "I remember you bought a sleeve of those earlier this summer. And considering this is the beginning of our school year and my friendship with all of you, think of this as a Hansel, a gift given for good luck."

Mrs. Yarbrough was touched. "You have a wonderful memory and thoughtful perspective."

"I'm probably guilty of being too much of an antediluvian; I am ridiculously old-fashioned," Miles said.

Mr. Yarbrough then looked over to his daughter and said, "Where are you two off to?"

Brooke admitted, "We haven't even talked about it. If we had discussed it, I would have known what to wear."

"I think I was so pleased she said yes that I hung up before we made a plan. You dressed perfectly."

Brooke then put him on the spot, "Why have you waited so long to ask me out? You've been coming over to my locker, seeking me out in the hall, the parking lot, but nothing."

Miles responded, "I move very slowly."

Mrs. Yarbrough smiled, "We like hearing that."

The first date was innocent enough. Miles took Brooke to Orchard Hills, where only three staff members remained to close the facility down for the night. Dano, the assistant pro in his late 30s, who had played collegiate golf at Mississippi State, was finishing up. He was rather funny, always laughing, always attempting to talk up his Bulldogs. Two older African American women, Esther and Beatrice, were cleaning up the 19th Hole, the snack bar. Miles borrowed a golf cart key from Dano to go retrieve a cart while Esther and Beatrice rolled out the red carpet for Brooke.

"Where are you guys going to eat tonight?" asked Beatrice, who was slightly overweight and nearing sixty years of age. Brooke wasn't sure, so she answered, "Not much has been said. We were going to go to a movie but couldn't find anything we liked. So, I suggested a putting contest if we could get here in time."

"A putting contest. That's excellent!" said Esther, thin and in her late 40s. "And I know you can win. I've seen you on the range. It took me a minute to recognize you, but you are the good golfer at Newnan High."

Brooke thanked Esther for her compliment, "The funny thing is, I don't believe Miles knows how good I am, but he is about to find out!"

Miles came back for Brooke, and Esther had some fun with him at his expense. "Miles, Miles, Miles. Why have you been hiding this beautiful young lady from us? We are taking this personally that you have kept her from us."

Brooke agreed, "He's had forever to ask me out. It took him years."

Miles, who towered over the other three, said, "Well, we are going to the putting green right now for some fun. Besides, I'm starting to feel four feet tall."

Brooke and Miles manufactured a putting competition. It was eighteen holes of torture for Miles but constant celebrations for Brooke. She shot two-under par while Miles carded a six-over, a full eight shots, in this case, putts back. Slender with the perfect build for playing golf, Brooke easily beat Miles even with borrowed clubs.

"I believe, looking back, I would rather have the security of not knowing you would kill me instead of the certainty of it playing out in front of me," Miles told her.

"What can I say? I'm a competitive player. And my short game is strong, too," teased Brooke.

"No kidding. Great speed with that putting," commented Miles.

The two parked the golf cart and headed back to the pro shop to return the key. They knew no one else was there because they had seen all three cars depart. What they didn't know was that Beatrice and Esther had left them water, grilled cheese sandwiches, and cheeseburgers at the counter. A note left for Brooke and Miles simply read, "Enjoy. And if one day you two have kids, the names Esther and Beatrice sound just right."

Miles read it to Brooke and told her, "I no longer feel four feet tall. It's more like three feet tall now."

CHAPTER FIVE

"I could not tell you if I loved you the first moment I saw you. But I remember the first moment I looked at you walking toward me and realized that somehow, the rest of the world seemed to vanish when I was with you."

Cassandra Clare

September 8, 2012

The University of Georgia was no longer in the lead when it came to Miles' destination to play college baseball. The visit to Stanford couldn't be properly gauged, but it was off the charts. Marquess showed him the campus and the baseball facilities and requested that Stephanie Wilson, a junior from Augusta, Georgia, introduce him to influential members of the Hoover Institution, including a meeting with Miles' hero, Victor Davis Hanson.

Stephanie walked Miles to the Hoover Institution, pointing out a couple of buildings as they passed. They would have an interesting exchange. Three years his senior, she was beautiful and tall with long dark hair and brown eyes. For the tour, she wore a lightweight Stanford sweatshirt, shorts, and tennis shoes for comfort. She had on her official nametag, wore a pair of Ray-Ban aviator sunglasses, and had her hair in a high ponytail.

As they walked, she started with some small talk, "So, a baseball player?"

"Yes, baseball," he said.

"You will fit right in."

He was curious, "How's that?"

"Baseball players, they are the players on campus, if you will, and plenty of girls are going to want a swing at you. Looks, southern accent, and all!"

He was shocked. "I have a girlfriend."

Stephanie stopped and looked at him. "Look, here's the deal. Stanford baseball players are known here as the princes of Palo Alto. They are the kings of campus. Every girl wants one, and every guy here wants to be one."

"How about you?" he asked.

She laughed, "I don't know any," then added, "I got this assignment today due to my dad's connections to the Hoover Institution."

Then, shockingly, for a guy who was not too long ago terrified to approach a girl, Miles stepped up to the plate. "All right then. Make me a deal. If I come way out here for school and baseball, you will go on a date with me."

She laughed, giving a 'no thanks' look. "I'm about to be twenty-one. You are seventeen. How about we wait ten years, and if neither one of us is married, then I will go out with you. At least then I won't get arrested."

They entered the Hoover Institution. Miles felt like he was surrounded by greatness.

Miles asked her, "How did you choose Stanford?"

"I didn't. Just look around. Stanford chose me. Miles, no one, no one who has had the opportunity to come to Stanford says no. These are the best of the best in every field. You know the saying, "At Stanford, we don't *think* we are better than you. We *know* we are!"

Miles and Hanson spoke about the current political climate for nearly ninety minutes. At the end of their conversation, the man Miles thought could explain politics better than any other offered him an internship. It would be limited in hours, but Miles was honored.

But that wasn't all. A phone call two hours later sealed the deal. The 2012 presidential election was less than two months away, and on the other end was the Republican nominee and challenger to incumbent Barack Obama, former Stanford student Mitt Romney.

Because of Miles' interest in economics and politics, Marquess had asked Romney to give the star recruit a quick call. He and Romney had been roommates when they were freshmen. Romney may not have been Miles' favorite politician, but he knew the country needed an economic expert like Mitt or Stanford alumnus Alvin E. Roth, Ph.D., to get America back on the road to financial prominence that so many desired.

At seventeen years old, Miles wasn't even old enough to vote. Nonetheless, the conversation was impactful and productive. The best was the final part. The last thing that Romney did on the call was extend an invitation for Miles and his parents to join him in New Hampshire on the eve of the November 6 election. "It will be my final rally," said the presidential hopeful.

Without ever asking his parents, Miles confirmed, "We will be honored to be there. May I bring a guest?"

Over the next several weeks, a favorite date night spot for the two turned out to be Orchard Hills Golf Club. Miles felt better about making out with Brooke in a golf cart at the back end of the golf course than spending hours parking and charging them. Brooke had recently made birdie on her favorite hole, which included a nice place to park a cart on a small bridge overlooking a lake. It was now October. The temperatures were dropping, and it was her favorite spot on the course. "I know it's appropriate to use vernal as a word in the spring, like the vernal freshness of spring. But when I'm here with you, there's something fresh, something appealing about this lake. It smells better. It's cleaner, just more fitting for us," Brooke said to Miles. As she leaned in, she realized she preferred the intensity of a late October kiss over a kiss in the hot summer.

Miles chose the morning of November 2, 2012, as his day to reveal his commitment. Privately, he had told Marquess that he was committing to him, the program, and the institution.

The finalists were Stanford, early front-runner Georgia, and Auburn, where his parents graduated, as well as where Brooke planned to play golf following her high school days. Brooke preferred the close location of Auburn to Newnan. She was interested in studying human sciences, but what enticed her was the Auburn Women's Golf Team.

Miles and Brooke had been dating for two months. He cared for her, but her decision to choose Auburn was not an influence on him. He had loved Auburn all his life, but today was decision day, and it would not be Auburn's day.

Miles was joined at the podium by his head coach from Newnan, Kenny Morris; his parents, Celeste and Greg; his pastor, Joel Richardson, of Central Baptist Church; and family friend and Newnan enthusiast, Norma Haynes. "Mrs. Norma," as she was called, was a Newnan legend and was a big University of Georgia supporter. Also with him was someone he greatly respected with roots at LSU and in the state of Louisiana,

Dr. Harry Barrow, the pastor of Newnan Presbyterian Church. Completing the rather large gathering were three local law enforcement officers, Jay LaChance of the Newnan Police Department and his brothers, John and Jeff LaChance, of the Coweta County Sheriff's Department.

His parents and Coach Morris sat at a table with him. The rest demonstrated their support by standing behind them. Newnan Athletics Director Steve Allen welcomed everyone there and turned the proceedings over to the seventeen-year-old, who began speaking to cameras, no notes on hand. There were three caps in front of him: the iconic cardinal red with the white "S" was to his right, Auburn was represented in the middle with a navy blue cap, and a black UGA cap was to his left.

Miles began speaking, "Thank you, Mr. Allen. And I want to thank everyone for being here. It's not an insignificant gesture by all of you; instead, it's rewarding for me to see so many meaningful people in this room. Everyone here, sitting and standing behind this table, is already aware of my choice. They are the only ones I've told, outside of the head coach of the university I will soon choose."

"My sincere appreciation to all the schools who took an interest in me, recruited me, and contacted me in many forms and fashion. I know God has a plan for my life, and I am at peace with my decision. Today will be my final decision because I have been offered the opportunity of a lifetime; thus, my recruitment officially ends today. I know from the Bible that the sting of death is sin. It spreads its venom with the arrow of sin. The result of sin is death. Christians should not fear physical death. Christ took the sting of sin from us. If you are here today, chances are you are a believer like me. When you leave here, feel blessed that you are in the company of so many others who love Christ, and God will reward you with eternal life. It means so much to me to be in the presence of so many other Christians, others who believe as I believe."

"I can announce here today that I will be majoring in Economics, and it will be my honor to be a part of the 2017 graduating class of Stanford University, where I am humbled to accept a scholarship offer to represent the Cardinal baseball team. I want to compliment Cardinal coach Mark Marquess for his hospitality during a recent visit and his belief in me. I await with great eagerness to be a small part of a university with such high academic standards, practically a utopian society. It's imperative for me today to take time to sincerely thank the baseball programs and staff from Auburn University and the University of Georgia. I encourage all kids who dream of playing college baseball one day to consider the navy and orange and red and black of these two wonderful institutions."

"Finally, in closing, those who are eighteen and older get to do a remarkable thing on Tuesday. In four days, you get to say what you feel at the ballot box by voting for our president. Although I am not eligible to vote, I would like to remind all who are that you lose your freedom for anything when you rely on the government for everything."

With that, Celeste handed Miles the white Stanford baseball jersey that he had fallen in love with. He slipped it on over his long-sleeved navy blue shirt. Miles never put on the Stanford cap but did grab a bag from under the table to hand everyone at the podium a Stanford cap. Most of them immediately put on the caps. He also presented each of his Newnan teammates with a Cardinal cap, teammates he forgot to thank during his speech.

On second thought, perhaps he should have used notes.

Two Atlanta television stations were on hand, as well as three print publications. Mr. Allen said Miles would welcome any questions. The first reporter asked, "Stanford, from a geographical standpoint, is so far away compared to your other finalists. Was it the academics that pushed Stanford over the top?"

Miles thanked him for his question. "The academics were the most critical factor. Playing for a traditional power, when you couple them together, it was meant to be. Stanford won the national championship in 1987 and 1988, and I would like to help deliver coach Marquess another one," stated the Newnan senior.

The next reporter mentioned he had never heard of an announcement like the one today, citing your major first. "Was that planned on purpose?" Miles admitted it was, saying, "Yes, and perhaps if I would have gone the route of an abozzo, made a rough drawing of the speech, I would have properly thanked my current and past teammates here at Newnan, my parents, and my coaches." This comment drew chuckles from the audience.

The same reporter asked a follow-up question. "I'm impressed you already have decided on a major. Have you always wanted to study economics?"

"No, sir. But as I reviewed the possibilities, I discovered that one of my top three all-time favorite baseball players, Mike Mussina, graduated from Stanford with an economics degree. I may never have his baseball career, but that's the company I want to keep, and to wear the same jersey (pointing to it) and to take similar classes as "Moose" would be rewarding as well."

The first reporter asked, "Mussina wore the No.35 with the Orioles and Yankees. Did you ask about the availability of the 35?" Miles responded, "The baseball staff and I have decided on the No.14 jersey. I have been promised 14, what I wear here. Moose wore the No.25 for the Cardinal, but I requested the No.14."

The final reporter to ask anything wanted to know how he would celebrate such an accomplishment tonight. Miles shocked him a bit by saying, "Not really celebrating tonight. I'll work a short afternoon shift at the golf course. My girlfriend, Brooke, and I will get together with our parents tomorrow night, and then we plan to see a late movie on Sunday night."

The reporter followed up, "Late?"

"Yes, sir. I love a 9:00 or 9:30 movie on a Sunday night. If I'm at the theater, I embrace the feeling of the weekend not being over. Monday morning still feels a bit away. Brooke loves suspense movies, so that will be the genre."

With that, Miles thanked everyone again for being there, looked at his watch, and declared he had to go. "I can't be late for class," he laughed and added, "I can't afford to do that here and certainly not next year."

CHAPTER SIX

"Democracy is based upon the conviction there are extraordinary possibilities in ordinary people."

Harry Emerson Fosdick

November 5, 2012

There was nothing new about Celeste Fuller voting on election day. Any election day. She didn't miss one. "I think it's the most patriotic thing civilians can do," she liked to tell others. No way she was going to skip the 57th quadrennial presidential election. One of the two finalists calling her only child was a different story. That was a first. But that obstacle wasn't difficult to hurdle. All she had to do was stay silent.

The next hurdle to climb was more difficult, overcoming serious anathema the day prior.

was vehemently against flying, despite Greg, of all ,s, being a pilot. Yes, Celeste Fuller, forty-seven, married to commercial pilot for twenty-two years, had never flown before. Never. And that circumstance was not going to change since her childhood best friend died in the ValuJet Flight 592 crash in 1996. That tragedy and the memory of her friend had stayed with Celeste all these years.

It was the day before one of the most important elections in United States history. The Republican nominee for president of the United States had invited her family to be his guest at his final campaign rally at the Verizon Wireless Arena in Manchester, New Hampshire. Celeste did well in getting to Hartsfield-Jackson Airport in Atlanta. Shortly after entering the ticketing area, she stopped. "I'm sorry, I can't," she told Greg.

When Greg tried to convince her that everything would be fine, that didn't put a dent in her fear. Greg showed a bit of frustration. "Don't apologize to me; apologize to your son," he said a bit too harshly.

Miles, although let down, graciously decided to take the high road. "It's okay, Mom. I accepted this invitation with alacrity. I was ready, but I didn't consider you. Take the car home. It will be okay."

And then there were three. Greg, Miles, and Brooke made their way to the gate for their flight to MHT (Manchester Boston Regional Airport). The trio safely reached MHT, about which a local on the arriving flight told them, "We just call it the Manchester Airport." That statement made total sense when you consider the airport is only three short miles south of the heart of Manchester.

The Romney campaign had a car and two campaign workers waiting to take the now-reduced group to the arena. "Where is Mrs. Fuller?" asked the younger of the two, a dark-haired male about the age of twenty-five. Greg replied, "She's sick; she's very sick."

Miles and the others arrived at the arena a few minutes after 5:00 p.m. They were allowed to take a side entrance, entering a hallway that provided a path to three rooms, including a break room that looked more like a cafeteria area.

"I feel like I'm in a band, and they are bringing me backstage," claimed Greg. Moments later, the airline pilot turned around to see a gentleman in all dark colors with long hair who was about forty years old.

"Welcome to New Hampshire," said celebrity singer and performer Kid Rock, adding, "Mitt is going to be very late tonight." The first thing Miles thought was, *How late?* Romney had multiple stops in various states but had hoped to be on the scene by 9:00 p.m.

"Look, I can tell you guys are in for a long night. I'm about to do a soundcheck. There's no one else in the arena. I'm singing "Born Free" just before Mitt hits the stage. How about I let you guys get a sneak preview?" asked the singer with the long, straight hair.

Miles, Brooke, and Greg walked into the arena. An empty arena. They stayed just left of the stage. Ten minutes later, Kid Rock was singing "Born Free," just as he said. A short seven minutes following that, the check was over. He was good to go. But the wait had just begun. Romney didn't arrive in Manchester until about 10:30 p.m.

The traveling party from Georgia was allowed backstage with other politicians and dignitaries. They all shook the hand of the presidential hopeful. But there was no real conversation, just a greeting.

Miles, his father, and his girlfriend were escorted to their seats in the third row. Kid Rock appeared on the stage and started singing "Born Free," although the environment was different from the sound check. The arena was packed, and electricity filled the air.

The roof nearly blew off when Romney appeared. He had to

be exhausted, but the sixty-five-year-old former governor of Massachusetts didn't show it. Romney had to wait several minutes to speak. The crowd refused to stop cheering. He thanked Kid Rock for his performance and got a huge ovation when he said, "Obama likes to blame the previous administration. I'm not just going to take office on January 20. I'm going to take *responsibility* for that office."

Romney asked voters to look beyond all the attacks and to reach out to as many undecided voters as possible. He knew he needed New Hampshire if he was going to pull the upset.

Romney wrapped up his speech just after 11:30 p.m. Thirty minutes later, the residents of Dixville Notch, located less than three hours from Manchester, held its traditional midnight vote at the Balsams, a hotel and ski resort. Still, nothing was decided in this election. Obama and Romney split the precinct's ten votes, 5–5.

Romney had planned for Manchester to be the final stop. But the campaign made a late decision to return to Ohio and Pennsylvania on election day after he voted in his hometown of Belmont, Massachusetts.

Three weary campaign supporters were fortunate to catch the last flight back to Atlanta, a flight delayed nearly two hours due to a mechanical problem. Miles and Brooke were back in their respective beds just before 6:00 a.m., with no hope of getting any quality sleep before getting up for what would be nothing like just another Tuesday at Newnan High.

CHAPTER SEVEN

"And there autumn met with the loveliest of winds, but a heart blown asunder as her leaves would fall again."

Angie Weiland-Crosby

November 6, 2012

As Romney was getting prepared to vote in his home state of Massachusetts, Miles was trying to stay upright on his feet following perhaps thirty-five minutes of sleep.

The national pundits were all correct. Obama was a huge favorite to win a second term. But when you become part of the election, that adrenaline rush, that wanting to see something happen so badly, can force your mind to play tricks on you. Things start taking a life of their own. But it wasn't meant to be for Romney and his supporters. He and his running mate, Paul Ryan, took the state of Georgia, but it wasn't enough.

Miles tried to make himself feel better. "Hey, we will always have Kid Rock," he told Brooke, attempting to channel Humphrey Bogart in his favorite movie, *Casablanca*.

Miles continued to work at Orchard Hills for the remainder of his senior year. He continued to take Brooke there for dinner with Beatrice and Esther, and he lost every single putting contest to Brooke. Their relationship was as strong as ever as the spring sports season arrived. In her junior season, she dominated the links, eventually ending at Jekyll Island with a state runner-up finish.

Miles never wavered in his commitment to Stanford. Individually, he had a phenomenal senior season. Miles still lacked the hitting power people expect of a Division I player, but he hit over .375 and stole two homers from opposing competition by climbing the wall as a defender.

Being six feet four inches doesn't always have its advantages. Riding roller coasters can be a challenge; forget about being in the back seat of a car, and don't be alarmed if your feet hang off the end of some beds. But height also can help in sports. Immediately, one thinks of basketball, but height also helps in baseball.

Starting his sophomore year at Newnan, Miles began the tradition of studying the warning tracks and walls/fences of all the parks he played in. The thought was to get familiar and get comfortable with the turf, the texture, the wind, and the height of the wall. Miles was going to do all he could to help the Newnan High Cougar pitching staff.

The effort and the thought were admirable. However, the execution, coupled with injuries to pitchers and six position players, proved too much to overcome. Newnan managed to clinch the final region postseason berth. But the Cougars were quickly eliminated by Lowndes County of Valdosta, 9-1 and 4-2.

Miles, the Newnan High valedictorian, went 3-6 with two walks in the series. He weakly grounded out to second in his final high school at-bat.

A reporter asked how he felt. "I'm disappointed, severely disappointed. It's hard not to be when you look at your opponent acting with such schadenfreude behavior. To know we are out, and not only are they over there celebrating, but you know our rivals are getting great pleasure from our misfortune," explained the Newnan senior on the final day he would don the Cougar uniform.

CHAPTER EIGHT

"Conversations about politics can give you the somewhat errant impression that you can make a difference in people's lives by talking about what others should be doing."

Daniela I. Norris

For his valedictory speech, Miles implemented a different method from the norm. Teenagers can be selfish and self-centered, so to avoid any sign of solipsism, Miles spoke to several of his fellow graduates on what his speech should be about. He did not get serious feedback. At least, not constructive or sincere feedback. Unanimously, it was suggested to him to keep it short. The threat of unwanted storms surrounding Drake Stadium guaranteed that.

Miles donned the traditional navy Newnan High School cap and gown with the valedictorian stole and multiple gold honor cords. When it was time to give his speech, Miles walked slowly up to the podium with no notes in hand:

Good evening, and congratulations to the Newnan High class of 2013. Due to the incoming inclement weather, coupled with the desires of all those I stand here to represent tonight, this is certain to be the shortest speech in the history of Newnan High School.

On behalf of the class of 2013, we want to thank our parents, families, teachers, and friends for all they have done for us. We are grateful for all the support from them and this community.

Although I promised my classmates that I would be breviloquent, I would be remiss if I did not share a few words with them.

We are young right now, feeling invincible. However, one day, years from now, when our mnemonic abilities are not what they once were, senescence will set in. Let's not have regrets and face our challenges confidently. The aches and pains will come on, but before we deteriorate, let us take time to appreciate the process of life's journey.

We will all experience some form of an epoch, a signature stage in our lives. I promise this is down the road. Tonight does not define us and will not go down as our good old days. I believe in my heart that better days are ahead. I feel axiomatic about that. I am so excited to see what this class does in the future.

Miles paused for a few seconds.

I promised my parents that I would leave politics out of this tonight.

At this point, Greg and Celeste, along with any member of the school administration, shared a painful look of chagrin.

Greg leaned into Celeste. He sighed, "What is he going to say?"

She looked up at her son on the stage and softly whispered, "Don't do it, Miles. Not here."

Miles then continued:

But in a moment of personal preference, I ask all our graduates to think for themselves when it concerns politics. There is not enough original thought. Don't believe the media. Be aware of the harm of social media. Be aware of the media's agenda. I abandoned the main-stream media a long time ago because I couldn't detect when the media's coverage started and the Democratic party's talking points ended.

Miles then pointed to his classmates.

I know this group will make a positive impact in this county, our country, and in this world. You will be remarkable. I can't wait for our first reunion. Until then, Go Cougars!

With that, he was done and exited the podium to scattered but not thunderous applause.

When the ceremony finished, Miles shook hands with a few friends and then made his way to the far end zone, where he had been instructed to meet his parents and Brooke under the goalpost.

He got down close to the thirty-yard line, and he felt an arm reach across his chest. It was Cooper Allen, the injured senior centerfielder whom Miles had replaced his sophomore season.

"Hey, Coop," said a startled Miles.

"Good speech. All know how you stand politically."

Miles answered back, "It's good to see you."

"Miles, a couple of years ago… I just want to say I am sorry about a couple of years ago. I was not kind to you, and my friends acted poorly towards you, too," said Cooper.

"That's great of you to say, but no hard feelings," confirmed Miles.

"I appreciate that. I know you are a stand-up guy. Good luck at Stanford. They are fortunate to have you."

Following graduation at Drake Stadium, not much changed in the day-to-day life of the future Stanford centerfielder. Although he did make three trips to California, he remained employed at Orchard Hills until the first week in August.

He and Brooke continued to remain a couple, although unsure what distance was soon to do to their relationship. They attended seven Braves games, often with friends, a couple with Mike Furbush, a legendary youth baseball coach in Sharpsburg, right next to Newnan. Miles had played youth baseball for Furbush. He was an old-school coach who preached discipline and fundamentals. Furbush was also an avid Braves fan, the Braves being considered the best team in the major leagues. He rarely missed a home game. It must be nice to have the "life of Riley."

Brooke joined Miles on one of the three trips over the summer to Stanford. Much of her summer was spent on a family trip to Northern Ireland and, of course, working on her golf game and stepping up to tournament play. Miles even arranged for her to talk to the Stanford coaches. She was a bit curious if Tiger Woods might be in the building. Hey, if Mitt Romney can call Miles, perhaps she can meet the former Stanford great.

Brooke enjoyed her time discussing golf with the coaches, but no Tiger ever walked through the door. There also was no serious talk of her being part of the program and joining Miles one year later in Palo Alto.

Miles felt fortunate to land a housing spot in Mirrielees, an apartment residence a little outside of the main campus. Mirrielees is close to Vaden and the Gerhard Casper Quad and is reserved for juniors and seniors. But the freshman from Newnan, Georgia, never asked if the placement was a gift, a guerdon, a reward for playing baseball, or simply a clerical error. Greg advised him, "Don't say a word. Just keep your head to the ground and play dumb."

Miles discovered that Mirrielees offered him independence and time to himself. The residence is named after 1907 Stanford graduate Edith Ronald Mirrielees. She was the editor of *Sequoia,* a literary magazine, and was co-founder of the women's honor society Cap and Gown. Edith joined the faculty in 1909 and remained until she retired in 1944. She later became a mentor and trusted friend to John Steinbeck. Edith passed away in 1962, and the Eastside campus was built in 1972.

The Escondido Road residence featured two- and three-bedroom apartments. Miles was placed in a two-bedroom, with a senior civil engineering major, Blake Zhu of Los Angeles. He had dark hair and was five feet ten inches with a slight build. Blake was not an athlete, and Miles was pleased that this living arrangement would provide a break from baseball. Blake didn't mind rooming with a freshman, although all other residents of Mirrielees were upperclassmen.

The two first met on July 29, before Miles even officially moved in. Zhu was at his table with fifty to sixty postal stamps in front of him. Miles impressed him immediately by saying to him, "With all of these stamps, you must think of philately as a hobby?"

"I do. Not many people know about that or even care," admitted the senior.

"We all have our things. I love classic movies," Miles said.

"I tell you what. When you come back next month, we will talk movies."

Miles responded, "And you will share with me your love for collecting stamps."

Zhu was still curious, "How did you know about philately?"

Miles replied, "Phil comes from the Greek word for love, coined in 1864 by the French stamp collector George Herpin."

His future roommate offered the incoming freshman some confidence and said, "You are going to fit right in here!"

"I'm looking forward to it, so forward to it," admitted an eager Miles. "Although baseball is hard enough, I am concerned about the adjustment to these classes and the challenges I will face."

"I didn't know my new roommate was a baseball player," said Blake. "What position?"

"Centerfield."

Blake was impressed. "I look forward to talking baseball with you."

Miles asked, "Who is your team?"

Blake quickly said, "The Dodgers. Is there another team? Who do you like?"

"The Braves, the Atlanta Braves," said the Southerner.

CHAPTER NINE

"And a voice of a multitude being at ease with her: and with the men of the common sort brought Sabeans from the wilderness, which put bracelets upon their hands, and beautiful crowns upon their heads."

Ezekiel 23:42 *KJV*

July 30, 1982

The Atlanta Braves were solidly in first place in the National League West. The Braves were 10 1/2 games up, and fans were already looking forward to the postseason.

Atlanta management, on this fateful day, opted to do away with the Chief Noc-A-Homa teepee. The Braves then lost nineteen of their next twenty-one games, blowing that huge lead. Braves management discovered that selling more seats wouldn't be worth it if the decision to remove the teepee was a curse. The teepee returned, and the Braves recovered. Greatly aided by a Joe Morgan homer for the Giants against the Dodgers, Atlanta, with a record of 89-73, outlasted Los Angeles by a single game.

The Braves, managed by future Yankees skipper Joe Torre, fell in three games in the NLCS to eventual World Series champion St. Louis. 1982 was also the year that Braves slugger Dale Murphy, who lived on a 500-acre farm in Grantville, Georgia, just minutes from Newnan, won his first of what would be two consecutive MVP awards.

Murphy hit 398 career home runs, won five Gold Gloves, and was the fifth Atlanta player to have his jersey retired, joining the ranks of Hank Aaron, Warren Spahn, Eddie Matthews, and Phil Niekro. Somehow, the slugger is not in the Hall of Fame. And it's a shame!

Miles returned to Newnan the next day. He was relieved to have met his future roommate. He would be returning to Stanford in two weeks for good. Miles continued to live life day to day, picking up each possible shift at Orchard Hills. Like other incoming college freshmen, he wanted to take as much cash to the beginning of the school year as possible.

Miles had already decided to major in economics. He read as much as he could to prepare him for the road ahead, but he also wanted to see his parents and Brooke as much as possible. One of his favorite outings of the summer of 2013 was when he caddied for Brooke in a 36-hole women's tournament at the legendary Druid Hills Golf Club in Atlanta. Druid Hills opened in 1912, and the 101-year-old course was a welcome sight to Brooke's game. The two felt a unique closeness on a course that was 101 years old and had hosted both the 1951 U.S. Women's Open and the 1921 presidential visit of Warren Harding.

Brooke played very well, closing with a seventy and securing a top-five finish. It was the time together on the course she cherished the most. Miles made her feel at ease. At times, he would hold her hand, share Bible scripture for strength, and even attempt to sing to make her laugh. The two had now been together for almost a year.

It had been another whirlwind sixty hours for Miles. He flew back on the thirtieth. Mike Furbush picked him up at the airport, and they went straight to Turner Field, seeing another Braves win. When the game was over, Mike dropped Miles off at a nearby hotel, where Brooke picked him up the next morning to caddy for her at Druid Hills. The first day, the temperature was well over ninety degrees and Miles crashed back at his hotel one hour after Brooke's first round of 74. The next day, the sun was scorching, the heat nearly unbearable, with no breeze, but Brooke's score of 70 made the hectic sixty-hour experience worth it.

The remainder of their days before his departure were sweet and innocent. Twice, they made time to return to Brooke's favorite location at Orchard Hills.

"Stand over there and let me look at you," she instructed.

"Why?"

"Because all of next year, when I'm here without you, I want to remember you here as you are today." He then kissed her as passionately as ever, hoping, too, she would recall that over her senior year. She then softly asked, "Why couldn't your parents have waited a year to have you?"

CHAPTER TEN

"Elite colleges like Stanford are extremely inaccessible. They're failing in their mission to provide access."

Sebastian Thrun

Stanford University is an elite 8,180 acres of global prestige.

The private institution, founded in 1885, is still on the quarter system. Miles was one of a little more than 8,000 undergraduate students in the fall of 2013. Move-in day was two days before the first day of class. Miles was almost shocked that he got away with residing at Mirrielees.

He followed his dad's instructions: Remain silent and hope for the best. He didn't feel he was being legerdemain in his behavior. He wasn't untruthful; he wasn't deceptive. He just wasn't forthcoming. What he was was eager to see some of his new teammates. But on night one, two days before his first class,

Blake surprised him with a welcome spaghetti dinner and a viewing of *The Godfather*.

"James Caan is brilliant in this movie. And to think, he was a conservative in Hollywood," noted Miles.

"Certainly not the norm in Hollywood. Robert DuVall has similar beliefs. I would love to work in the film industry," said the senior.

This confused Miles. "Why are you getting a degree in civil engineering?" asked the freshman.

"I ask myself that every day. I am going to work for a sports firm. My older cousin has one in Pasadena. He wants me to represent professional athletes. Why do you think I have such an interest in you?" laughed Blake.

When the epic film had concluded, Miles inquired, "How did you end up here at Stanford?"

"I had no choice. My parents met here. My father told me it would be the ultimate act of tergiversation if I didn't attend their alma mater."

"Thanks for the movie. I'm going to amble around campus and hopefully let go of some of this agita," Miles said.

Blake wanted to put his new roommate at ease. "Miles, we are just getting to know each other. You are far from home. But remember what I told you when I first met you. You belong here. This is your new home."

Miles appreciated Blake's thoughtfulness and his attempt to dulcify the stress and anxiety the eighteen-year-old couldn't conceal.

Miles used the next day to locate all his classes and check in at the baseball offices. He was pleased to discover several of his older teammates were also living at Mirrielees. On his walk around campus, he thought of those who came before him.

Related to baseball, he thought of Mike Mussina, Jack McDowell, and Ed Sprague, Jr.

Miles also felt that the presence of some of the most prominent alumni: notable individuals like Bill Hewett and David Packard, the co-founders of Hewett Packard; Nike co-founder and chairman Phil Knight; Yahoo co-founders Jerry Yang and David Filo; and the Google founding duo of Larry Page and Sergey Brin. Of course, he asked himself if he belonged with such greatness. Probably not. But, then again, none of them likely took four home runs away with over-the-wall catches in the outfield as he did. Not even Knight-wearing Air Jordans could do that!

The night before classes started, Miles gathered with his teammates in the baseball complex. He was now officially a Stanford Cardinal. He didn't know it then, but most of his next four years would be spent in that complex with his teammates.

There were couches, recliners, televisions, refrigerators, and tables. Whatever a player needed was at his disposal. Each player had his own laptop and iPad. Because of these attractive amenities, baseball players congregated at the complex and developed close bonds with teammates.

Brad Hampton, a senior starting pitcher, took Miles under his wing that first night. "We pick each other up here. Thirty-five guys, and we play for each other. Coaches don't believe they should monitor us or be forced to. The upperclassmen here are in charge."

It was clear. At Stanford, you must be self-motivated. Miles learned that many of his teammates were civil and mechanical engineering majors. Some were economics majors like him, and many were management science and engineering (MS&E) majors. These guys were the best of the best.

About half the team was from California, the other half from all over the country. Scheduling and time management were of the utmost importance. If you had class in the morning, you were expected to be with the team in the afternoon for baseball and fellowship. Miles learned early that if you didn't get the work in with the team, you must do it individually. Once again, it was about scheduling, discipline, and self-motivation.

Known for his speed and defense, Miles took a greater interest in research, specifically warning track research. He had already established a habit in high school of studying home and away warning tracks and walls. The truth was that he didn't know exactly how tall he was. He knew he was somewhere between six feet five inches and six feet seven inches, likely short of the latter. But Miles had hops. He could climb a wall. More importantly, his speed enabled him to find a baseball and quickly zone in on it. Although he only played sparingly his freshman season, Miles made mental notes that were later logged into an iPad on every park in which Stanford played.

As Miles met the challenges of his first year at Stanford, Brooke breezed through her final year at Newnan High School. The two initially remained very close, but those frequent phone calls began to slow down after a couple of months.

Things were strong again when Christmas break arrived. Miles spent three weeks back home, working eight shifts at Orchard Hills for Dano and head pro Wyatt Detmer. The course wasn't doing as well financially. The offseason was always a challenge, but it was even harder this time around. The course would eventually close its doors well before Miles graduated from Stanford.

The days working at Orchard Hills helped Miles become the man he was. He respected all his co-workers and was thankful for how well Dano and Wyatt treated him. Esther and Beatrice continued to be devoted to the club all the way to the final day.

The Newnan High golf team continued to host golf matches

there and at Newnan Country Club. The owners, to prolong the life of the club, even designed a frisbee golf course.

It wasn't meant to be. One can still see remnants of the great Scottish Links layout from I-85. And for many, when they closed their eyes and thought about the course, they could recall great shots and beautiful birdies.

CHAPTER ELEVEN

"What defines us is how well we rise after falling."

Bob Hoskins

Miles failed to make the Stanford starting lineup as a freshman. This was no surprise. He did, however, see action in forty of their sixty-one games.

The Cardinal finished 35-26 but were just 16-14 in the conference. Miles hit .288 in 2014 as a freshman. The Cardinal qualified for the NCAA tournament as the No. 3 seed in the Bloomington, Indiana regional. Stanford opened with an impressive 8-1 victory over No. 2 seed Indiana State. The Cardinal bats went silent one day later as host Indiana University got the best of them, 4-2.

Stanford's hope of reaching Nashville and facing Vanderbilt in the super-regional looked bleak. The Cardinal would have to beat Youngstown State the next afternoon and then defeat

Indiana that night and again the next day. Miles saw his only action of the Bloomington regional in the contest against Youngstown State. In a reserve role, Fuller went 1-2 with a single in the Stanford 12-4 victory. That night, the Cardinal bats came alive, and Stanford staved off elimination, winning a squeaker over the Hoosiers, 5-4. The victory set up a winner-take-all contest the next day.

Typically, when a team is forced to play five games in four days, the pitching staff becomes pretty thin. But Marquess managed his staff well, and every Cardinal left it out on the field. The regional final was a nail-biter, going to Stanford, 5-4. The victory sent Stanford to Nashville with a berth in Omaha at the College World Series on the line. The Stanford players felt confident. They had already dispatched the No. 4 overall seed, Indiana.

Tim Corbin was building a national power at Vanderbilt. But the Vandy boys, despite a pitching staff that included Walker Buehler, Tyler Beedee, and Carson Fulmer, had only won seventeen of thirty Southeastern Conference games.

Greg and Celeste were more than anxious that Stanford was coming to Nashville. While Greg frequently flew to Stanford games, Celeste had not seen her baby boy since he was home for Christmas. Miles missed them so much that he stayed with them in their hotel room on Wednesday and Thursday. Game 1 versus the Commodores was on Friday.

Everything seemed in place for Miles, with one exception. There was no Brooke. She had already graduated from Newnan, enjoying her moment at Drake Stadium. But when Miles couldn't get back for her prom, there was a definite change in the relationship. Technically, the two were still a couple. But only because they had not yet had "the talk"—not yet.

Miles was too occupied with the assignment at hand to put too much thought into the Brooke debacle. All college baseball players dream of Omaha. Miles and his Stanford teammates were now two wins from living out that dream.

Despite playing some of its best baseball of the season, over these last two weeks, Stanford came up one game short of realizing their dream of returning to Omaha for the first time since 2008 when the Cardinal lost in the semifinals.

The Vanderbilt offense was mighty, putting up eleven runs in Game 1 and twelve more in Game 3. Stanford enjoyed its moments as well, thrillingly winning Game 2 with a score of 5-4.

It was a bitter defeat for the Cardinal team. Miles couldn't watch the College World Series. It hurt too much. Adding the proverbial insult to injury was Vanderbilt winning the national championship over Virginia in three games.

When the series was over, Miles had two serious conversations. The first was with his parents. "I can't explain how badly losing to Vanderbilt hurts. To see them win it all, we know we were good enough to win," said the reserve outfielder. His parents attempted to console him. "You've got three more shots at it," said Celeste, still pleased that a short trip to Nashville was all it took to see her son in uniform.

Celeste asked Miles what he learned about himself during his first year at the prestigious university. "Being conservative in that atmosphere is not easy. I mainly stayed silent, which, in a way, contradicts what I suggested to my classmates on graduation night. I wanted them, encouraged them, to think originally," said her son.

Celeste nodded her head but was looking for more. "Miles, what about your growth in your walk with God or handling being that far from home?"

Miles hesitated, "With my relationship with God, nothing has wavered. I don't mean to maunder or obfuscate my explanation. Do I belong at Stanford? I believe so, though it has been a challenge. I do love my team, and the guys are great."

She applauded his grades. "You made a 4.0; that is what impressed me."

Miles appreciated the praise. "Like I said, it was a challenge. Balancing the athletic aspect of college life, like baseball, working out, and meetings is one thing. Think of that as the first four miles of a marathon. The academics present the other 22.2 miles of the equation."

Celeste wanted more intel regarding his relationship with Brooke. "The workload has put an end to you guys, so it seems."

Miles agreed, saying, "It certainly didn't help. Brooke has her priorities. We are about to have that talk."

His mom looked for something positive to say. "There are plenty of beautiful girls in California."

"No doubt, but I'm not positive a Stanford girl is for me. They are bon vivant women with parents who provide a lifestyle I am unfamiliar with. They expect to have a secure standing in this world. Get the degree, do little work, yet have enormous financial gains. I don't believe dating is a priority for me."

The second serious conversation was with Brooke. It was not easy. "What did you expect would happen to us when you went all the way to California for college?" she asked. Miles recognized her tone and took the high road. He feared fueling tensions any further, so he kept his remarks as anodyne as possible. She had been a dedicated girlfriend for a long time, and if she needed to blame him for the breakup, he was man enough to take it.

"Miles, I want you to understand. Although I'm not interested in anyone else right now, I need to get more serious about golf and make my path at Auburn. I even plan to go through Rush."

Miles offered back, "This doesn't have to be goodbye."

Brooke chimed back, "Hey. We will always have Kid Rock. We will always have New Hampshire."

CHAPTER TWELVE

"The most terrifying words in the English language are: I'm from the government, and I'm here to help."

Ronald Reagan

Although Miles played a more critical role in his last three years at Stanford, that super-regional loss at Vanderbilt in 2014 was as close as he ever got to Omaha and the College World Series. His sophomore season of 2015 was an absolute challenge. He remained a resident of Mirrielees, but his roommate, Blake Zhu, had graduated. Although he spent most of his time studying at the baseball complex, generally in the company of his teammates or tutors, Miles appreciated his time with Blake. The two, despite one being a senior and the other a freshman, had great discussions, sharing opinions on politics, life, and sports. Miles didn't mind talking about the Dodgers, but when Blake brought up his love for the Lakers, Miles attempted to zone out.

Miles' complex schedule didn't allow much time to work or to visit the Hoover Institution. It wasn't an internship or even a part-time job. It ended up being about two hundred twenty hours of work over his final three years.

The highlight was talking about policy with Victor Davis Hanson and Condoleezza Rice, the future director of the Hoover Institution and the former United States Secretary of State and U.S. National Security Advisor.

Notable past Hoover personnel include Henry Kissinger, Milton Friedman, Newt Gingrich, James Mattis, George Shultz, and the respected economist Thomas Sowell. The Hoover Institution is steadily ranked in the top 10 of the most influential think tanks in America. Its research teams work on many policies, including law, history, economic policy, and education.

The institution's first honorary fellow was Ronald Reagan, who was named in 1975. For his campaign for President in 1980, Reagan had thirteen Hoover employees working in different areas of the campaign. When Reagan took office in January of 1981, thirty current or former Hoover Institution employees joined the Reagan administration.

Miles didn't have the chance to visit the magnificent library at the Hoover Institution as much as he would have preferred. Being a baseball player at Stanford was once again about scheduling, being disciplined, and being self-motivated.

Miles' most challenging season on the diamond was his sophomore year in 2015. The Cardinal plummeted to a 24-32 record. It was the first losing season for the national powerhouse since 1993, and that squad finished only one game under .500, 27-28. This edition of the Cardinal finished eight games under .500, tenth in the conference, with a poor 9-21 PAC 12 record. Miles hit .291. It was better than the year before but not good enough for a player not providing power. He was playing elite defense while providing little offense, hitting seventh in the lineup.

Sitting in an Economic Policy Analysis class during his junior year at Stanford, Miles thought about what a potential professional career might look like if he never made it to the majors.

Finance? No, thank you. He looked around the room and decided the guy three rows over would be suited for a career in investment banking or private equity.

Corporate law? That wasn't for him. If he enrolled in law school, it would better his chances of one day running for President of the United States. He glanced at his classmates and thought to himself, *"Maybe I will run to keep one of these people from being president."*

After all, Miles had once fielded a phone call from Mitt Romney. Maybe Peter Thiel, the billionaire entrepreneur and venture capitalist known for donating to conservative political candidates, would bankroll a fellow Stanford graduate's candidacy. *"I need his phone number,"* Miles told himself, *"The PayPal creator doesn't need to know I have no account."*

An economics degree from Stanford University could help land him a position as an economic advisor for another individual running for president. No, Miles would rather be president. Plus, he always had heard that height helped those running for office.

How about a career in academia? He could one day be a professor and devote himself to researching topics and helping to create policy. He gazed around the room again. Not here at Stanford. He loved and appreciated his time at Stanford, but his politics and ninety percent of the others on campus didn't match. He got about as excited as the next guy about quantitative methods and regulation, but he had no desire to teach it.

About this time, the class was dismissed. Miles had ten minutes before his Econometric Methods for Public Policy Analysis and Business Decision-Making class began. He thought about how daunting the next hour would be. He silently prayed to the Lord, *"Please let me have a baseball career. On that large stage, I can lead others to You and Your Kingdom. And, in doing so, I won't lose my mind with a career in humanities and sciences. It will be a win for all!"*

Usually excited about being in class, Miles was restless. He secured his seat inside the Ralph Landau Economics Building classroom located at the corner of Galvez Street and Serra Mall. One more hour of class. One more hour until baseball practice. One hour closer to graduation. One hour closer to discovering if he would have a professional career playing in stadiums across the country or one in finance, academia, or corporate law. He threw his head back and thought the former sure sounded more appealing than the latter.

Stanford University baseball players were expected to exhibit character beyond reproach. However, the members of the team knew how to have a fun time. But just as in studying and practice, they held each other accountable related to their conduct and behavior.

Looking for a distraction so he didn't have to think about his career or his future, Miles agreed to meet his teammates on a Friday night at The Patio @ Rudy's. The establishment was in downtown Palo Alto for more than fifty years before it relocated to Emerson Street in 2014. The team enjoyed the atmosphere, with twenty-one flat-screen televisions, outdoor seating, live entertainment, and the best gourmet burgers and custom wings. The Old Pro sports bar and NOLA were other popular nightlife destinations for members of the team.

On this "throwback music" night, it was the wings and

burgers that drew the players to The Patio @ Rudy's. Miles walked by five beautiful girls, dancing to "Rock and Roll Girls" by John Fogerty, on his way to join his teammates. Seeing his curious look, one of his teammates set him straight, "Miles, they are visitors from UCLA, here for the basketball game tomorrow night."

Miles nodded, "I knew I had never seen them before. If they wanted to impress me, and they had to hear a Fogerty song, they would be dancing to "Centerfield" instead."

The other three guys laughed, with one confirming, "I bet," then suggested, "I don't think it's about you, baseball, or your position on the field. Tonight is about them."

As the players admired the girls and their dancing abilities, Miles remembered that Fogerty was from nearby San Francisco. "Awesome. Perhaps Fogerty will come in tonight," Miles muttered sarcastically.

As Miles turned back to look at his menu, he noticed that one of the five, an attractive blonde, smiled at him. He didn't think too much about it, but four or five minutes later, that same girl sat next to him, handing him a Michelob Light.

She had long blonde hair and wore a sheer black long-sleeved cropped top and jeans with huge rips at the knees.

He looked at the beer. "Michelob Light. How did you know?"

"Just a guess. I'm Whitney, by the way."

A server then stopped by and handed him water and a Red Bull sugar-free can.

"I'm Miles."

"And apparently, you don't drink since the waitress just gave you a Red Bull," she noted.

"Ah, you are stunning *and* perceptive. Why can't they all be California girls?" he asked her.

"Hey, you've got one here. I'm from Newport Beach."

"I'm sure you are. And, a good dancer," said Miles as a teammate grabbed the Michelob Light.

"With twelve years of formal training, I've been dancing all my life," she said. "Often the feature dancer."

"So, as a high school senior, your terpsichorean routine was probably the closing performance of the spring show?"

Whitney had a lost, then bemused look on her face. "I have no idea what that means, but your friend told me that you were in the televised finals of the Scripps National Spelling Bee. I'm assuming you are the most intelligent and best-looking guy here. Plus, you have an adorable accent, too."

"So, UCLA?" Miles responded, attempting to deflect the compliments.

"Los Angeles. Is there any other place?" she asked.

"Of course. How about Atlanta?" he said.

"You are from Atlanta? You are a long way from home," she said, smiling as she stated the obvious.

He decided to go back to his impressive vocabulary. "A California girl, a Georgia boy. Yet, we sit here in such propinquity."

Whitney started laughing. "Propo-what?"

"Propinquity. The state of being close to another, like best buds."

Whitney was honest, "When I saw you walk in, I didn't think you would be just a new friend."

Miles was curious. "What did you think I would be?"

Whitney put her entire left arm on his shoulder, pulled him close to her, and then passionately kissed him. Miles, not one to be at a loss for words, was, in fact, speechless. She was then curious and asked, "Where do you see yourself in five years?"

Miles responded, "Playing centerfield for the Atlanta Braves."

Whitney put her hand up against her face, her elbow resting on the table, her blue eyes looking right at him, and she started laughing.

"What's funny about that?" he asked.

"I'm sorry. But when a guy tells me he is going to play a sport professionally, it's like when someone tells me he's in a band. I just start laughing."

"Thank you for the extra motivation," he said.

"You're obviously attracted to me. Tell me. What's your biggest turnoff, Miles?"

"Democrats. Specifically left-wing lunatics."

Whitney responded, "My gosh, my parents would love you. I should have known you were conservative since you had on khakis and a quarter-zip sweater from Peter Millar. Wait, you picked a strange place and state to come to school."

"I don't speak about politics in class or on campus. And these guys, our team, we are a brotherhood. I couldn't care less if one of the guys is a Democrat or a Republican," explained the centerfielder.

"I don't think I can date a Republican," said Whitney.

"But your parents..."

"I said *they* would love you. They are conservative. I have more liberal views. You know, I had to rebel."

By this time, "Dream On" by Aerosmith was playing.

Whitney got up to join her friends on the dance floor. As she was leaving, she shouted, "Listen, Miles. Steven Tyler croons, 'Sing for the left,' the *left*, Miles, and 'Sing for the tear.'"

He politely corrected her, "That's actually 'Sing for the laughter,' not *left*, and 'Sing for the tear.'"

A teammate looked over, "You let her get away. She's the hottest person here."

Miles laughed, "It's the risk we all must take. And she's from Los Angeles and didn't even ask me what I do or what kind of car I drive."

Miles continued to smile, grabbed his water glass, and clinked the pitcher's beer mug in a toast, "To California girls."

"To California girls."

CHAPTER THIRTEEN

"When you get your opportunity, you have to be ready. You need good assistants, you need a mentor, you need help. There aren't any good coaches who don't have that support."

Mark Marquess

Marquess challenged his junior centerfielder and forced him to beat out a couple of incoming freshmen to keep his job. Miles responded, although the team didn't. Miles hit .326, up one slot in the lineup, batting sixth. He still was delivering little power but utilizing his speed to help manufacture runs. There was the before-mentioned huge hit at rival California and his theft of a Washington State home run in a game at Pullman. But the Cardinal could do no better than a tie for sixth in the PAC 12, splitting thirty conference games. Stanford concluded its season with a 31-23 record but no postseason appearance. That meant no chance of the College World Series. No chance at Omaha.

The 2017 season provided one final opportunity to reach that magical destination, which is Omaha. Greg continued to travel to see his son play. Celeste still refused to get on a plane. "I'm just scared of heights. I can't even get on the elevator," she tried explaining to friends.

Miles and Brooke had little communication. They had not seen each other since Christmas after the breakup. When he was in Newnan, Miles met Beatrice and Esther, the former Orchard Hills employees, for coffee. He told them, "We decided to see each other that time at Christmas. But it was different. All she did was talk about drinking, partying, and her sorority friends. She didn't even talk about golf."

"And she lived for golf," noted Esther.

"We always hoped you guys would end up together. But if you don't, God's got someone in mind that is even better," added Beatrice.

Esther then asked Miles about his final season and upcoming graduation. "My time out there has flown by. I've matured a great deal as a person, but I'm constantly playing catchup, putting out fires," said Miles.

"Unfortunately, welcome to the real world," laughed Esther.

There was immense pressure on the Stanford baseball team in 2017. Mark Marquess, the legend, who had been at the helm of the program since 1977, had announced this would be his forty-first and final campaign.

As his retirement approached, Miles had one more shot at Omaha and one last chance to get his legendary coach back there. Marquess, generally known as No. 9, had lifted the trophy in 1987 and 1988. He also had the best team in 1990.

They reached Omaha but failed to win a third title in four years.

Marquess moved Miles to second in the lineup, and the senior responded, hitting .336. Stanford finished the season with an improved 42-16 record, good enough for the overall No. 8 seed in the tournament.

That No. 8 seed enabled the Cardinal to host the regional and super-regional. The Cardinal also took second place in the Pac-12, with a respectable 21-9 record, six games better than the season before. And they were on fire heading into the regional, having won twenty-one of their last twenty-three games.

The Cardinal welcomed Sacramento State, Cal State Fullerton, and Brigham Young University (BYU) to Klein Field at Sunken Diamond for the NCAA Regional.

Stanford cruised to a 10-0 win over Sacramento State in the opener. The winner of the next game against Cal State Fullerton would be in the driver's seat, even better than the pole position of a huge race. Cardinal starting pitcher Andrew Summerville pitched well in almost five innings of work, but the Stanford bats were silent. Cal State Fullerton starter Josh Gavin yielded only one run in seven innings of work as his Titans defeated the host team 4-1. The Cardinal managed only one extra-base hit.

Saturday arrived, and so did Blake Zhu from Los Angeles. "When you guys lost last night, I wasn't about to miss today and hopefully tonight," said Zhu. Blake, like all else cheering on the Cardinal, knew Stanford would have to beat BYU in the afternoon and Cal State Fullerton at night and then take down Cal State Fullerton again tomorrow night. Blake had graduated three years ago, moved back to Los Angeles, and was now working in Pasadena. But he had returned twice a year to Palo Alto, once in the fall for a Stanford football game and once each spring to see Miles patrol centerfield. And every time, Blake stayed with Miles in that same residential room in Mirrielees.

In the contest with Brigham Young, Marquess handed the

ball to senior economics major Christopher Castellanos of Long Beach, California. Castellanos, a lefty, was a fierce competitor with a great desire to win. He wasn't about to allow No. 9 to go out on his watch. Castellanos threw a complete game four-hit gem, surrendering only a single run. With Brigham Young designated as the home team, the solo shot provided by Cougar designated hitter Colton Shaver gave BYU a 1-0 advantage.

Stanford had twelve outs remaining in their season. They wouldn't need them. The Cardinal responded to the Shaver long ball with three runs in each of the sixth, seventh, and eighth innings for a 9-1 win. The Cardinal hit three bombs, the biggest one being a three-run blast by senior Jack Klein. The communications major from San Francisco put the good guys on top, 3-1. Junior Quinn Brodey, who would be drafted in the third round by the Mets, and freshman Daniel Bakst hit back-to-back shots in the seventh to push the lead out to 6-1. But the real star of the game was Castellanos, who saved the bullpen, keeping those guys fresh for hopefully two games against Cal State Fullerton.

Freshman LHP Erik Miller of Wildwood, Missouri, got the ball in the nightcap against Cal State Fullerton. The science, technology, and society major, who stood six feet five inches, was 5-1 on the season in thirteen starts and four relief outings. Cal State Fullerton entered the contest with a 36-21 record. Stanford was 42-15, needing a win on this night and another the following night to host a super-regional.

Miles, who had grown two inches since Blake first met him, now stood at six feet six inches tall. The two had a chance to quickly visit ninety minutes before the first pitch. "I always forget you are a giant," said Blake. "Well, I've continued to grow. That whole 'you stop growing at fifteen' is bogus," explained Miles.

Blake then looked over to Greg, who had joined them.

Greg attempted to explain, "We believe there was a mix-up at the hospital when he was born."

Miller gave up a two-run shot to Scott Hurst in the second, giving the Titans a 3-0 advantage. Stanford got one run back in the home half of the second to cut the lead to 3-1. The star of the contest was Titan pitcher Colton Eastman, who went one out short of seven innings, giving up only two hits and a single unearned run. Chris Hudgins added a solo shot in the ninth for Cal State Fullerton, providing a little more cushion. The homer came off All-American Colton Hock.

Stanford wasn't about to go down quietly. They were fighting for their No. 9, for themselves, and for their university. The Titans went to their stud closer, Brett Conine, in the eighth inning. But he was good for another inning of work, seeking his fourteenth save of the season. The Cardinal mounted a rally against Conine, who gave up only six runs all season. But Brodey led the inning off with a triple down the right-field line. Bakst brought Brodey in on a grounder to short, reaching when Titan first baseman Dillon Persinger couldn't hold the bag. But Stanford could get no closer than 4-2, and the contest ended on a Klein groundout. Klein knelt just past the first base bag. Everyone understood his emotion; everyone understood his pain.

Nine's career was over, but not before he got a standing ovation from the Stanford crowd. The Cal State players and coaches also showed their respect with an ovation and tips of their caps.

Marquess was still proud of his team, a squad that had missed the postseason each of the two previous years. "I am very proud of the kids. I don't believe I've ever had a team win twenty-one of twenty-three games. They were so dedicated, had a great work ethic, and they got better and better."

It also marked the final appearance of Miles Fuller at Sunken Diamond. "I can't take this uniform off," he told his father. "I know I'm never going to put it on again, so I don't want to take it off."

Miles was going to stay back at the hotel with his dad but was pleased to see his Uncle Phil, who had also flown out from Sandy Springs, Georgia. Phil and Greg would share that room, and Miles would sleep in his bed if he slept at all.

His uncle tried to console him, "We didn't want this to end tonight, not like this. But you played four years for one of the greatest programs and got one heck of an education. And now you are going to play professional baseball," said Phil.

Marquess left the field with his wife, Susan. His glorious forty-one seasons included 1,627 wins and two national titles. Former Cardinal and current San Francisco 49ers general manager John Lynch summed things up best in a tweet. "Thank you, 9. The numbers are legendary, but the lessons you taught all of us who had the privilege of playing for you will last forever."

CHAPTER FOURTEEN

"There are no secrets that time does not reveal."

Jean Racine

The 2017 MLB Draft was held between June 12 and 14 in Secaucus, New Jersey. There were thirty-six first-round selections and 1,215 total selections. The first selection was Royce Lewis for the Minnesota Twins. The Twins selected first after finishing a league-worst 59-103 in 2016. Lewis was the California baseball high school player of the year and had been committed to UC-Irvine before signing with Minnesota.

Miles, now a Stanford graduate, knew he would be drafted but was unsure when. His poor play in his last four games of college didn't help his anxiety going into the draft. He was able to collect only one hit in the four regional games. He had attempted to see Brooke the day before the draft, but she had already left for the Bahamas with some sorority sisters.

Brooke was not the same person he knew before. Her partying at college continued to escalate. She sought more prominence and more recognition from her peers. She attempted to control the lives of those who were closest to her. For reasons unknown to Miles, she had developed a real problem with sincerity and honesty.

Miles was selected in the tenth round of the 2017 draft by the Milwaukee Brewers. He was assigned to the Carolina Mudcats in Zebulon, North Carolina, a Class A – Advanced team that played home games at Five County Stadium. The team began play in 1991 after the Mudcats relocated from Columbus, Georgia, to Zebulon, a suburb of Raleigh. The Mudcats received great support from the community, and a strong contingent of North Carolina State students and faculty regularly attended the games.

Miles remained with the Mudcats for the remainder of their 2017 season, failing to crack the starting lineup. The most single-game activity he experienced was as a defensive replacement in center field in the seventh inning of a road contest. He returned to Newnan in September, excited to be home for what seemed like the first time in four years. Orchard Hills was now closed. He planned to live with his parents during the offseason and train in nearby Peachtree City, Georgia.

Things did not work out well for Brooke at Auburn. Her life came to a crashing end six weeks into her senior year. But the downhill spiral started before the final night of her life; while drunk, she made a fatal decision to leave a bar with another intoxicated friend, Grace.

Brooke had so much promise as she entered Auburn. But she never jelled with her collegiate golf teammates. Her game never flourished. After three years of quality opportunities and tremendous instruction, her scores failed to improve, and remaining stagnant as the competition improves is not a good thing when it comes to golf.

As she was getting lapped on the golf course, her grades remained solid, but her performance in the classroom didn't do anything to lessen her desire for control over anything or other people. Because her golf game continued to unravel, it appeared she desperately tried to control other areas of her life.

Despite being in a top-notch sorority, Brooke struggled to make many friends. Her golf team commitment meant that her schedule was different from those in her sorority. She was aloof, distant from her parents and teammates, often crying herself to sleep. She had little self-confidence, and as her social life suffered, her golf game couldn't provide any pick-me-up. To overcome her feelings of isolation, her drinking continued to increase.

Brooke made bad decisions after bad decisions. The twenty-one-year-old decided in late September to leave the golf team. It was on that night that she made another horrible decision, putting her trust in Grace, a pretty blonde but the most dishonest person in her sorority. The most common thing Brooke and Grace shared was the love of manipulating others. A close second was alcohol. And it would cost them their lives. Despite the plea of Ellie, a far more responsible roommate of Grace, Brooke put her trust in a completely inebriated Grace. Ellie, honest and sincere, scared of potential danger, did all she could to prevent disaster.

Although Brooke told her not to, Ellie was leaving the apartment in her car en route to the bar to pick them up while on the phone with Brooke. "I can be there in four to five minutes," Ellie said, trying to convince the two to stay put. Ellie was valiant in her attempt to rescue the two girls. But like other previous behavior displayed by Brooke, this night was no exception. She liked to call the shots and have the control. Brooke had turned into a person who thought she knew what was best for her, resisting others' advice and dismissing even a caring gesture from someone with an exemplary character such as Ellie.

It was later discovered that Grace had a blood alcohol level of two and a half times the legal limit of the state of Alabama. That was obviously why she went the wrong way on a one-way road, a road she had traversed hundreds of times. If the two had just waited for Ellie, they would be alive today, with the potential to right their lives, give back, and do good in this world. Instead, Grace and Brooke took two others to hell with them, one instantly and another a few months later. University employees Alex and Jack were on the other end of the head-on collision. Jack, a male in his 40s, was killed instantly. He suffered massive head and chest trauma. Alex, a female in her mid-30s, was fortunate enough to survive the impact her Toyota withstood. But her spinal cord suffered damage beyond repair. Alex would never walk again. Complicating her recovery was the discovery that she and Jack had been embezzling money for years, taking bribes from parents of students for certain favors. Ashamed of the publicity after being caught and refusing to show remorse, instead of living her remaining days in a wheelchair, Alex opted to cowardly end her life with a single gunshot to the head. It was the loss of power and prominence. The loss of money as well. It was a reminder that people are brave when they have power. When they lose it, the truth comes out about who they are and what they value.

When Miles became aware of the tragic death of his former girlfriend, his only girlfriend, he was crushed, and certain memories of Brooke were triggered in his mind. He reminisced about the first time he saw her, the first date they shared, and all the time they spent on the phone, at the movies, and on the golf course.

Miles also thought back to the time the two were in his bedroom, and Brooke asked about a picture on his wall. The large photo was of someone he greatly admired, the amazing

Louis Zamperini. At the time of the photo, Zamperini was running track for the University of Southern California. It's odd how Zamperini's courage impacted Miles Fuller. As he faced USC baseball throughout his Stanford University career, he always thought of Zamperini, and it made him appreciate and respect the team and the university he was competing against.

Miles wanted Brooke to read the book *Unbroken* by Laura Hillenbrand, a wonderful look at Zamperini's epic life. Unfortunately, Brooke never got around to it. It was just another missed opportunity Brooke wasted in her short life.

The book did a great deal for Miles. Whenever he was in a bind or up against the wall, he drew inspiration from the perseverance that was required of Zamperini to survive. Louis Zamperini was an American treasure. He passed away in 2014 at the age of ninety-seven. A World War II bombardier in the United States Air Force, he survived forty-seven days adrift at sea following the crash of his B-24 due to mechanical failures. Zamperini, who finished eighth place in the 5,000 meters at the 1936 Berlin Olympics, was captured by the Japanese. He was moved to several different prisoner-of-war camps. Although resilient, he had no power. That dominance belonged to Mutsuhiro Watanabe, nicknamed "The Bird," a sergeant in the Imperial Japanese Army. Watanabe tortured American soldiers, especially Zamperini, due to his Olympic star status. Zamperini had to be remarkable to endure the pain just to survive.

Alex, in Auburn, did not have the courage of a Louis Zamperini. Like "The Bird," she was weak with no moral character. Watanabe couldn't face his punishment. When the war ended, he went into hiding instead of taking responsibility for his war crimes. Watanabe was a coward, and he had lost power and influence. Alex couldn't face the ramifications, joining Grace, Brooke, Jack, and Watanabe in hell.

Watanabe knew how to deliver torture on this earth. Unfortunately for him and the four others, they are now on the other end of the torment and for eternity in the lake of fire.

Zamperini has no bad thoughts of "The Bird" or any others. He resides now in a place where there is no death or sadness. His life changed forever in 1949 when he, at the age of thirty-two, attended a Billy Graham crusade. Zamperini became a Christian evangelist, devoting his life to leading others to heaven. Those who share his love of the Lord will be blessed to enjoy His presence in the new earth, the new heaven, the new Jerusalem.

CHAPTER FIFTEEN

"Enter through the narrow gate. For wide is the gate, and broad is the road that leads to destruction, and many enter through it. But small is the gate and narrow the road that leads to life, and only a few find it."

Matthew 7:13-14, *NIV*

Miles attended Brooke's funeral. It wasn't easy. It never is when things end like this. Too many things were left unsaid.

What was said by Miles was his failed attempt to witness to Brooke the final time he ever saw her. It was during the Christmas break of his sophomore year at Stanford. Brooke had only been in college for a semester but was a changed person. Her regrettable reaction to his attempt to speak about Christ shocked him. The romantic feelings he had for her were gone. It was clear to him that the two had no future, even as friends.

He attempted to console her parents. Death is inevitable. Sudden death is tragic and hard to comprehend. It's hard to fathom you will not see that person again. But Miles accepted, in his heart of hearts, that he was never going to see Brooke again. She wasn't in heaven, and he knew it. A survivor then lives with the guilt of not delivering the deceased to Christ.

It was also hard for Miles to forget how close he was to seeing her one last time, having just missed her before she took that sorority trip to the Bahamas.

Miles talked to twenty to twenty-five people at the funeral service, but ten minutes later, he couldn't recall any of the conversations. He was in a daze.

He wasn't alone. Those who spoke at the funeral struggled as well. The preacher started strong, but his words devolved into incoherent logorrhea that was hard to follow.

Miles returned home and was joined in the living room by his parents. It was hard for him to stay still. But nothing he could do was going to change the circumstances. Brooke was dead.

He told his parents he needed to be alone for a little bit to think and reminisce. What he needed was some sort of closure. At Stanford, when he needed to concentrate on his studies, he would seek out the library at the Hoover Institution or retreat to the baseball complex. Those venues served as a phrontistery, a place for thinking. The baseball complex offered a sanctuary for all members of the team to gather to study different assignments.

After a few minutes, he knew where he needed to be. He phoned Wyatt Detmer, his old boss at Orchard Hills.

"Wyatt. I know this is an unusual request, but do you still have the four-wheeler and trailer you once kept at the course?"

"I do," confirmed Wyatt.

"May I borrow it?" asked Miles.

"Sure. What's up?"

"I need to take it to the back of Orchard Hills, Brooke's favorite spot," explained Miles.

"That's pretty rough terrain," stated Wyatt.

The grass, weeds, and bushes had grown considerably since the course closed. Wyatt met Miles in the parking lot with the key to the four-wheeler. Wyatt had called the former assistant pro, Dano, to join him.

Wyatt asked, "Do you want company?"

"This is something I have to do for myself," Miles said.

"Just go slow," warned Dano.

Miles went slowly, trying to follow the old cart path as best as he could. He only had about forty-five minutes of daylight remaining. He was already shaken, but seeing the course in its current state of disrepair saddened him even more.

He stopped at the short bridge at the back of the course, overlooking the lake that he and Brooke had always visited. It was their spot when he was a senior, and Brooke was a junior at Newnan High School. Miles then got out and walked over to the area where she had once requested that he stand. She had wanted to remember him in that spot each time she played the course.

Now, it was time to pull the reverse. The baseball hitter in Miles viewed this as a pitcher attacking the batter in the opposite manner. The fastball pitcher gets ahead of the count with a first-pitch curveball. Miles looked back and could see them all those times in the golf cart together. He stared at the spot on the bridge for a good three minutes.

Then he reached into his Stanford windbreaker and pulled out a small white card. It was an old Orchard Hills course scorecard. He had kept this scorecard in his bedroom upstairs at his parents' house for five years. He and Brooke had used this as a makeshift scorecard from their first putting contest at Orchard Hills. The putting green was long gone. But this keepsake didn't belong on the practice putting green. It belonged on the corner of that bridge.

He folded the scorecard in half and placed it inside a plastic sandwich bag. He placed a rock he spotted nearby on top of the bag. He left the bag and the rock up against the front of the bridge. The scorecard showed Brooke -2 under par and Miles +6 over par.

He had written, "Just wait until next time."

She had added, "See first results. Same outcome."

And Brooke was correct. She would win each time.

Miles jumped back on the four-wheeler, thinking about his words on that scorecard, "Just wait until next time."

And once again, he was left to accept that there would be no other time. He was never going to see her again.

CHAPTER SIXTEEN

"I have not failed. I've just found 10,000 ways that won't work."

Thomas A. Edison

Robin Yount won two American League MVP awards in 1982 and 1989 for the Milwaukee Brewers. He spent his entire twenty-year career with the Brewers, playing shortstop and centerfield.

Yount was drafted in 1972 and made the Brewers the next year. Unfortunately for Miles, this centerfielder was not on the same career path. In fact, through 2019, Miles was still in Zebulon playing for the Mudcats. He wasn't playing every day, failing to hit above .260.

He told Greg after a game, "By the time I figure out the answer, the question has changed."

Miles never went into a deep slump, but he rarely got hot at the plate, either. He did have a talent for making the pitcher work. His keen eyes at the plate, his ability to foul off pitches, and his excellent defense finally led to a promotion in 2020 to the Brewers AA club in Biloxi.

As it turned out, Miles never played an inning in 2020 in Biloxi. The start of the 2020 season was initially delayed, and the season was canceled on June 30 due to the COVID-19 pandemic.

To limit travel in 2021, minor league teams played six games a week in the same stadium against the same opponent. Most teams had Mondays off. Opponents were those that were regionally close.

The Biloxi Shuckers were placed in AA South. After a rain-out, Biloxi opened the season in Birmingham on May 5 but was swept at Regions Field. The highlight of the 2021 Biloxi season was a combined no-hitter against the Mississippi Braves. Biloxi finished the season with a disappointing 45-69 record.

Miles once again failed to produce at the plate. He hit no homers and finished the year with a .234 average. Possibly feeling the pressure of being released from the organization, his frustration began to build.

Neither Greg, Celeste, nor his Uncle Phil could recall a time that Miles complained about balls and strikes. But toward the end of the 2021 season and for the majority of 2022, Miles questioned calls and disputed umpires' strike zones.

He got some strict advice from his Biloxi manager. "Your job, Miles, is to be a hitter, not an umpire."

He was now twenty-seven years old and fearful that the Brewers would soon cut him. He made the mistake of telling a local writer that he deserved more playing time. "I'm still progressing at the plate. No one on this team is better than me defensively. I deserve to be out on that field every day."

The manager read his comments in the paper and left Miles a note in his locker. "The performances of the players dictate who is going to be in the lineup." Miles understood the message. He didn't start another game and was limited to being a defensive replacement and only sparingly used as a pinch-hitter for the remainder of the season. His final appearance for Biloxi came on the last day of the 2022 season when he was to pinch-hit in the bottom of the ninth with his team trailing 3-2 with two outs and a runner on first base.

With the count 0-1, the opposing pitcher missed with consecutive sweepers way outside. The game was televised, and a commentator said, "Fuller, he's so tall. He's six feet seven inches. His shadow has been here for three days."

The other announcer countered, "I believe he could light a cigar off of a volcano."

As they continued to laugh, Miles drove a 91-mph four-seam fastball to the right field bleachers for a game-winning home run, his first homer in his final at-bat of the year.

In the spring of 2023, the Braves invited Miles to spring training as a free agent. Braves scout Alan Butts, who lived about ten minutes from the Fuller house, pushed for the opportunity. Miles had nine hits in forty-one plate appearances for the Braves in spring training. He listened to every bit of advice, every bit of information a veteran would share.

Although a hitter, he loved talking pitching, especially with Braves pitchers. He had just missed playing against Will Smith in high school. The lefty was four years older than him, also from Newnan, a graduate of Northgate High School.

Smith greatly helped the Braves win the World Series in 2021 over the Houston Astros. Smith didn't give up a run in the 2021 playoffs and won each of the first two NLCS games against the Dodgers.

But Smith, who had just won a ring with the Astros, was now signed to play for the Texas Rangers. Miles was no lock to make the Braves, but thought it would have been amazing to be teammates with a player from his hometown.

Miles' best spring training moment of 2023 came in Tampa against the Yankees at George Steinbrenner Field. The Braves took only two notable players to the road contest. Miles had nine hits in the spring, but four of them occurred that day in Tampa as the Braves beat the Yankees 5-2.

Although he failed to hit .250 in the spring, Miles remained hopeful that the Braves would sign him. The Braves had injuries to two key outfielders, and another was facing recent domestic abuse allegations, aggravated assault allegations, and a charge of DUI. The injuries, coupled with the questions concerning such destructive behavior from other players, gave the tall outfielder great hope. However, just three days before the season started, the Braves let the outfielder who played high school ball just down the road from Atlanta go. For the first time since he was four, April arrived, and Miles Fuller was not on a baseball squad.

CHAPTER SEVENTEEN

"Did my heart love till now? Forswear it, sight! For I ne'er saw true beauty till this night."

William Shakespeare (Romeo & Juliet)

Miles had earned enough money during his Biloxi playing days to comfortably rent a two-bedroom condo. No longer with the Brewers, he did not need to retain it.

The soon-to-be twenty-eight-year-old moved back in with his parents. "I've got to be the oldest child living in this neighborhood," he told one of his former Newnan High teammates.

Most of his Stanford teammates had moved on from baseball. Several had played minor league baseball, lasting one or two years before being cut. Others had made it four or five years. A few fortunate players had reached the ultimate stage.

Miles was down, dejected. But he wasn't willing to throw in

the towel just yet. But he also needed a purpose. Maybe baseball wasn't meant to be. After all, he had an economics degree from one of the most respected universities in the country. His craft didn't have to be limited to economics. Someone of his ability may have a degree in economics but be an autodidact when it comes to something else.

"Perhaps I will become a specialist in poverty or a master tennis player," he joked to his friend and East Coweta athletics director, Hap Hines.

One thing Miles could be was versatile. On the baseball field and off. He had protean skills that enabled him to adjust to many different things, and his intelligence helped him become a quick learner. He had strengths, like being able to discuss stamp collecting the first day he met Blake during his freshman year at Stanford.

Hap suggested substitute teaching while Miles was still training. To keep some cash coming in, Miles subbed two to three times a week. "I've got to be the only substitute teacher from Stanford in history," he made fun of himself.

He just didn't stop at East Coweta. He also filled in at Atkinson Elementary in Newnan and Smokey Road Middle School, as well as others in Coweta County.

The kids always couldn't get over how tall he was. Each time someone asked, "How tall are you?" the truth was that Miles really didn't know. He was somewhere between six feet six and six feet seven inches tall.

One crafty sixth grader told him, "Earthquakes and tornadoes have to go through his drills." Another student added, "I bet Santa Claus would wait in line to sit on his lap."

Substitute teaching turned out to be a blessing for the unemployed baseball player. Although Miles continued to train, believing God was not done with him in baseball, he was invited by FCA director Rob Brass to participate in Fellowship of Christian Athletes.

FCA distributed 230,247 Bibles in 2023 alone, staying true to their respectful mission of leading every athlete and coach to Jesus Christ. FCA has been delivering God's Word since its first camp in 1956.

Rob told Miles, "One of my favorite things I get to do is distribute Bibles. It is most rewarding, and I always remember how the kids appreciate them." Rob was a great mentor for Miles, and the platform for leading more people to Christ was given to him by Rob.

In addition to his work with FCA and the students he taught, the highlight of 2023 was a day trip with Hap Hines and two others to Augusta National for The Masters. The four went on Friday for the second round. The other two on the outing were Coweta County School Superintendent Dr. Evan Horton and Newnan High Principal Dr. Gamal Kemp.

The four decided to take a view from the bleachers behind the seventeenth green. Brooks Koepka completed his morning round, was the leader at the time, and had already finished before the bad weather arrived. The four chose to walk a few holes before heading out, hoping to avoid the inclement weather. They stopped at a concession stand for a couple of egg salad and barbecue sandwiches. Miles was paying the tab when he looked just over to his right and spotted a beautiful brunette, five feet nine inches tall and probably a bit too thin. Then it hit him. He had seen her before. It was the Stanford student who had given him a tour of the campus and the Hoover Institution when he was just seventeen years old. It was Stephanie Wilson, who, as he remembered, was from Augusta.

Without saying anything to his friends, he approached the woman, feeling confident it was Stephanie. "Hey, I hate to interrupt you, but are you Stephanie Wilson by chance?" She was shocked, alarmed. "Yes," she said in a volume that was a bit loud for a golf course. "Well, at least I was before I was married."

She still hadn't placed him. "I know you gave hundreds of tours at Stanford back in the day, but I'm Miles Fuller."

Stephanie interrupted, "The baseball player from Newnan."

The two then gave each other a hug, their previous interaction having been ten years prior.

Miles noticed she was not wearing a ring. "So, how is the married life?"

She answered, "The funny thing is my ex didn't understand when you got married, you are supposed to stop dating others."

"I'm sorry to hear that," said Miles. "And I have to say you are so thin, you could be used as a bookmark."

She laughed, "What can I say? It's the divorce diet. If you want to lose some pounds, get a divorce."

"I guess I'm glad I never got married," said the former Stanford baseball player.

Stephanie, now thirty, had married at twenty-four but divorced two years ago. Miles liked her quick wit.

She admitted, "I don't think I can lift one hundred pounds in England."

Knowing she was talking currency while poking fun at her struggles to eat with the stress of divorce made him laugh.

He looked back at the others, all ready to beat the incoming storm. "Hey, I've got to go. Can I get your number so we can get dinner or something?"

Stephanie smiled back, "How can I say no to a Stanford Cardinal?"

Miles agreed, "I have simple tastes. I only settle for the best."

Number in hand, he hugged her goodbye and then rejoined his friends. The four took about twenty steps, and then the horns sounded at Augusta National. The storm was minutes away, and play was suspended for the day.

CHAPTER EIGHTEEN

"Your talent is God's gift to you. What you do with it is your gift back to God."

Leo Buscaglia

A new relationship was good for Miles. It was only his second serious relationship. It was good for Stephanie as well. They traveled back to Palo Alto in May for a weekend baseball series just to enjoy the campus, the scenery, and the setting. There's an old saying out there that Stanford alumni don't believe they are better than you; they know they are.

Miles, now using the company Blake Zhu worked for as his representation, continued to engage in conversations with major league clubs. He also continued to substitute teach and traveled to Augusta twice a month to be with Stephanie.

He was stoked beyond belief to discover that her father,

Dale, was a member of Augusta National. Although he worked at a golf course, Miles wasn't a very talented golfer. Dale and Stephanie got him and Greg on the grounds to play two rounds in October. It was a gift few received. Greg, who had already met Stephanie, told Miles, "You have our permission to marry her."

Miles and Stephanie returned to Stanford in late October, just after the World Series. It was odd for Miles to see guys he had played with in spring training on such a national stage. The Braves were now the best team in baseball, competing in the N.L.D.S., and he could have been right there with them, but when given the chance the previous March, he failed to produce. And the Braves failed to advance past the N.L.D.S.

As their relationship grew and the calendar revealed Christmas was fast approaching, Stephanie suggested to Miles it would be fun if they each shared a Christmas tradition. Then, they could create new traditions as a couple.

So, on Friday, December 22, Stephanie decided it was time to put the plans for traditions in motion. While visiting his family in Newnan, she suggested, "It's time for you to decide what holiday tradition you want to share with me."

"I've thought about this for several days. I've thought about different options, and I've chosen for us to ride the Christmas Merry-Go-Round in Valley, Alabama, where my parents grew up."

"What's that?" she asked.

"A carousel. Reserved only for Christmas. It means the world to people who grew up there. Even if you move away, you do everything you can to get back and ride it each year. It's a tradition that people share with their kids and grandkids. It's festive. Some people even get engaged there," explained Miles.

"Are you going to ask me to marry you?" teased Stephanie.

He was quick to respond. "I guess you are about to find out. It's after 5:30 already. We have to go now to make it. It will take us a little less than an hour to get there."

"Yes, let's go tonight," said Stephanie, as if she wanted to get his part of the equation completed so they could get to her tradition. She would not reveal her decision until the visit to the merry-go-round had been completed.

The couple invited his parents to join them, but Celeste had already committed them to attend a neighborhood Christmas party hosted by the patriotic Norma Haynes.

Celeste did call her nephew, Jeff "Hack" Goodwin, to find out if he could meet them at the Christmas carousel. It would take Hack less than ten minutes to arrive in front of the old WestPoint Stevens' Langdale Mill, where the carousel was temporarily located each holiday season.

The Christmas Merry-Go-Round was given to the City of Valley in 1956 as a gift from West Point-Pepperell Inc. Greg and Celeste both rode it as kids when it was in nearby Fairfax, on a youth baseball field beside Fairfax First Baptist Church.

Seeing Hack, an older cousin of eight years, was a complete shock to Miles. Celeste was a good informant, notifying Stephanie by text that she had asked her nephew to surprise them. Stephanie kept it a secret, not revealing a thing.

The three rode the carousel twice, once on the horses and once on the sleigh, which was generally reserved for the older crowd. The crowd at the carousel was light, a low temperature of thirty-four degrees keeping a lot of people away.

When the night at the carousel was complete, the three went to Dairy Queen for some ice cream, specifically Blizzards. Hack chose Oreo, Stephanie selected chocolate chip cookie dough, and Miles took his usual M&M. After they finished the Blizzards, Stephanie suggested she and Miles return to Newnan.

"Why are you in such a hurry?" asked a confused Miles.

"This part, your part, of our tradition is done, completed. Now it's time for mine, and it's going to take us a good bit longer to get there."

Miles assumed they would be going to Augusta the next morning, but Stephanie had grander plans, "We are going to Munich tomorrow, actually Kitzbühel, Austria. But we fly first to Munich, then take the train to Kitzbühel."

Miles was not too willing of a participant. "Munich, then Austria...what? I can't be away at Christmastime," he emphatically told her, adding, "My mom will never understand."

Stephanie was one step ahead of him again. "I've been texting with your mom, and she's cool with it. She negotiated a deal with me."

"A deal with you?" asked Hack as Miles tried to process the events of the last few minutes.

Stephanie explained the details of the deal. "Celeste gave us her blessing, but we have to spend Christmas next year in Newnan."

Miles rocked back in his chair and paused for a few seconds, looking at both. "I guess I better find my passport," he said.

Stephanie beat him again. "Your mom already has it and has packed a few items for you too!"

"So, you are telling me the only person I know who is afraid of flying located my passport and has started packing my bag?"

Stephanie suggested, "I think she is pleased for you."

Miles looked over at Hack. "I thought it was peculiar back in April when, for the first time since I was four, I was not on a baseball roster. Then, a week later, I'm in Augusta, and I see Stephanie while I'm the only twenty-eight-year-old Stanford alumnus living at home. Now, I'm going to Germany and Austria for Christmas. Can you make sense of this?"

Hack didn't vocally answer but pointed to the five-foot-nine-inch Stephanie. Miles already knew the answer, but he asked anyway, "I don't guess we can take your dad's jet?"

She quickly replied, "Definitely not! But don't worry, he's paying for us to fly first class, just me and you."

He needed more assurance. "Are you sure there are first-class seats available?" asked Miles.

"One hour ago, there were four. Now there are two."

Miles responded, "Well, I guess I'm going to Munich tomorrow."

Confidently, she replied, "You haven't heard "O Holy Night" until you have heard it in German."

Then Hack wrapped up the conversation, singing a part of one of his favorite Christmas songs. "Sounds like you are going to *have a holly jolly Christmas. It's the best time of the year."*

Stephanie and Miles celebrated their first Christmas together in Austria. For the second time in his life, Miles was in love.

Stephanie's father, Dale, owned an updated and upscale cabin in Kitzbühel, one of the most famous ski destinations in the world. Kitzbühel is a favorite of the European wealthy, located just over sixty miles from Innsbruck and a short ninety minute train ride from Munich.

Miles and Stephanie spent five days in Kitzbühel, enjoying fine food, shopping, and meeting many English-speaking Germans who owned homes in the popular Austrian resort. Miles and Stephane enjoyed Kitzbühel so much that they planned to return the following month when the Hahnenkamm mountains would host the annual World Cup ski races, including the Hahnenkamm Downhill, the Super Bowl of ski racing.

Stephanie was right about the German rendition of "O Holy Night." The couple may have been in Austria on Christmas Eve, but the German version—sung at the stunning gothic Stadtpfar-rkirche Kitzbuhel Catholic Church—was about as beautiful as it got. In fact, it may have only been matched by the enchanting charm of the church, which sat comfortably on top of a small knoll, looking mirific with the mountains looming in the distance.

Kitzbuhel was founded in 1271, with the Stadtpfarrkirche constructed between 1435 and 1506. It featured a bright hue and a domed tower, and Miles found the high altar, large church hall, and pulpit extremely appealing.

Miles was moved by two imperative instances of the quick trip. He had a difficult time defining how rewarding it was for him to be that far away from home yet worshiping his Lord and Savior with so many other believers. Secondly, as he held the candle in front of him while "Silent Night" was sung, he later told his father, "If non-believers could experience that, I believe they would feel the presence of the Holy Spirit. If someone can't feel it at that time, that emotion, that electricity, I don't believe one ever will."

Miles and Stephanie were in Austria, but they discovered it was a small world after all. Walking in the downtown district of Kitzbühel, Miles was alarmed to see a familiar face. It was a former college opponent, Chris Duck.

Always outgoing, it was Duck who started the conversation. "I looked down the street. I thought it was you. The Stanford centerfielder, right, Fuller, something?"

Miles was alarmed and impressed to be remembered. "Yes, I'm Miles Fuller."

"You were the fastest player I ever played against."

"I appreciate that. It didn't help me when you hit that bomb out of Klein Field. What brings you here?"

"Last minute Christmas shopping. I practically live in Düsseldorf. I've traveled to Germany for my job over fifty times, and I've probably got almost that many trips to go."

Miles was curious. "What about baseball?"

"Serious back injury."

"Sorry to hear that. You were a hitter."

"And you?"

"Probably done. But wonderful to see you."

Another high point of the European outing was two stops at Schatzi Kitzbühel, where the two spent a combined four hours talking and drinking coffee. They shared the same corner table, which was tucked just past a window, offering partial privacy. The latter of the two visits occurred after the two had attended the Christmas Eve service.

"You know, Miles, there are other coffee shops in Kitzbühel," Stephanie told him.

"Of course. But I like this one. This is our spot," he said.

"I'm okay with it. That's that. This is our spot."

Then Stephanie suggested they wrap things up and walk back to the cabin, located less than a mile away. "This can very well be our spot, but I suggest we get going."

Miles was curious, "Why's that? Are you afraid to miss Santa?"

Stephanie laughed. "No, but the snow is picking up, and it's already after 5:00. The locals will tell you that you shouldn't be on these streets on Christmas Eve."

"Why is that?" he asked.

"I'm sure you know about the legend of Krampus."

Feeling relieved, Miles replied, "I do. Are you scared of Krampus?"

"No, I'm not. But Frau Perchta is a different story."

"Frau what?" he asked.

"Perchta. She goes back a thousand years. She's still a mystery; some believe a goddess, and most see her as a witch or as a demon. She holds a cane, but she tortures people at night during the holiday season."

Miles responded, "You remember when we were with Hack in the Valley just days ago? He started singing that we were going to have a holly jolly Christmas. You didn't say a thing about this Frau Perchta character. That was the time to mention this witch."

Stephanie made him feel even more uneasy. "Her nickname is the 'Belly Slitter.'"

Miles then agreed. "You are right. If this thing is coming out tonight, I don't want to meet her."

Like frightened kids, the two showed dauntless determination, traversing the snow and bitterly cold conditions and safely reaching the cabin.

"Be sure you lock that door," Miles told her.

Christmas morning arrived, and no Santa Claus had shown up. But more importantly, Frau Perchta had not visited either.

As shaken up as Miles was being in a foreign country and thinking about Frau Perchta, Stephanie was thankful she didn't share similar tales of other haunted holiday Austrian figures.

Stephanie woke up on Christmas morning, smiling as she watched her boyfriend sleep, telling herself, *"I will save "The Night Folk," "The Knocking Knights," and the legend of "Straggele" for other Christmas Eve trips to Kitzbühel. One Christmas Eve villain a year is one too many for this sweet boy lying beside me."*

Then, while he continued to sleep, she went to the Lord in prayer, thanking God for another shot at happiness, thanking Him for delivering a Savior on this, His birthday over 2,000 years ago. She completed her prayer with a request that, if possible, Miles be given one more shot at baseball so that he could use that platform to lead others to Christ.

Stephanie Wilson was no stranger to the oldest and most glamorous Austrian ski resort. She had been visiting Kitzbühel all her life, and following her divorce, the resort had served as a haven.

As Miles continued to sleep, his girlfriend decided to go on a short hike that would eventually take her to the Hotel Tiefenbrunner. The Tiefenbrunner is where her family stayed before her parents decided to purchase their place.

Stephanie had twice entered and completed the Kitzbühel cycling marathon held in early September, once while married and once after the divorce. The cycling marathon was a demanding 216-kilometer challenge across Brandenberg and the Alpbachtal Valley over the three mountain passes of Kerschbaum Saddle, Pass Thurn, and Gerlos Pass. It required an elevation gain of 4,600 meters, finishing at the summit of Kitzbüheler Horn.

Stephanie was fit, so the eleven-kilometer round trip walk to the Hotel Tiefenbrunner was not taxing. Since she had twice defeated the cycling marathon, she was contemplating entering the Kitzbühel Triathlon, which will be held in June.

In Austria, it was easier to get dinner reservations on December 25 than on the more celebrated December 24, and Stephanie wanted to book the restaurant at the Tiefenbrunner for dinner on that night.

It was late in the season, and the couple had missed the annual performance of the Wilten Boys' Choir. They were too late to take in most of the Christmas villages and had missed the Christkindl, the main gift-bringer, after the child for whom Christmas was named.

Initially, Stephanie wanted to take Miles back to the main square of Kitzbühel, where they could take a ride on a horse-drawn carriage or pay for a walking tour. The illumination from the holiday lights only enhanced the atmosphere of the walking tour.

This world-renowned ski resort had plenty to offer everyone. Stephanie arrived at the Tiefenbrunner and was pleased to book a dinner reservation at the Goldene Gams for 6:15 p.m. She walked around the venue and was reminded how much she missed the pool and sauna. It was still cold out, so she went to the bar to warm up with a Glühwein, an orange-infused spicy drink, best mixed with a dry red wine such as a Chianti or cabernet sauvignon.

Established in 1665, The Gasthof zum Pfandl was a historic alternative to the Tiefenbrunner. Hallerwirt and Skialm were quality places to eat and share fellowship. But the Hotel Tiefenbrunner felt like home. Just before Stephanie left the bar, a server informed her that there would be a 5:15 glockenspiel performance. This means "to play the bells." The glockenspiel produces a high-tuned sound that is bright and penetrating. It is played by striking the bars with plastic or metal mallets. Often confused for a xylophone, the glockenspiel is popular with orchestras and marching bands.

Stephanie could be convinced to skip the downtown walking tour so they could be back in time to hear "Carol of the Bells" on a glockenspiel, especially if the performance was accompanied by a piano.

Stephanie returned to her parents' place to find, alarmingly, that Miles was still sleeping. She leaned into him and shook him aggressively on the shoulder. It completely startled him. "What the heck are you doing?" he asked as he checked his pulse.

"Checking to see if you were alive. I wanted to make sure there wasn't some dead guy in the bed," she explained.

"Some dead guy?"

"Yes," she laughed.

"And if I were dead?" he asked.

"I would call your parents, make that your dad, and tell him to come get you."

"Gee, thanks."

The glockenspiel performance at the Hotel Tiefenbrunner was everything Stephanie had hoped it would be. After Miles ordered cream of mushroom soup and medium roasted beef for both, *he wasn't about to order the waiter-suggested venison,* he asked about Stephanie's history with the hotel.

"The first time I came here, I was five. I felt like this place was magical. There was all this snow. Look back to your right. The scenery is breathtaking. Those mountains are gorgeous," sighed Stephanie, looking the part of a local wearing an ivory cashmere sweater with black wool pants.

"I agree with you. I have enjoyed looking at that copse in the background, blowing slightly with the wind," he said.

"I am just glad you decided to wake up," said Stephanie as she sipped from another Glühwein.

"You mean harshly awakened. I could have slept all day in my torpid, lethargic state. I feel like an animal that needs to hibernate. It is so cold."

"Well, I am glad you went to California for college, though nights were not warm at Stanford."

"I am cold all the time. I may have never made the majors, but at least that saved me from freezing in Detroit or Boston."

"So, say you are done with baseball. We never talk about this, but what will you do long-term? You are too educated to be a substitute teacher. What is it that you want to do?"

"I haven't given up on baseball. So, that, as you know, is my priority. God will lead me where He wants me to be. It may not come straight from Him, but it will come, perhaps as a sign or advice from a Christian friend," said the baseball hopeful.

"This is kind of fun. A one-on-one press conference with you."

"Yes, the more you drink, the more you talk," he noted.

"Is that bad?" she asked.

"No, it is cute. That was probably an anomalous response and not what you expected."

"Speaking of cute, there are times when I just want to wrap my arms around you and hold you and never let any other girl get to you."

Miles smiled, but at that moment, the salad and entrees arrived at the same time. Then, the snow caught his attention, and he spotted a large terrace outside. "I bet that terrace is hard to beat when the weather is warmer," he said.

"Everyone wants to get out there. It gets booked first. We think we saw Hansi Hinterseer out there a few years ago."

"Who is she?" he asked.

"HE is probably the most famous resident of Kitzbühel. He is a former alpine ski racer turned singer, actor, and entertainer."

"Well, he may be the most famous resident, but once I am President of the United States, I will be the most famous visitor."

Stephanie started laughing. "Even if you are President, you might not be as popular as him here. They all but worship ski racing here, and he and Toni Sailer are locals."

"Ever seen this Toni Sailer on the terrace?" asked Miles.

"No. He died fifteen years ago, but he won three gold medals at the 1956 Winter Olympics."

"You know your ski racing."

"I know Kitzbühel. I love it here!"

He agreed, "I love being here with you."

"I am glad because I think you will be back many times."

With a gorgeous girl who loved Jesus and thought the world of him by his side, coupled with the beauty that Kitzbühel offered, it was not difficult to fall in love. Marriage, however, was not on the horizon. Stephanie was still not far enough removed from her divorce and not feeling the desire to be married again. That was okay with Miles. He adored her and was thankful for their time together but was still hopeful for one last shot at the majors.

To honor his commitment to FCA, Miles and Stephanie flew back to the States on December 27 so Miles could join Rob, the regional FCA Director, for an event in Atlanta. In a stroke of luck, Stephanie and Miles were in seats 1A and 1B. They were able to rest on the return flight, which ended up being helpful as the next few days were a whirlwind.

On Thursday, December 28, 2023, former NFL player David Pollack served as the keynote speaker for the 2023 FCA Bowl Breakfast, held at the Atrium Ballroom of the Atlanta Marriott Marquis. "I just know I'm not done with baseball," repeated Miles to Rob during the event. "But, if I'm wrong, it's worth it just to see one student accept Christ and say no to Satan."

On New Year's Eve, he received the most fortuitous news possible. The New York Yankees reached out and offered Miles an opportunity to attend camp as a non-roster invitee. The Yankees needed outfield help, and perhaps it was his impressive showing the year before in Tampa against the Yankees that registered with the most successful franchise in the history of sports. This was probably his last shot at making the show. The longer one is away from the game, the easier it is to miss one sort of like lending a friend money. The longer one goes without paying it back, the easier it becomes to forget about it.

Miles reported to Tampa on Valentine's Day. He was thankful it was the Big Guava. He knew Tampa; he was very comfortable there. He had been visiting his friend, Fred Blatchford, in Tampa for years. Fred had season tickets to the Lightning hockey games, and Miles was a frequent guest. Fred, in his early 60s, insisted he move in with him. "You can stay until they cut you. It won't be long," he joked with Miles.

Fred was rarely at home. If in town, he was training for the Ironman Triathlon, deep sea diving, or teaching others to scuba dive. He was one of the small percentage of individuals who have looked into the eyes of a shark. Not just a lemon shark or a nurse shark but also the unique hammerhead and the perilous bull shark.

The Yankees were going to give Miles a serious shot, a deep look. New York needed outfield help. Aaron Judge was all-world but had missed significant time in 2023.

Yankees outfielders had let too many opportunities pass them. Aaron Hicks was now in Los Angeles, Harrison Bader was now with the Mets, Giancarlo Stanton was struggling, and others that were given shots had come up short. The youngsters who had been called up in 2022 and 2023 were also inconsistent. The Yankees needed a speedy outfielder who could patrol centerfield so that Judge could play elsewhere.

New York opened its 2024 spring season in Lakeland against the Detroit Tigers. Lakeland is beautiful, especially the charming downtown district. Almost as gorgeous as that old English "D" on their classic uniforms. Miles was issued the No.14, took his customary walk to the warning track in center, and then returned to the clubhouse.

The new Yankees manager, Willie Randolph, had posted the lineup. Miles took a quick dekko at the lineup as Randolph walked up behind him. Miles was three months short of being twenty-nine years old, but Randolph still called him a kid.

"So, what do you think about the batting order, kid?"

"I think I'm playing centerfield for the New York Yankees!"

"Make the best of it," instructed Randolph.

"I will be setting the table for these guys, skipper."

Miles made the best of his opportunity, going 3 for 3, two

doubles and a single. One double should have been a single, but he noticed the lackadaisical approach of the Detroit left fielder. "It doesn't take talent to hustle," he later told reporters.

Miles continued to produce throughout the spring, hitting .322. His biggest mistake was a glaring base-running error against Pittsburgh. He was 4-4 swiping bags, but an adrenaline rush got the best of him on a sweet bunt down the line to third. Miles easily beat the throw to first, and the ball bounced behind the Detroit first sacker. Second base was in his vision, and he had it secured. But he tried to extend it to third before he saw the third baseman catch the oncoming ball a good fifteen feet before Miles arrived. The base running miscue did not escape his teammates.

"What were you thinking? Did you get confused? Did you think you were back in Little League, and you would just keep running until they tagged you?" asked a veteran player, laughing.

Take away that mistake, and it was an impressive spring. Miles, as he approached twenty-nine, was getting quicker. His sprint speed to first was 30.4 feet per second. "He's home to first in three seconds. How many extra hits is that speed worth?" Randolph asked general manager Jason Giambi. "He goes thirty feet in a second." The major league average for a competitive play was twenty-seven feet per second.

On March 26, Randolph called Miles into his office. The Yankees would be leaving the next day to open the season in Houston. "Miles, we are signing you, placing you on our forty-man roster. But I'm sending you to AAA Scranton to start the season. Coach Al can do great things for you there," said Randolph.

Miles was frustrated.

"Don't get down about this. You are still progressing; you will be in pinstripes soon," said Randolph.

Publicly, Miles took it better. He told a reporter, "I had the best spring of my life. Persistence is the key to success in every area of life. Today is part of the process. Gaining experience in the minors, there's a learning curve when it comes to this."

Miles called his parents. They could tell he was down, rather deflated.

"It can be a humbling game," said Greg.

Miles responded, "I have to be positive. Last year, I thought I was likely done. One day, I will reach the apotheosis of what I can do in this game. I believe it in my heart to be true."

Celeste replied, "That's an outstanding perspective."

After their phone call, Celeste turned to Greg and said, "Pennsylvania is a long way to drive."

Greg answered, "That's why we have planes."

CHAPTER NINETEEN

"You have to dream, whether big or small. Then plan well, focus, work hard, and be very determined to achieve your goals."

Henry Sy

March 27, 2024

The New York Yankees traveled to Houston for their 2024 season opener with great expectations for the upcoming season. With Randolph at the helm and Giambi as the general manager, the organization was determined to be back in the playoffs after the disaster that was 2023.

Division rival Tampa got off to another nice start, although not in the neighborhood of their 2023 start when they opened with a phenomenal 20-3 record.

A month into the season, the Yankees were down a couple of starting pitchers. The team had two of its top prospects, Victor

Hayes and Clint Parker, both in the lineup, but neither were hitting above .240. Hayes and Parker were not new to the majors. Both had been called up in 2022 and placed on the post-season roster. Both failed to contribute, as Houston swept the Yankees in four games. It was the Yankees' fifth straight ALCS defeat, the first team to unfortunately reach that mark.

Two months into the 2024 season, the Yankees were in third place. Management felt like they needed a boost. Ownership knew they needed one. Scouts were on the phone, working the iPad, and going to games across the country, seeking a player to give them a punch.

Another month went by; New York was still weighing options. The team was still looking up to others in the race for the East.

Miles wasn't hitting as well as he had hoped in Scranton, just .252 with two home runs. He was now hitting sixth in the lineup. Scranton was home on July 4. He arrived at the park at noon, talking with a couple of teammates he faced while at Stanford. One, starting pitcher Cole Crawford, invited him to join a couple of others at the Scrantastic Spectacular.

"What's the Scrantastic Spectacular?" asked Miles curiously.

"Big event to these people here. A concert tonight at 8:00 p.m. Fireworks follow at 9:30. I went last year. You'll enjoy it."

"I don't have plans. Count me in," replied Miles.

Coach Al then brought out the lineup card for the 3:00 p.m. matinee. Starting at center, hitting sixth, was No.14 Miles Fuller.

Miles had a great time at his first Scrantastic Spectacular. He got in at about midnight and phoned Stephanie to tell her good-night. Stephanie, who ran her dad's foundation, was nice but had to remind Miles that tomorrow was a workday. "Talk to you tomorrow, Miles."

Miles picked things up a little after the Fourth. He was bunting more, attempting to put pressure on opposing defenses. Coach Al also allowed him to swipe more bases. It's a heck of a thing to see a six-foot-six-inch-tall player with that much speed. As one visiting broadcaster noted, "He's so tall. His barber likely gets a nosebleed."

Miles had become a professional base runner. He gave himself an edge, attacking the ground. He knew he couldn't allow his feet to get underneath himself. It would hamper his performance.

A month after the Fourth of July, Miles had a twenty-one-game hit streak. It was now August 6. The Yankees, the big club, were struggling and looking up at Toronto, Baltimore, and Tampa in the standings.

The 2023 season got away from the Yankees. They did nothing at the trade deadline to help their chances outside of acquiring a decent reliever from the White Sox.

2023 also saw the end of another New York milestone. Domingo German had thrown a perfect game in Oakland. The Yankees had won the World Series every year that they had a pitcher throw a perfect game. Don Larsen in 1956, David Wells in 1998, and David Cone in 1999 all delivered perfect games. The 1956, 1998, and 1999 Yankees went on to take the ultimate prize.

To add insult to injury, German would soon be gone, seeking treatment for alcohol issues. The 2024 version of the Yankees was slipping in the standings. It was time to make a move. Past time.

CHAPTER TWENTY

"I didn't pay attention to times or distance, instead focusing on how it felt just to be in motion, knowing it wasn't about the finish line but how I got there that mattered."

Sarah Dessen

August 9, 2024

Following a disappointing blowout loss to Syracuse, Miles was asked to report to Al's office. It was a moment he would never forget.

Coach Al was not in the best mood. While his boys were playing poor baseball, some moments never got old for a manager in the minor leagues. Miles slowly walked in, and Al sat up, extended his right hand, and said, "Miles, I've loved having you here this season, but the big club called. Judge got hurt tonight against the Royals. He's lost for the season. Miles, this is your time. Congratulations!"

Miles was too shocked to celebrate. Plus, he, like everyone else, was a fan of the face of baseball. While he was pleased and deserving of this enormous honor, Miles also understood the significance of what Judge meant to the team, to the game, and to the state of New York.

Al told Miles to get his belongings because he would be headed to the airport soon. "Whatever else you need will be shipped to you. I'm going to hug you because you won't be back," said the Scranton manager.

Miles was a punctilious individual. He showed great attention to detail. Generally, his minute attention to detail was well-served and expected. On this night, he was still trying to process the moment. But this felt different. Did he hear Coach Al correctly? Rarely did he feel confused or incoherent.

It took him ten minutes to locate his cell phone, although it was in the same spot as always in his locker. When he arrived at the airport, he got his parents on the phone. "Mom, put me on speaker. I'm going to the show! I'm going to be a New York Yankee!"

As his parents attempted to grasp the moment, Miles felt a tap on the back of his left shoulder. "Mom, Dad, I need to go. I will call you right back."

The tap on his shoulder came from Brendan Beck, the younger brother of Tristan Beck, a teammate of Miles at Stanford. The Beck family is a Stanford legacy. Brendan, now a part of the New York organization, was also a Stanford graduate, playing four years for the Cardinal. A right-handed pitcher, Brendan had just been called up to Scranton.

"I hear the No.14 will be available," said Brendan.

Beck finished his Stanford career with 289 strikeouts in 289 innings pitched, winning twenty-two of thirty-two decisions with an ERA of just over 3.00. Brendan's mom and sister were also Stanford alumnae. He was now only one step from joining his brother, three years his elder, and currently performing well for the San Francisco Giants.

Miles phoned back his parents, got news to Stephanie, and talked to Blake. His Uncle Phil was the first to phone him. After that conversation, he knew he needed to call his high school coach, Kenny Morris, and his youth baseball coach, Mike Furbush.

As he was boarding, he got his former Orchard Hills boss, Wyatt Detmer, on the line. Detmer then used three-way calling to reach his former assistant, Dano. Miles then had to go, but he asked both to call Esther and Beatrice. "I will tell them the great news," said Dano.

Upon his arrival at Yankee Stadium, Miles was greeted by two equipment employees. The first stop was the locker room. It's almost impossible for a first-time big leaguer to define the feeling of seeing his jersey hanging in his locker. Miles was stunned and slowly approached the locker. The centerfielder softly touched the sleeve of the No.14 uniform, almost testing to see if it was real. He said out loud, "No jersey has ever looked this good."

Yankee reliever Clay Holmes was the first teammate to officially welcome him to the club. "I see you don't need to shave. When I got word that I was traded here from Pittsburgh, I remember telling my wife I needed to go buy a razor," said the Yankee closer. Holmes' wife, Ashlyn, was an Auburn graduate, and since Clay was once committed to playing college ball at Auburn, considering the connections Miles had to Auburn, it became easy for the two to bond.

Miles was then told to go see the skipper, as in Willie Randolph, the much-maligned first-year manager of the struggling pinstripes. Back in the spring, he liked Randolph from the start. Randolph played twelve glorious seasons for New York, winning two World Series (1977, 1978) as a player and then four more on the staff of Joe Torre. After eleven years as a Yankee assistant, Randolph was hired in 2004 to manage the Mets. He lasted less than four years, although he compiled a record of 302-253. He had coaching positions with the Brewers and Orioles, but outside his involvement with the United States in two World Baseball classics and another international competition, Randolph had not been in coaching since 2011. As far as his character, he was a good man, a family man, with ideal morals and values.

The native South Carolinian told Miles, "I know you are highly intelligent, a Stanford alum. I need you to be a smart, smart ball player. We need something or someone to ignite us."

Miles responded, "I'm honored to be here, thrilled to play for you. I have family in Orangeburg right by you. I want to make an impact and be that catalyst you speak of. I won't take this opportunity for granted. I will be ready. When I'm in center, our scouting report becomes my Bible. I'm always erudite and informed."

Randolph replied, "To that point. You are not in the lineup tonight, but be ready offensively and defensively."

"And Miles, be careful with the vocabulary. Remember, this is a locker room, and I expect the press will love you," he said sarcastically.

"Yes, sir."

As he started to walk away, the manager admitted. "Miles, I'm going to be honest with you. We seem to find new ways to lose all the time. Now Judge is gone for the season. You are an academic. If lessons are learned in defeat, our team is getting a great education, like a Ph.D."

Miles returned to his locker and shook hands with a few of his new teammates. Then he just looked up at 'Fuller' on top of his locker. It was a moment he would not forget.

Then he noticed a note inside his locker, no bigger than the scorecard he left up against that bridge at Orchard Hills. It was folded over and brief. It simply read:

Hey, welcome to the club. Now have fun.

Hope to see you tonight. Nice to have another local in the show.

Will

The Will was Will Smith, the closer of the Royals, who had graduated from Northgate High School, just off I-85 North, where he had played for the legend Greg Hamilton. A nice gesture from the opponent. A thoughtful gesture from a friend. Smith made baseball history in 2023, becoming the first player to win three consecutive World Series with three different clubs, capturing the title with the Braves in 2021, the Astros in 2022, and the Rangers in 2023.

Six weeks remained in the summer. Seven weeks were left in the season. Autumn was just around the corner, and scoreboard-watching was a nightly ritual. The Yankees were not contending in the American League East.

Compliant with tradition, during warmups, Miles rushed out to the centerfield fence at Yankee Stadium. He studied it, the grass, the warning track.

If the Yankees were going to contend for the playoffs, they were going to need to make a comparable push to the level of the 1934 Yankees. This team was going to need Miles to make a similar impact to that of New York outfielder George Selkirk in 1934. To this point, their paths were eerily parallel. Selkirk made his major league debut in 1934, finally called up to the majors after seven years in the minors. In just forty-six games, with only one hundred ninety-two plate appearances, Selkirk contributed thirteen extra-base hits and thirty-eight RBIs. The outfielder hit over .300 in five of his nine major league years, appearing in six World Series while winning five (1936, 1937, 1938, 1939, and 1941). His only loss was in his last one, 1942.

Selkirk was twenty-six when he made the majors. Miles was now twenty-nine. Selkirk got the call in late July 1934 after Yankees left fielder Earle Combs sped after a deep ball at Sportsman's Park in St. Louis, hitting the concrete wall and fracturing his skull.

The Canadian also is noted for saying one year after reaching the majors, in 1935, that there should be a cinder path at least six feet from the outfield wall. It would serve as a signal to let the outfielder know he was off the grass and dangerously close to the wall. Major League Baseball implemented the warning track in 1949. Selkirk's 1936 Yankees went 102-51-2 and won the American League pennant by an astounding 19 ½ games. As Miles looked out at the current standings on the scoreboard, it hit him. The Yankees had almost as big of a deficit as the 1936 team triumphed.

CHAPTER TWENTY-ONE

"I want to thank the Good Lord for making me a Yankee!"

Joe DiMaggio

In March 2021, when a tornado ravished his hometown of Newnan, then Braves reliever Will Smith did all he could to help the area begin to heal and recover. Smith is a class act, and he modeled that behavior following the World Series win of 2021. He signed as many autographs as possible, even joking with a friend, "I'm saving everybody's Christmas!"

Smith was now out on the mound, needing one out to secure a Royals 3-1 win at Yankee Stadium. He had his back to home plate when he heard, "Now batting for the Yankees, No.14, Miles Fuller." It was time for Miles to make his long-awaited debut, and what a moment for Newnan and Coweta County, as Fuller's first plate appearance would be a face-off against another local in Will Smith.

This was an apropos moment for Smith. He made his debut at Yankee Stadium as the Royals starting pitcher in May 2012. The first batter he faced was Derek Jeter. Yes, that Derek Jeter. Smith induced Jeter to ground out.

In a class move, as Miles approached the box, Smith tipped his cap to Fuller. The Yankee did the same, though it shocked him. Miles didn't even see the first sweeper that fortunately stayed outside. He was too busy reflecting on the tip hat exchange and how it reminded him of the gesture by the Cal State Fullerton team done in honor of Stanford coach Mark Marquess in 2017.

The second pitch was a curve low and outside. Miles wasn't ready for it either. That moment in 2017 reminded him that he had failed to call the Stanford great, a man known as 'Nine' after Miles' promotion.

Miles, known to take a great deal of pitches, was hoping Smith would serve up a gopher ball for a hometown friend. But he also knew the Yankees needed a base runner to bring up the tying round.

Miles fouled off the next two breaking balls, one high and the latter down the middle of the plate. Smith wasn't going to make it easy on him. The next pitch, a slider, missed inside. The count was now full, and Smith had gone high, low, inside and out. Miles had plenty to think about. Smith threw his best curve of the sequence next. Miles saw it, was on it, and drove it opposite field to right, but it came up thirty feet short of the warning track.

Miles and Derek Jeter had something in common. Both failed to reach in their opening at bat against Will Smith. But the similarities ended there. Miles had played one game in pinstripes with one plate appearance. The great Jeter ranks first in Yankees history with 2,747 games played, 11,195 at-bats, 3,465 hits, 358 stolen bases, 544 doubles, and 29 leadoff home runs.

The following day went no better for the Yankees or the offense as Kansas City left town with a 7-2 victory. Miles did not play.

Randolph, knowing the team was in dire need of turning things around, showed agitation when talking to reporters. "Our goal, we aim to win every game. We just aren't getting it done right now."

Then, he was asked to comment about the struggles of the offense. "We have to hit better; we have to pitch better."

The Yankees were now headed to Chicago to face the White Sox. The team was thirteen games out of first place, injury-riddled, and struggling to score.

Yankee ace Gerrit Cole was asked about what he expected over these next six weeks of summer, seven weeks of the season. "We are going to turn things around. I have no doubt in my mind. At times, it's good to get out on the road. I'm looking forward to getting to Chicago."

Miles had limited time to see his father after the final out was made. "I know this is not how you envisioned things, beginning 0-2 after two games," said Greg.

Miles shook his head. "No, but this is the real world. I'm an adult, and you and Mom can't provide those halcyon times from my childhood. Those are happy memories, free from the pressures of adult life."

His father gave him something to think about. "Don't get caught up too much in this that you miss the moment. You have made it to the highest stage. You have gone from subbing in for teachers last year to now playing for the New York Yankees."

Miles hugged his dad. "Thank you, and thanks to both you and Mom for getting me here."

Writing notes and cards, often sending them in the mail, was important in the Fuller household. "There's not a day that goes by in your life that you shouldn't write something down, whether it be in a journal or a note for someone," Miles remembered Celeste telling him when he was about thirteen years old.

Her advice to him when he was beginning high school still resonates to this day. "As a Christian, Miles, you have a responsibility, a duty to lift others. We have enough people in this world trying to tear people down, so encourage others. Always encourage others." Celeste instructed her son to read 1 Thessalonians 5:11: "Therefore encourage one another and build each other up, just as you are doing."

Miles took her advice to another level. He decided to handwrite that scripture and place it on the wall just to the right of his bed. Not a day went by that the baseball hopeful wasn't reminded to encourage and lift others, practicing epistolography, much to the delight of his mother.

Many of his cards in his senior year of high school had gone to Brooke. Since the breakup following his freshman year in Palo Alto, it was Celeste, his father Greg, Phil, and those LaChance brothers (all officers of the law) who received the most.

Before he departed for Chicago, Miles had an assignment for his father.

On this night, Miles handed his father the following note to be given to his mom.

Mom,

Thanks for all the practices you got me to and back. Thanks for the ice cream, the bubblegum, and all the times you washed my baseball jerseys. See, I am still writing notes, thanks to your influence.

Love,

Miles

Miles embraced Greg again. "I love you, Dad," said the Yankees centerfielder to his father.

Greg responded, "I am so proud of you, Son. You are The One!"

CHAPTER TWENTY-TWO

"I need to make sure that when I am finished playing baseball, I can provide for my family. I don't want to be just a dumb jock. I want to be a businessman, somebody that understands the economic ways of the world, and I can use baseball as a way to launch myself into my next career."

Thurman Munson

August 12, 1987

Every Atlanta Braves baseball fan should celebrate this day. Annually. Why? The Braves made their best trade in franchise history on this day.

The Braves sent veteran pitcher Doyle Alexander (5-10, 4.13 ERA) to Detroit for an AA pitcher named John Smoltz. Smoltz was 4-10 at the time with an ERA of 5.68, playing for Glenn Falls. Smoltz would debut at Shea Stadium against the Mets on, of all days, Tom Seaver Day. Smoltz was outstanding in his debut, tossing eight innings and yielding only one earned run while striking out two and walking one.

Smoltz would win 213 games over his twenty-two years, saving 154 games. He was the first pitcher in Major League history to win over 200 games and eclipse the 150-save mark.

Smoltz, the first-ballot Hall of Famer, shares the same birthday with Miles Fuller, both born on May 15. Smoltz was born in Warren, Michigan, in 1967, while Fuller was born twenty-eight years later in 1995, the same year Smoltz won his only World Series title.

The former Atlanta great is also known for being a remarkable golfer and national baseball broadcaster and for giving back to the game of baseball by instructing youth. Miles once attended a clinic Smoltz performed at Fayette County High School in Fayetteville, Georgia.

The 2024 version of the Braves was just as dominant as many of those wonderful Atlanta teams of the 1990s. On August 12, the division was secure. Most believed it would be either Atlanta or Los Angeles representing the National League in the World Series come October.

Ronald Acuña Jr. was the reigning National League Most Valuable Player. Despite the fireworks of the 2023 Braves, the 2024 team was even more explosive, with a healthier pitching staff. The Braves were determined not to exit the playoffs early this time around.

The Braves also acquired sensational lefty Chris Sale in the off-season and added 2024 All-Star starter Lawrence Hamberlin from the Padres at the trade deadline, bolstering a loaded lineup. Braves closer David Hodo had only twenty-two saves, mainly because Atlanta was rarely in three-run games or less.

The biggest addition to the 2024 Braves was catcher

Hernando Fernandez, a Yankees killer when he played from 2015 to 2023 for the Kansas City Royals. For years, different Yankees speculated that Fernandez was using performance-enhancing drugs. Yet, Fernandez, loved by the team he suited up for but hated by all others, never failed a drug test.

On August 12, 2024, thirty-seven years after Smoltz made his Atlanta debut, the Yankees were in Chicago watching highlights of another Braves win before they took the field against the White Sox. Rumors were rampant about Fernandez cheating. Miles told Yankee shortstop Jorge Lopez, with whom he became close in the spring of 2023, "If Biden and the Democrats want to get serious about fentanyl and the border, they should speak to Hernando. Who better to talk about the ongoing drug problems facing our nation? He's got a direct line to the cartel."

Lopez agreed with him. "We call him a counterfeit Casanova in Mexico. His friends drive themselves into catatonic stupors."

Miles was in the lineup, hitting ninth, after not getting a hit in his MLB debut against Kansas City and Will Smith. Facing hard-throwing Stormy Weathers of the White Sox, Miles crushed a 2-0 fastball down the right field line in the fifth inning of a scoreless game, with the New York dugout securing the souvenir for Miles. Fuller would finish the night 2-3, adding a seventh-inning single in the 3-1 Yankees win.

New York needed to win *every single game*. The Yankees' offense woke up a night later, posting four runs before Miles even came to the plate. Miles would extend his hitting streak to two games with a two-run double as New York cruised to a 7-1 win in support of Yankee starter Jason Harbison, who went six innings for the win.

The Yankees leaned on ace Gerrit Cole the next afternoon. Cole, coming off his Cy Young Award from 2023, had spoken about being ready to get to Chicago. Cole knew what he was talking about, throwing seven shutout innings. The New York bullpen was a bit shaky, but the Yankees prevailed 4-3 to sweep the series.

Randolph gave Miles the day off. Considering the team had an off day the following day, Miles didn't like it, but he wasn't about to address it with the Yankee skipper.

The Yankees were now 11 ½ games behind Toronto, still eight out of the final A.L. wildcard.

Miles spent a great deal of his offseason time over the last seven years in Auburn. He first met former Auburn mayor Bill Ham when Miles was still in high school. Newnan was playing at Auburn High in a baseball game, and Fuller complimented the mayor's ability to throw his ceremonial first pitch right down the middle.

"Can you help us tonight?" asked Miles.

"I wish I could," said the mayor.

Following the Auburn High 4-3 win, Miles decided to ride back to Newnan with his parents. As fate would have it, his parents suggested dinner at Amsterdam Café, and they were seated in a booth next to the mayor and his wife, Carol. A friendship began that night that has only strengthened through the years. Miles also grew close to the couple's son, Forrest, now forty-one, a successful businessman himself. Forrest, Bill, and Miles have taken guys' trips over the years to Auburn sporting events, beach outings, and other adventures, preferring to travel in the skies. Stephanie had joined them on one of the beach trips and, in return, had invited father and son to join her and Miles in a round of golf at Augusta National.

So, as the team arrived in Detroit to take on the Tigers in two days, Miles had an idea of a worthwhile off-day activity. He called Forrest, who was in Detroit to see Miles play, to inquire about taking his plane to Canton, Ohio. "Is it possible? We would like to go over to Canton for the afternoon," he explained.

"Let me check into it," said the frequent flyer.

Miles, pitcher Jason Harbison, and shortstop Jorge Lopez were interested in flying to Canton to pay respects to former New York Yankee captain and legend Thurman Munson. Munson was killed in August 1979 when the Cessna Citation he was piloting crashed at the Akron-Canton Regional Airport while Munson was practicing takeoffs and landings with two others. Munson had bought the plane so he could fly home on off days. On this day, Munson had completed three touch-and-go landings. However, on the fourth landing, the flaps were not extended, and the aircraft sunk too low, hitting a tree and falling short of the runway.

The other two passengers survived, but they were unable to extricate the Yankee catcher. The Yankees honored Munson the following night at home against Baltimore, rallying for a 5-4 win on national television. The Yankees immediately retired the No.15, and his jersey remains hanging in his locker at the Yankees Museum. Munson was the American League MVP in 1976 and helped the Yankees win it all in 1977 and 1978, the twenty-first and twenty-second titles in team history.

Miles would admit there was some trepidation, flying into the same airport where Munson lost his life. But he had complete confidence in Jerry, the pilot, and Jerry delivered a beautiful landing.

Miles, Jason, and Jorge took an Uber ride to Sunset Hills Burial Park on Everhard Road in Jackson Township. Fans frequently visited Munson's grave, often cleaning the marker with towels, rags, and window cleaner. On this day, several baseballs and a bat were at his grave, Lot number 6 in Section 1. The stone includes a topper piece with an image of Munson in his Yankees pinstripes, holding a bat in his left hand. Inscribed below is "Thurman Lee Munson, captain of the New York Yankees from 1976 to 1979". On the back is his jersey number. As Miles saw that, he couldn't help but think he was next to Munson numerically. The base of the stone shows his birth and death dates. Then, as the three read the inscription at the top of the base, they all got chills. It reads, "Thurman Munson was exactly what he wanted to be. A devoted husband, a loving father, a respected man, and one very fine ball player."

To this day, the Yankees remain close to his widow, Diana. On the flight back to Detroit, Harbison suggested, "Do you know how we honor Mr. Munson and his family?"

Neither of the other two responded, thinking Harbison was being like a college professor, asking a question and then waiting a couple of seconds to reveal the answer.

"We just don't make the playoffs. We win the East; then we win the ALCS; then we win the World Series."

Miles and the two others returned to Detroit just as it was getting dark. Speaking of people with private jets, there was a surprise waiting for him, the best surprise.

Right there in front of him, in the lobby of the Westin on Washington Boulevard was Stephanie Wilson herself. What single twenty-nine-year-old American boy wouldn't want a striking brunette waiting for him at his hotel?

After getting over the initial shock, he approached her, arms pointing out to her, and recalled one of the signature lines from his favorite movie, *Casablanca*. A raconteur he was not, but he gave it his best shot. "Of all the gin joints in all the towns in all the world, she walks into mine."

CHAPTER TWENTY-THREE

"The time is a critical one, for it marks the beginning of the second half of life, when a metanoia, a mental transformation, not infrequently occurs."

Carl Gustav Jung (Symbols of Transformation)

Miles Fuller and Jason Harbison knocked on the door of Yankee manager Willie Randolph the next morning at 10:00. Jason told Randolph about the epiphany the three Yankees had the evening before.

"We don't want to just make the playoffs. We want to win our division and take it from there," Harbison told him. "We want to win it for Munson and his family. You played with the man. He always went all out. Right, Skip?"

"He was our leader. He was our heart. Thurman loved our team, and he loved being a Yankee," confirmed Randolph.

"Will you say something to the guys today before we take

the field? I'm not even a rookie, so I don't feel like I have much clout in the room to say anything," offered up Miles.

Randolph started laughing. "Aren't we a trio? I was born in Orangeburg, South Carolina. Miles, you lived in Orangeburg for several years. And Jason, you are from Cullman, Alabama. If our schoolteachers could see us now, constructing schemes, strategies, and all."

Miles responded, "I would rather be from the Deep South than from up here any day. It's too close to Canada. It's too like Canada. It's cold and easy to forget that it exists."

Randolph smiled, "I will speak to the team."

Miles came back, "Give them a metanoia, a change in direction. Instead of changing the direction of our lives, we are on a mission to turn our season around. God will be with us!"

Harbison said to both, "It sounds good to me, the metanoia."

Randolph hesitated, then asked, "If that doesn't work?"

Miles suggested, "Then we present them with an organon."

Jason was honest, "I'm afraid I'm not sure what that means."

Miles cleared things up, "We offer them an instrument of thought, a system of logic, a means of reason."

Randolph paused, "Let's just win some ball games."

Miles started to walk out of the room, "How about operant conditioning? It's a learning process in which behavior becomes modified by reinforcement, usually associative."

The coach had the best advice yet, "Let's just take it one game at a time."

Harbison and Fuller were walking down the hall, Harbison two years younger at twenty-seven. Harbison said, "You know, you would think as smart as you are, you would have gotten here, to the majors, before the age of twenty-nine."

The two had bonded, perhaps due to their southern roots, in

the one week Miles had been with the club, so Harbison felt comfortable saying something like that.

Miles answered, "You see, the thing is, when I'm at the plate, no one tells me before you pitchers throw it if it's going to be a fastball, curve, or change-up."

Harbison chuckled, "Isn't hitting, at least half of it, guessing?"

Miles agreed. "Like I've said to others in the past, by the time I figure out the answer, the pitcher changes the question."

Miles and Stephanie went for a walk, sat in a nearby park, and caught up over coffee. Stephanie was learning to enjoy baseball. "I had watched maybe two games before this time last week. In the last six days, I've seen five games," she said.

"Hey, it beats the heck out of watching depressing news or unrealistic movies," responded the baseball player.

"And I've got a surprise for you tonight," she teased.

"What is it?" he anxiously asked.

"Now, if I told you, it wouldn't be a surprise."

He was thinking of black lingerie or something seductively red. That covers two of the three Stanford colors. Lingerie, something seductive? He was so far off; he wasn't even in the ballpark.

It was August 16, the 76th anniversary of the passing of the immortal Babe Ruth, who died in New York at the age of fifty-three. Ruth was so popular that thousands of locals kept vigil outside the hospital over his final few days. There was such a demand to see Ruth that the slugger was placed in an open casket in the rotunda of Yankee Stadium for two days.

Nearly 80,000 people paid tribute to him at Yankee Stadium.

Another 75,000 waited outside his funeral service held at St. Patrick's Cathedral. His 1948 funeral was led by Cardinal Francis Spellman. Ruth is buried next to his second wife in Hawthorne, New York.

The 2024 Yankees were hoping to bury the Detroit Tigers. The 2023 Yankees were reeling when they went to Detroit for four games over the final four days of August. The Yankees won the first three, and a dramatic three-run homer by Anthony Volpe in the top of the ninth tied the last game at 3-3, forcing extra innings. With the home run, the young Yankee star made history, becoming the first Yankee rookie to hit at least twenty home runs with twenty stolen bases. The Yankees lost in ten innings, 4-3, denying New York its first four-game sweep at Detroit since 1926.

After a spirited locker room discussion, something seemed different about the 2024 version of the Yankees. They were almost arrogant after Randolph and Harbison talked about Munson, and this team had no reason to be arrogant.

But that air of confidence carried out to the field. Miles Fuller went hitless, but on the anniversary of the passing of Ruth, the Yankees blasted Detroit 9-3.

It was still a winning night for Miles because before the contest, as he walked in from checking out the Detroit warning track, he glanced over to the New York hospitality seats.

He spotted his stunning girlfriend, Stephanie. No, she wasn't wearing any black lingerie, nothing red. She looked sexier. She had never looked better. There she was in a pinstripes jersey, quickly turning around to showcase the No.14 and the name Fuller on the back.

The diapason of the moment registered with him. Like a young child being stampeded by a herd of Heffalumps, it overcame him. He stopped in his tracks. For the first time, he could hear the sounds of the ballpark and smell the hotdogs and spilled beer. He took his dad's advice. He took it all in. Miles could grasp the entire range, the scope of his achievement. Miles Fuller was a Major League baseball player. Miles knew then he was never going back to the minor leagues. He was here to stay.

CHAPTER TWENTY-FOUR

"If you meet a thief, you may suspect him, but virtue of your office, to be no true man, and, for such kind of men, the less you meddle or make with them, why the more is for your honesty."

Dogberry, William Shakespeare (Much Ado About Nothing)

The Yankees extended their winning streak to five the following night with a thrilling 2-1 victory. It was only fitting that Anthony Volpe was the hero. As mentioned, in Detroit the year before, on August 31, the New York Yankee cranked a game-tying three-run homer in the ninth, becoming the first Yankee rookie to hit twenty homers and steal twenty bases in a season.

Later that night, Ronald Acuña Jr. of the Braves stole his thunder. The top talent in the National League hit a grand slam at Los Angeles, becoming the first player in Major League history to hit thirty home runs and steal sixty bases. The National League MVP was an astonishing talent.

Volpe was outstanding in his own right. His two-run homer, this time in the seventh, propelled New York to a 2-1 win. The 2023 Yankees couldn't complete that four-game sweep on the final day of August, but this edition, the 2024 team, finished off a three-game sweep of Detroit the next afternoon, 6-3.

Once again, Miles was given a day off, a day game that followed a night game. He didn't mind. The Yankees had now won six in a row, trailing first-place Toronto by 9 ½ games.

The team had another off day the next day, then would welcome Cleveland and Colorado for three games each at Yankee Stadium. In baseball, you take things one game at a time. But there wasn't a single Yankee on that Sunday evening flight back to New York who couldn't wait for Tuesday because, like the old Herman's Hermits song, this team knew they were "Into Something Good."

Stephanie and Miles said goodbye in Detroit following the Yankees' win. She was flying home to Atlanta and, in forty-eight hours, would be headed with her parents to Europe. Those two flights gave her something to consider, especially the trip to Munich. Maybe she was wrong before. Maybe, just maybe, she would consider getting married again. Perhaps she could think more clearly at her parents' European getaway in Kitzbühel, Austria.

The Yankees got into New York around 9:30 p.m. on Sunday. Miles arrived at the hotel room the team had assigned him. He had barely seen it when he was in town before, just called up from Scranton. He was most pleased to see more of his equipment and personal items were waiting for him. Coach Al in Scranton was correct. The team had shipped all his belongings to him.

The room was spacious, with a California king bed, a huge sofa, a large screen TV, and a table with chairs. He looked around the room. There was only one thing missing. That pretty brunette who was with him in Detroit. And she was getting ready to travel to Europe.

During the Monday day off, Willie Randolph reflected on the discussion he had in his hotel room with Jason Harbison and Miles Fuller. Was it possible to win the division? He knew it was. Randolph had lived it. The 1978 Yankees went to bed on July 19 a full fourteen games behind Boston. Going into September of 1978, the good guys still trailed Boston by 6 1/2 games.

Then, in a four-game series that became known as the Boston Massacre, New York clobbered Boston 15-3, 13-2, 7-0, and 7-4. Of note, New York scored fifteen runs in the opener without a home run.

The winning New York pitchers were Ken Clay, Jim Beattie, eventual Cy Young Award winner Ron Guidry, and Ed Figueroa.

The first win on September 7 came against former friend, Mike Torrez, a righty, who was on the mound as the Yankees captured the 1977 World Series title.

Guidry was already 20-2 on the season when he shut out the Red Sox on September 9. Guidry finished the season with an incredible 1.74 ERA. He struck out 248 hitters and threw an impressive nine shutouts.

New York would eventually pull ahead by 3 1/2 games, but a loss to the Cleveland Indians on September 23 cut the lead to only one game. The Yankees rebounded to win six consecutive games, but Boston did one better. New York now needed to defeat the Indians in the final game of the season. They failed to do so, setting up the most famous 163rd game in MLB history.

Guidry, now 24-3, got the ball against the former Yankee, Torrez. Leading 2-0 in the seventh, Torrez, the Game 7 winner of the 1977 World Series, now pitching for Boston, gave up consecutive hits to Chris Chambliss and Roy White. Torrez then retired Jim Spencer, setting up Bucky Dent for one of the most memorable home runs in MLB history. Dent, who had homered once in his previous sixty-three games, stunned the Boston crowd with a three-run shot over the Green Monster.

Thurman Munson would add an RBI double and Reggie Jackson a solo homer, giving the Yankees a 5-2 lead.

Yankees closer, Goose Gossage, replaced Guidry in the bottom of the seventh, but the Red Sox touched him for two runs in the eighth, climbing within 5-4.

The Red Sox had runners on the corners with two outs in the ninth, but Gossage saved the season, retiring Carl Yastrzemski, who had previously homered and singled, with a pop-out caught by third baseman Craig Nettles.

New York had little time to celebrate. The ALCS was to begin the next night in Kansas City. The Yankees rode the wave of momentum, eliminating the Royals and then defeating the Dodgers in a rematch of the 1977 Fall Classic.

So, could it be done? Yes. But the Yankees were going to have to be better than good, and Randolph was going to need to be precisely strategic.

Following road trips, teams tend to struggle the first game back home. Randolph had a fresh bullpen and Clarke Schmidt, another Georgia boy and a product of the University of South Carolina, on the mound. Schmidt, the second most reliable starter in 2023, gave New York six strong innings in the opener against Cleveland. The game was tied, 1-1, when Miles came up in the home half of the sixth, bases loaded and two outs. The home plate umpire was Jordan Baker, at six feet seven inches, the tallest umpire in MLB history.

Miles finally figured out that he was not quite six foot seven, since Baker was a hair taller. The Cleveland catcher was having fun with both. "You guys are so huge I bet you have both been banned from pony rides since you were in kindergarten."

With the count 1-1, the Cleveland left-handed pitcher threw a slider in, but Miles was way out in front, fouling it off. Miles then fouled off a couple of quality pitches.

The Cleveland catcher again attempted to get in his head. "Be alert, Mr. Baker. Miles gets startled by unfamiliar noises like applause."

Miles had remained silent but asked for time, telling the catcher, "When you talk about 4.0, you aren't talking GPA. You are referring to your blood alcohol level."

Maybe he shouldn't have said anything at all. Miles got a breaking ball down and away, swinging through the off-speed pitch.

"What did I tell you? I told you he was scared of applause."

Randolph, as stated, was going to be crafty. He had to be to get his team back in the race for the playoffs. They were on a streak, but what could he do to help give the team a lift in this contest? He had spoken to Cole about potentially entering this contest in a relief role, then closing out the six-game homestand on Sunday, on full rest.

So, when Yankee closer, Clay Holmes, worked a scoreless seventh, clearly something was going on. Cole warmed up during the stretch, and as the Yankees hit, gave it away. Credit Cole for being willing to accept the strategy. This move of Randolph could have been unwelcome, backfiring, and unpleasant. But Cole gave his team the best chance to win.

Cole pitched a scoreless eighth and ninth, gaining the victory, when Jasson "the Martian" Dominguez powered a walk-off two-run shot to right.

In talking to reporters after the contest, Miles was asked about the winning strategy. "I thought it was brilliant. Life is interesting for all of us, even the reporters. No one can escape the vicissitudes of life; we must all adapt to the changes the obstacles bring," he told them.

Then one of the reporters asked him why he thought they (the group that covered the game) had interesting lives. "Today your job is to be here, to watch us perform. But look around, which one of you is willing to take a challenge if asked? Would you move to the newsroom if your newspaper needed you or if your website asked? Could you report on news, political figures, entertainment, or stocks?"

One of the reporters confirmed that he could. Miles closed his locker, "I'm glad to hear that. These days it seems that everyone understands the role of a journalist except the journalist. I have to go shave, but any of you could do better than those representing your media outlets."

A second reporter said to the group, "Do you ever get the idea Fuller believes he's the smartest person in the building?"

A third reporter replied, "Yes, but probably because he is."

The original reporter then chimed back, "I like Fuller when he is relaxed, convivial, even wistful."

Then Roger, the oldest blogger at about age sixty-five with a gray beard said, "I believe he's an arrogant prick, a guy who thinks he's going to be up in the big leagues for ten years. He accuses us of being elite. I could warm up to him if he either turned off Fox News or earned the right to be here."

Although the win streak was snapped one night later, Miles arrived the next day recalling what his older cousin Jeff "Hack"

Goodwin of Valley, Alabama, told him over and over as a kid. Hack was the biggest Braves fan. "Just win every series. All the Braves need to do is win every series."

Brilliant minds think alike. When Miles looked down on his phone, he had a text message from Hack. "If you win tonight, you win the series. Just win every series." The Yankees did just that, and Miles had the most impactful game of his brief MLB career, going 3-3, with two doubles. He also swiped a bag, and the Yankees won, 6-1.

Cleveland headed out, and Colorado came to the stadium for three games. It was August 23 and the good guys now trailed East-leading Toronto by six games. The Yankees dominated the three-game sweep. Although Miles was productive at the plate, he brought the house down when he leaped up over the center-field wall and brought back a ball that had cleared the wall by a foot. Jasson Dominguez ran over from right, put his arm around Miles, and the two ran in from centerfield together. Miles tipped his cap to the Yankee faithful standing and applauding from behind the dugout.

Was he Don Mattingly with the glove? No. Mattingly finished with a career fielding percentage of .9959. That meant for every 1000 times the ball came his way, he made four errors. Mattingly won nine Gold Gloves, second most of any first baseman.

Miles wasn't Mattingly. But he was a stellar defender. Miles hit safely in all three games, scoring Jorge Lopez from second, with a game-winning two-out single in the bottom of the seventh in the series finale on Sunday.

The Yankees went 5-1 on the homestand. It wasn't even September yet, and the good guys had cut the deficit to five games.

Miles returned to his locker after the Sunday victory. Stephanie had called from Europe and requested a short note to be left in his locker. It simply read:

"Congratulations on a great week. I thought you looked good in the road uniform.

Then I saw you in pinstripes. I miss you. I love you!"

He sat down at his locker, unable to disguise the smile on his face, loud music all around him. Jorge Lopez, the Yankees shortstop/second baseman, was curious. "What's that?"

"A note from Stephanie."

"Good news, I hope."

"The best. I have no idea why she is all about me."

A reporter then approached Miles at his locker. "Hey kid, you got a second?"

Miles, not a fan of the reporter or his employer, made a quick excuse. "I skipped lunch, so I'm feeling esurient now. But my hunger aside, what do you need?" asked the centerfielder.

"Look, this now is why I'm here. I'm just going to give you a heads-up. A great deal of the press…"

"What, a great deal what?"

"Let me just say, they aren't big fans. They feel like you are talking down to them. Part of it is the Stanford vocabulary. I just thought I would tell you, sort of warn you," said the sixty-year-old newspaper veteran.

Miles responded, "I don't understand you guys. Some barbs you deliver toward me are arbitrary, but others are driven by personal animus. Am I a blatherskite? Do I say a bunch of foolish things? Am I Dogberry in Shakespeare's *Much Ado About Nothing*, talking nonsense?"

The reporter sincerely tried to advise him, "You speak a great deal about Christianity, yet you treat us in the manner you do. You enjoy talking down to us."

"Let me explain something to you. God is not impressed with our philosophy or our rhetoric. He is impressed with our faithfulness and our commitment to Him," said Fuller.

"I guess you don't get it," said the reporter.

Miles finished the conversation. "I have a plane to catch to Washington. How's this? Why don't we just agree not to speak to each other?"

CHAPTER TWENTY-FIVE

"Age and glasses of wine should never be counted."

Anonymous

Though not as attractive as his surprise in Detroit, upon his arrival in D.C., Miles got another jolt. Waiting for him in his room was a note from his Uncle Phil. It read:

Miles,

I'm here at the hotel. I wanted to surprise you. I've already gone to bed. I will call you in the morning. Let's win some games!

Uncle Phil

Miles was pleased but then thought, "I hope he doesn't call me too early."

The opportunity was at hand for the Yankees to gain ground. They had just won all but one game the previous week. A rest day was coming Thursday. The Nationals were improved, but New York was capable of sweeping and had to win the series.

Cole had pitched brilliantly the day before, but he wouldn't be available until Friday night back at home against the Cardinals.

After sitting downstairs with his uncle for over two hours, with Phil wearing a Yankee pullover for the first time in his life, the two joined Jason Harbison for a cup of coffee at Starbucks. Jason was scheduled to pitch, but the skies were ominous. The three sat around for two more hours, talking about pitching and hitting.

Jason was trying to save what had been a lackluster season to this point. "Formerly, I thought I was bad in obscurity. Then I got on social media and realized the whole world knew I was a loser," said the pitcher.

"I'm going to tell you what Micky Mantle said to Roger Maris in the movie *61**, 'Don't pay attention to that junk. People are stupid,'" said Miles.

The centerfielder rarely used any social media, explaining, "I don't want to know what people are saying about me. We have enough negativity in this world. We should be trying to lift people and encourage them. Here we are in the most corrupt place possible, Washington, D.C. They don't call it the swamp for nothing."

At that time, thunder shook the building, and Jason peaked around the corner. "Speaking of the swamp, it looks like one right now. We aren't playing tonight."

Phil said, "I've got an idea. Let's go see the movie *Speak No Evil*. I will see how much it will cost to rent the entire theater. Ask a few of the guys if they want to join us. My treat," said the supportive uncle.

The rain never went away, and a doubleheader was scheduled for the following day. Jorge Lopez and pitcher Jose Alvarez took Phil up on his offer. Jason called a car service, and the five enjoyed *Speak No Evil*.

Jorge tried to buy the popcorn. "It's all been taken care of, even your Coke ICEE," Phil said as he pointed to his nephew. The theater employees delivered popcorn, candy, and drinks. Then Jorge looked at Jason, "How do we do this?"

Jason believed he understood, "Where do we sit? I don't know. I've never been to a private movie showing in a theater. This is a completely different experience."

Phil stood to the left for the first twenty minutes of the film, sipping on a Dr. Pepper. The four players shared two rows, a couple of seats in between them.

Jorge and Jason sat in the third row, with Jose and Miles in the fifth row. They were in the second section with a table full of refreshments separating the bottom seating and where they sat.

Miles knew a Coke ICEE was one of his few guilty pleasures in life. If he ever was left on that deserted island, he would need everything necessary to make an M&M Blizzard from Dairy Queen, a Coke ICEE, an endless amount of grape-flavored Big-League Chew, and a Red Bull Sugarfree drink.

The movie was good, perhaps one that could be considered at awards season. The five returned to the hotel and had the Dr. Pepper and Coke ICEE replaced with other beverages. They gathered in a large sitting area in the lobby. Phil was delighted when he asked the bar manager if he had any Jones Family wine, and the manager confirmed two unopened cases had been stored untouched in the back. Phil was fifty-two years old, but he felt like a kid at Christmas. "You just can't find the stuff anymore," he explained to the others. "I want all of you to do me this one favor. Just try it."

They all did. Eventually, Jason switched to beer, and Miles cut things off after one glass. But Jorge and Jose assisted Phil in finishing off the two bottles.

The baseball players, always willing to heighten their knowledge of some of the finer things in life, asked Phil for advice on purchasing wine and building a collection. Phil did his best to explain some of his favorites. "This wine is an exceptional red. If you like it as much as I do, may I also suggest Quilceda Creek, the 2020 'Palengat' Cabernet Sauvignon, or, say, the 2013 Tom Eddy Cabernet Sauvignon Stagecoach." The players leaned in to hear more. Phil reached down and showed them a bottle of the Tom Eddy. The others handled it like a kid would handle a signed baseball from Aaron Judge or Juan Soto.

Phil attempted to explain a few significant qualities of this cabernet sauvignon, "Tom's 2013 and 2016 releases of this wine were awarded the International Sommelier Competition Domestic Wine of the Year. No other wine has achieved that type of recognition." Phil opened the bottle, pouring small amounts into five glasses. "I want you guys to picture the power and the nuances of the Vaca mountains on the eastern side of the Napa Valley. This is a thick and rich wine. It coats the mouth and provides a liquid luxury."

Everyone in the group approved, and then Jose asked to be excused.

"Where are you off to?" asked Miles.

"I'm off to my room to order this wine online!"

With that, the group called it a night.

The Nationals did the baseball world a big favor. The rain moved out, the temperatures dropped, and the Nationals scheduled a twilight doubleheader—none of that split doubleheader stuff. Give the fans two games! And they did, with the opener starting at 4:35 p.m. The crowd continued to trickle in throughout the evening.

When Miles arrived at the park, he knew something was up.

He was told Randolph wanted to see him. "No way he's sending me back to Scranton," he told himself.

He arrived at his office. "Miles, I'm making a change. I know you have enjoyed hitting at the bottom of the lineup. And we may go back to that, but I'm moving you up to leadoff today, both games. You work the count and put pressure on the defense. I need you; we need you on base, stealing bags," the manager told him.

Miles went back to his locker and softly played "Centerfield" by John Fogerty on his phone. Just a little something to pump him up. He then went out to centerfield and checked on the wall, the warning track. Thank you, George Selkirk.

It was now fifty-four degrees, the coolest start date of the summer. Autumn was nearing. It felt wonderful outside. The ball was not going to carry in the hot air because there was no hot air, just winds at seven to ten mph blowing out to left.

Randolph patted him, and Miles stepped to the plate. The first two pitches were breaking balls, both away. This pitcher was known to throw a great deal of off-speed pitches. Miles then got a 95-mph four-seamer that was a bit low. This at bat was working out just as Randolph had hoped. Get on base, steal a bag, or perhaps some old-school hit-and-run.

If the pitcher is consistently missing low, it's a mechanical issue. It's on the pitcher to change the eye level, down 3-0, and give the hitter a high fastball. National starter Dalton Whitlock failed to do so. Miles was guessing the slider, and he was correct. Randolph was in disbelief when he saw his leadoff man swing. The slider wasn't a bad pitch, but it was just off the plate, right where Miles was anticipating it to be. The Yankee centerfielder got all of it, driving it opposite field, through the cold air, bypassing the slight wind that was pushing in, with it eventually landing on the twelfth row.

It was caught by a native New Yorker, now living in D.C., who had graduated from Auburn University, of all places. It's a small world, after all. Steve Segerlin was never a Yankees fan, but he was glad to hand over Fuller's first home run ball in exchange for a Jasson Dominguez signed bat.

"I like this lead-off stuff," Miles told Randolph as he walked back to the dugout past his manager.

"Where do you go from here?" asked utility player Kevin Downes from Texas. "Are you going after Jeter's team leadoff homer record?" The two laughed it off.

Miles would add a third-inning single, a steal of second base, scoring on Anthony Volpe's double. Dominguez ended Whitlock's day with a three-run bomb one inning later, pushing the lead to 5-0.

Harbison was good until the sixth, striking out four before he was touched for three in the home half of the sixth. With the Yankees up 5-3, Randolph called on Jose Alvarez, who at this time yesterday was in an empty theater with the four others.

Alvarez turned into a version of Goose Gossage or Sparky Lyle, going multiple innings and saving the bullpen for the nightcap. Alvarez got the final ten outs, only giving up a run, and the good guys took the opener 5-4.

Miles went back to his locker, sat down, and grabbed his phone. There were over fifty text messages congratulating him on his first big league home run. He then recalled the conversation from yesterday about social media. He checked the only social media he ever had: a Facebook account established during his freshman year at Stanford.

Miles had not been on the app since being called up to the Majors. He wasn't sure if it was the defensive stealing of the home run ball back at Yankee Stadium or today's first career homer, but Miles had 3,864 new Facebook friend requests. The only one he immediately accepted was Steve Segerlin's, who then tagged Miles, holding a picture of his first home run ball, a beautiful ball now resting in his locker.

Temperatures fell below fifty degrees for the second game on

Tuesday night. Miles had to put his heroics of the first game, his first Major League home run, behind him. As promised, he was in the leadoff spot again.

He was facing lefty Brandon Hughes, the Nationals' best pitcher. Washington had decided to retain Hughes at the trade deadline despite his pending free agency. Hughes had been a dependable starter for the Nationals for almost five seasons.

It was almost 9:00 p.m. ET when the second game got underway, 8:57 p.m. to be exact. Before the clock turned to 8:58 p.m., Miles was on base again, plunked on his left shoulder by a 97-mph four-seamer on the second pitch of the game.

It took Fuller a minute to get down to first base. Hughes never acknowledged him. The Nationals' pitcher threw over to first, a token throw, ahead 0-1 to Kevin Downes, getting a start in the second game. Fuller was off on the 0-1 toss, a slider that stayed down. Fuller got the bag with ease.

Downes then gave the good guys a 1-0 advantage with a double off the wall. Hughes decided to go to the slider again, and Downes showed he had seen it one too many times.

Hughes gave the Nationals five innings, but it cost him ninety-one pitches. He left trailing 2-0. The Nationals would score twice in the home half of the sixth, tying the game 2-2.

Fuller then came to the plate in the top of the seventh, catching up to a 93-mph fastball, landing two feet just inside the line in right. Miles had third on his mind but then got the stop sign from third base coach Jorge Posada. Two pitches later, Miles was standing on the bag, having swept third for the first time in his career.

It was then that the player from Newnan, Georgia, was given the nickname "Grand Theft Awesome," and the Yankees players loved it. "He's Grand Theft Awesome," Posada yelled back to the dugout.

Miles would score what turned out to be the game-winning run as catcher Austin Wells drove him home with a deep ball to center. Yankee reliever Scott Brand worked two scoreless innings, and Holmes notched the save, securing the double-header sweep.

It was late when the team returned to the hotel. Miles made plans to see his Uncle Phil once more in the morning before the 1:00 p.m. matinee contest.

The Yankees and the Nationals were now about to face each other for the third time in approximately twenty-one hours. Both teams were exhausted. The Yankees needed the game far more than Washington. New York also had a much-needed day off tomorrow, returning to New York to host the Cardinals.

New York would also be watching the waiver wire, seeing if the Nationals might unload Hughes or if the White Sox would put the hard-throwing Stormy Weathers on waivers. The trade deadline had passed, but if a player was on a roster before September 1, they were playoff eligible.

Miles had his concerns. After breakfast with Phil, he reported to the trainer, complaining of increased shoulder pain stemming from being beamed by the ball the night before. The trainer inspected it and didn't believe it was too serious. The X-rays were negative, but the trainer, Randolph, and Miles all agreed it would be best to have the day off.

The rest of the Yankees also took the day off, as Washington prevented the sweep, 6-0. The Yankees trailed Toronto by seven games. They didn't talk about it, but they were now only three games out of the final wildcard.

The Blue Jays were slumping, and the Orioles had pulled within two games of the East leader. Tampa and Boston were doing nothing to help their causes. This was a winnable race, but outcomes like the finale in Washington were unacceptable.

The rain followed the Yankees to New York. It was

announced on the off day, August 29, that the game for Friday was postponed because of too much rain.

A split doubleheader was scheduled for Saturday the 31st, with game times of 1:05 p.m. and 7:05 p.m. On Saturday, it would also be revealed if the Yankees had put any player on waivers or potentially had claimed some.

CHAPTER TWENTY-SIX

"Have I not commanded you? Be strong and courageous. Do not be afraid; do not be discouraged, for the Lord your God will be with you wherever you go."

Joshua 1:9

August 31, 1959

Los Angeles Dodgers ace Sandy Koufax struck out eighteen San Francisco Giants in a 5-2 win against their rival on August 31, 1959. The Giants moved from New York following the completion of the 1957 season. The Dodgers would finish four games up over the Giants, sweep the Milwaukee Braves, then defeat the Chicago White Sox in six games for the World Series title.

The Dodgers, playing home games at the Los Angeles

Memorial Coliseum, set a then-home record for attendance, bringing in more than two million fans in their second season since leaving Brooklyn.

The World Champs were led by a talented pitching staff that included Koufax, Don Drysdale, Johnny Padres, and Roger Craig, who managed the Giants from 1985–1992 and passed away in June of 2023 at the age of ninety-three.

Sixty-five years after the 1959 title-winning team, the Dodgers seemed to be the only serious obstacle to preventing the Atlanta Braves from winning the 2024 National League Pennant. The Dodgers had a great bullpen and a potent top-of-the-order, including Mookie Betts, Shohei Ohtani, and Freddie Freeman. The Dodgers had already put away the Padres and the other National League West division challengers with a month still left in the season. The entire baseball world wanted to see the Braves and Dodgers meet in October.

August 31 was also the day players who had been put on waivers discovered their destinations. The Yankees had put zero players on waivers, and, much to the chagrin of the team, they had claimed no individuals either. More alarming, they had passed on Stormy Weathers of the White Sox and Brandon Hughes of the Nationals. Both went to the East-leading Blue Jays.

"Are you kidding me?" declared New York reliever Scott Brand. "You would think we would have claimed one or both to at least keep Toronto from getting them."

Miles was a free agent and open to signing with anyone when the season was over. This time last year, he thought he was done with baseball. When his old Stanford roommate, Blake Zhu, reminded Miles that he could have been part of the Braves' 2023 postseason run, Miles had to admit the obvious. "I had my chance in the spring. I didn't do enough; I didn't perform well enough. It was my fault." He had hoped the Braves would have been interested in offering the centerfielder a minor league contract, but, once again, his performance in the spring prevented it.

He was so thankful that the Braves placed him in the lineup for the game in Tampa against the Yankees. The performance on that one day, that single game, placed him where he was today. And that place was the cathedral that is Yankee Stadium. The team was back in New York for a short three-game series against another member of baseball royalty, the St. Louis Cardinals.

Miles had turned in a paper in his Newnan High days stating that his three favorite baseball uniforms of all time were the Detroit white jersey, the New York home pinstripes, and the gorgeous gray St. Louis road uniform, with the two cardinals placed on the bat. He had felt so blessed to have worn one so similar in college, the Stanford gray. Now, each home game, he was donning the pinstripes.

The Yankees have policies that include players having no long hair and being clean-shaven, although a mustache is allowed. Those requirements were not an issue for the outfielder. Miles had never even come close to having a beard and didn't care for long hair. He had told his parents, "I feel like we are the face of the organization. We need to look like gentlemen." His father, Greg, had always been clean-shaven, as had Phil and all his cousins, including Hack Goodwin. "It's just what we do," explained Greg to his son Miles when he was in ninth grade.

While at his locker, Miles was reading Joshua 1:5-9 in his Bible when he heard an Atlanta game playing in the background. He turned around to see them celebrating a walk-off home run from Lane Anderson, with teammate David Brewer pouring bottles of water on him as he touched home plate. They were both two of the Braves Miles enjoyed getting to know in the spring of 2023. Miles was with the Braves as an unsigned spring training attendee but bonded with several of the Atlanta players, including dependable pitchers Matt Trucks and John Perkerson.

As he watched the Braves in the 2023 postseason, it was easy to pull for them, yet he felt like he had missed out on a wonderful opportunity. Now, it was 2024, and Atlanta was certainly the favorite to win the World Series. He went back to reading his Bible, and then a few seconds later, his phone notified him of a text message.

It was Braves shortstop David Brewer, a fellow believer, a brother in Christ. The message simply read, "Good luck tonight. Let's meet up in October. There is still time."

He then got up and walked over to Yankee teammate Brad Litkenhous. They were looking over at the Braves postgame show. "Hernando Fernandez hit two more home runs today," said Litkenhous. That gave the Braves catcher fifty-one, and he was hitting an outstanding .352, all under the speculation of cheating.

"He could hit a pelota ball out of the stadium, the way he is seeing the ball right now. It's unreal. He's determined to break the single-season home run record of Judge," said Miles.

Litkenhous, the funniest Yankee of them all, replied, "And no one likes the guy. Raccoons avoid eating his trash. Black cats avoid Fernandez for bad luck."

It was time to take the field. "Let's finish off August with a bang," instructed Randolph.

Gerrit Cole, defending Cy Young Award winner, got the ball for New York. No matter the circumstance of the season, the Yankees liked their chances when their stud got the ball.

Cole worked a 1-2-3 first inning, and the players could feel a little more electricity in the air. The Yankees crowd was excited this Friday night, counting on Cole to be Cole, expecting a Yankees victory.

Miles led off and was immediately in the hole 0-2. He fouled off a couple of mistake pitches, but on the fifth delivery, weakly grounded out to third. Making things more frustrating, the shoulder pain was back. The training staff looked him over. He took his position in the outfield in the second inning, but when he returned to the dugout, he told Randolph he needed to be removed.

Miles would undergo more testing and treatment the rest of the evening. Cole didn't need his help on that night. He went eight innings, the Cardinals could only mount one insignificant run, and the Yankees won 6-1. The nightcap was rescheduled for the following day after a two-hour delay.

Tomorrow was September 1, the first day of autumn, according to meteorologists and climatologists. Summer had three weeks remaining, the season only a month more. A feeling of fall was in the air. By the reaction of the Yankees' fans at the game tonight, a feeling of potentially being in the postseason was a possibility, a circumstance that had no chance three short weeks ago.

CHAPTER TWENTY-SEVEN

"I wandered with dear autumn as far as I could go, and in the end, I didn't leave. I kept her in my soul."

Angie Weiland Crosby

September 1, 2024

Randolph stood in front of his team before the newly scheduled doubleheader took place. "Welcome to autumn, guys. It is sixty-seven degrees, and clear skies. We are in this race. I don't want to talk about the division, the wild card, how many games we trail. I don't want you to think about Toronto or Baltimore. I want your mind on the Cardinals. Let's get these two today and get to Texas."

On the strength of three hits from DJ LeMahieu and a towering home run from Juan Soto, New York won the opener, 6-4. Scott Brand and Clay Holmes both pitched an inning of scoreless relief. The win came with a cost. Soto was hit in the left wrist by a 100-mph fastball and was lost for the season. The Yankees would play the remainder of 2024 without their top two offensive threats, Aaron Judge and Juan Soto.

Miles once again was held out, but Randolph told him he would play him after five innings of the second game. In the first game, the teams swung the bat like they were late to a flight. Only four times in the game did the count go full.

The second game was much the same. Jason Harbison got the start for New York and outside a two-run laser by Paul Goldschmidt in the top of the third, Harbison had a strong outing. The Cardinals' approach at the plate was good for his pitch count. New York trailed in the bottom of the fifth by a single run, but a three-run blast by Anthony Rizzo to left gave the Yankees the lead for good.

Miles was indeed placed into the field in the sixth. He made two plays from the field with no discomfort. He got one plate appearance, a single in the eighth, then Grand Theft Awesome stole second.

Yankee reliever Jonathan Loáisiga got the final four outs in support of Harbison, which gave the Yankees not only a sweep of the doubleheader but also a sweep of the series.

Stephanie, watching the second game of the doubleheader with her parents in an American sports bar in Munich, was slumping in her seat until she noticed her boyfriend inserted in center in the sixth inning.

She didn't have any euros, but her mom, Julie, did. Stephanie walked over to the jukebox and played "Centerfield" by John Fogerty. She didn't care that she was three years older than Miles. When he came to the plate in the eighth, she declared to Dale and Julie, "Mom, Dad, that's the man I'm going to marry."

Dale said, "If you do, be sure he knows the difference between being single and being married."

"He gets it, Dad."

"Can he handle an older woman, what, three years older?" asked her mom. She paused, then said, "It's a fair question."

"I'm not even concerned about that," replied Stephanie.

"It's only three years, not twenty," said her dad.

Stephanie, sitting at the table watching the remainder of the game with her parents, looked like a twenty-three-year-old instead of a thirty-two-year-old, hair back in a ponytail, wearing her signature navy Yankees cap. She wore a sage down jacket from Lululemon and navy wide-leg pants, which she paired with her favorite Golden Goose Mid Star sneakers.

Her father told her, "I never thought you would remotely care about baseball. Even your friends in high school who were into baseball couldn't interest you in the game."

Stephanie's mom cleared things up. "They weren't as cute as No.14."

Then Stephanie replied, "They just weren't No.14. Period."

Miles got back to the clubhouse and took out his phone from inside his locker. He had anticipated hearing from Stephanie. There were no new messages from her, and considering the time difference between New York and Germany, he knew none would be coming on this night.

He had been told by the public relations staff to expect a text from a magazine writer. The text from Meghan Andrews of *Single in The City* was in his inbox. The two would soon conduct a phone interview when he was in Texas. The rest of the team was packing for Texas as New York pitcher Jason Harbison stopped off at Miles' locker.

"Are you ready to get to the bus to go to the airport?" the pitcher asked.

"Yeah. Do you know anything about *Single in The City*?"

"For sure, the magazine. It's a major publication here.

There's not a woman in her 20s or 30s in New York who doesn't read it," explained Jason.

"Okay, I feel good about this. They want to feature me, and that doesn't sound controversial," replied Miles.

"Not at all. It will be positive."

"I could use a panegyric piece for a change," said the centerfielder.

"What in the world does that mean?"

"It means a published work that praises someone or something, often a public speech, but this will be in a magazine. This will be a significant change from the norm. The media here hate me."

Miles then looked over his right shoulder and saw Jorge Lopez dressed differently than usual. Lopez was in an impressive dark gray suit.

"Look at Jorge. He must know some haberdasher in town because he is dressed to kill. You can read a little more about a haberdasher in Chaucer's *The Canterbury Tales*. The wives in the story wanted their husbands to run for office and improve their social standing. Aren't you glad you have an amazing wife?" asked Miles.

Speaking of running for office, the two then looked over at a clubhouse television that was showing Joe Biden. "Hey, our President looks sharp. I guess he has a haberdasher as well," said Harbison.

Miles agreed, "Yes, he does. The difference between Jorge and Biden is that Jorge understands denial is not a river in Russia. Mr. Biden believes it is."

The Yankees had fulfilled the wish of Randolph, sweeping the vital doubleheader. Rain had wreaked havoc on the series, and now the Yankees were going to be arriving in Texas about the same time the sun was coming up.

Rain can create trouble in baseball. And this was bad timing for sure, but not even as close to the headaches the 1982 New York Yankees endured. Opening day that year was scheduled for Tuesday, April 6, versus the Texas Rangers. The game was snowed out due to a blizzard of more than a foot of snow. Conditions didn't allow for a game to be played until Sunday, five days after the scheduled opener. By then, the Rangers had exited town. The White Sox were the opponent for the Sunday doubleheader, and Chicago swept, winning 7-6 and 2-0, with Goose Gossage and Tommy John being handed the losses.

Now, forty-two years later, Coach Randolph, a member of those 1982 Yankees, was relieved to get a Sunday doubleheader sweep, a complete reversal from forty-two years ago. He chuckled when he thought back to the scheduled 1982 opener against the Rangers. How fitting it was that they were about to spend the next three days facing the Texas Rangers. What he wouldn't do for another sweep!

Those 1982 Yankees finished 79-83, sixteen games back of the Milwaukee Brewers, only a year after New York had reached the 1981 World Series.

As Randolph tried to get a few hours of sleep on the plane, he smiled, telling himself, *"We missed the playoffs in 1982. We are going to get there this year. I know it. I can feel it."*

CHAPTER TWENTY-EIGHT

"It's not about reducing pressure it's about building the capacity to embrace more."

Jonah Oliver

It was after 6:00 a.m. when the Yankees got to the hotel. Miles was supposed to talk to a writer from the New York magazine *Single in The City,* but he had to postpone the 10:00 a.m. phone interview for twenty-four hours.

Miles never slept on the plane, so he immediately crashed at the hotel. His father, Greg, had left him a message that he could make the final game of the series in Texas on Wednesday.

Miles woke up at 2:00 p.m. and was pleased to hear from his dad. He looked forward to seeing him in forty-eight hours. But the best news was discovering no soreness in his shoulder. The inflammation was gone; there was no pain, no discomfort. The treatments had worked. The Yankee rookie centerfielder was good to go.

Often, when a Major League team is delayed on a travel day, it's not the opening game in which they struggle and are unable to overcome the scheduling conflicts. It instead tends to be the second contest, when there is potentially no benefit from the adrenaline rush, which was with them in the opener.

The host Rangers had faded the prior August, eventually losing the division by tiebreaker to the Astros, but rebounded, catching fire in October and winning the World Series. This August had been better, and they hoped to continue a positive ride now that September ball was underway.

New York may have been drowsy in the opener, but the bats were ready. The good guys plated two runs in each of the first three innings to take a commanding lead. Three different Texas pitchers struggled to command the fastball. The Yankees led 8-3 after six, winning 8-5.

Miles returned to his hotel room and fell asleep watching a replay of the game in which he had just gone 1-4.

He awoke in plenty of time for his interview with Meghan Andrews, a writer from Single in The City magazine.

After a brief greeting, Meghan got right to business.

"So, Miles, here's the question all our female followers want to know. You are not married. Is there a girlfriend?"

The Yankee outfielder paused, then laughed briefly. "There is. Her name is Stephanie. She is from Augusta, Georgia."

"How long has this been a thing?"

"If it were a baseball game, we would be in the second inning," explained the ball player.

"How did you meet?" asked Meghan.

"I first met her when I was going into my senior year of high school. She was a junior at Stanford University, and she gave me a tour of different buildings on campus."

"So, Stephanie is an older woman," joked the writer.

He responded, "She is three years older."

"Do you typically choose older women for relationships?"

"I've only had one other relationship. She was a high school girlfriend and was one year younger. It lasted until the completion of my freshman year at Stanford," said Miles.

"Did you break up with her to date Stephanie?"

"No, no. Not at all. My high school girlfriend is now deceased. Like I said, Stephanie and I have only been together for a short period."

The writer was curious. "If it's okay to ask, how did the high school girlfriend pass away?"

"A car crash. A deadly car crash," said Miles. "It happened her senior year in college. Three people were killed in the crash."

Meghan started to put a few things together. "So, you guys had been broken up for a long time. Has her death played a role in preventing other relationships?"

Miles thought for a while. "No. I just didn't meet anyone I wanted to invest my time in. I don't want to waste my time or God's time. And the answer to the former, at the time Brooke died, we had been broken up for over three years."

Pausing the interview, Meghan said, "Can you give me a moment to stand up just a second? I have some back pain."

After about forty-five seconds, she returned.

Miles then asked, "Have you been sitting down at your computer for a time?"

"Yes, frequently, especially the last few days."

He had a suggestion. "There are truncal stretches and exercises you can try. They can help your back and relax those nerves. When we finish, I can e-mail you some examples."

The interview continued, and after asking some questions about being a Yankee and living in the city, Meghan attempted to discuss politics. "There is a pretty strong belief that you are very conservative politically. Is that true? There seems to be a solid story of you with the Mitt Romney campaign twelve years ago. We are about to come up on another election. What is your stance?" she asked.

"I appreciate the question. I appreciate all your questions. I can confirm that I attended a Romney rally in 2012, but I wasn't part of his campaign. As far as being conservative, I will just say right now I have concerns about both Democrats and Republicans. And I wish we had an honest and impartial media. But, for our team, although the election is closing in, we have decided not to discuss politics or policy during the season. We are focused on making a run at the playoffs."

Meghan then pivoted from politics. "When in the city, where do you like to eat? Where do you visit?"

"I honestly haven't done too much of that. There was a TV show in the 70s, long before our time, *Kojak*, and a few of us like to seek out places where they filmed. I guess that's an answer for the latter. As for the former, I haven't gone out to dinner often, but Carmine's has been a favorite."

"Okay, when you and Stephanie break up, I will meet you at Carmine's. I like it as well, and it's close to work."

She continued the interview, which felt weird to Miles since he did not comment about whether he would ever break up with Stephanie.

Meghan then asked about his parents, "Do your parents come to most games?"

"No. My father makes a few, but he has a full-time job. My mom is scared to fly, so she will be in the stands when driving distance allows."

"What does your father do?"

"He's a pilot for Delta," said Miles.

Meghan, age twenty-seven, single herself, then said, "There is a deeper story here. I just want to make sure I have this straight. Your father is a commercial pilot, a captain, and your mom is afraid to fly?"

"That is accurate. My mom lost her best friend in a December 1996 air disaster that crashed in Miami. She hasn't flown since."

"Oh, my goodness. That is tragic. Do you have a fear of flying?"

"When I was younger, I was fearful. Having a father in the business has helped. Don't get me wrong. I have no desire to ever be a pilot," Miles replied.

"Let's shift gears and talk about the team. Who are your closest friends on the team?" she asked.

Miles replied, "We all get along well. Hard to single out a few, but a guy like pitcher Brad Litkenhous has been invaluable to me. His walk with Christ resembles mine. We pray together, and we share scriptures. Jorge Lopez and Jason Harbison are frequent dinner companions. Scott Brand also is strong in his faith. Scott is going to lead several of us in a Bible study this afternoon."

"What's the best time you've had on the road?"

"No doubt about it, in Washington. That makes sense, right? The corrupt capital of the country! But we had a rain out, and my uncle, who has a huge avuncular relationship and friendliness with me, rented out a theater, and a handful of us went to see James McAvoy in *Speak No Evil*."

"Is he your dad's brother?"

"Correct, Uncle Phil. Phil Fuller. He's very kind and gracious and shares his experiences. He's a great resource for me and a true epicurean, especially when it comes to wine," said Miles.

"Is that your drink of choice?"

Miles laughed, "No. A Red Bull sugar-free drink and bottled water are one and two. I don't drink alcohol often. But if I do, since I love coffee, I enjoy Bailey's Irish cream coffee."

"What's it like being the so-called new Yankee?"

"I'm honored to play for this organization. It's a dream come true. So many people have told me, those obviously older, that Mickey Mantle was their favorite player. Well, now I'm wearing those same pinstripes. It's a very humbling feeling."

The reporter asked him to name a pitcher he feared facing.

"I don't want to have anything to do with Brandon Veasey with the Blue Jays. I faced him eight times in the minors, and I went hitless," said Miles.

"You were almost out of baseball. A free agent. I'm told you will be a free agent again at the end of this season. What do you contribute to this run you are on?" she asked.

"I put my life in God's hands. I would like you to include this in the publication. Whatever the reader is going through, remember when the waves are over your head, they're under His feet."

"I respect the religious aspect of your answer. Let me ask this. How have you remained mentally sharp? No one can question your mental toughness," she said.

"I've been persistent. Persistence is the willingness to move forward in your goals, being able to overcome hurdles, putting in relentless hard work, picking yourself up even when you face unanticipated obstacles and unexpected setbacks."

"Solid answer. I think I've got it. Almost done here. I don't believe you will like this. Some of the media that have covered you have spoken under the condition of anonymity, saying to me that you have been borderline disrespectful to them in the locker room. They feel like you believe you are better than them, more intelligent than them. They respect you were a Stanford University scholar, summa cum laude, but they are under the impression that you haven't paid your dues yet to either say some of the things you have said or give the impression you are a leader in the clubhouse."

Miles hesitated. "There's a great deal to unravel there. I believe some anodyne comments I made were instead taken out of context and thought to be inflammatory. I also know they didn't appreciate it when I stated everyone understands the role of journalists but the actual journalists themselves."

Meghan sought some clarification. "So, you feel like some of your words were not insensitive but more misinterpreted?"

"Probably so. But if my friends in the media want to switch roles with me for a night, just let me know. I'm confident I can write up a game story. I'm not so sure one of them can hit a 97-mph fastball. Is that me being rude or insensitive?"

Meghan responded, "I think you are being honest, brutally honest, but these days, too many people are soft."

Miles answered back, "I am here to be the best teammate I can be. I want to do all I can to help us win each game. Our goal is to make the playoffs and bring another title to our city!"

The interview was now over, and Meghan had grown a little curious about her subject. "So, will you hit a home run for me tonight?" she asked.

"I'm not much of a long ball hitter," he admitted. "But how about a single? A single for my favorite writer from *Single in The City*?"

"That will work. I will be watching. Go Yankees," she said.

"Go Yankees!"

Miles read briefly in Lamentations. You can't exactly read for a long time in Lamentations, although the book is pivotal. Then he thought to himself, *"A single? I can do better than that!"*

It was September 3, and the Yankees were not dead, far from it, three games back of the bleeding Blue Jays and Orioles. No one was going to confuse Miles Fuller with former New York sluggers Mickey Mantle and Roger Maris, but it was on this day in 1961 that Mantle smacked two home runs to give him fifty.

Maris hit fifty-three, and the two became the first teammates to hit more than fifty in the same season. They are still the only teammates to accomplish this feat. Maris would finish with a record at sixty-one, a record that held up until 2022 when current Yankee Aaron Judge hit sixty-two that left the park. Mantle finished with fifty-four in 1961. The 1961 Yankees won the World Series in five games over the Cincinnati Reds, with the clutch pitcher, Whitey Ford, capturing MVP honors.

That World Series victory by the 1961 Yankees helped extinguish demons that remained from the 1960 World Series. The Yankees outscored the Pirates 55-27, but Pittsburgh won the seven-game series with a Bill Mazeroski walk-off shot, the first time a World Series ended on a home run. The MVP of the series was Yankee second baseman Bobby Richardson of Sumter, South Carolina. Richardson is the only MVP in World Series history to have played for the losing team.

Miles was inserted into the lineup for the second game in Texas, right where he wanted to be, hitting ninth. Hitting lead-off was difficult. It took him an inning, even longer, to feel his feet on the ground.

He was once asked at Stanford if he ever got nervous in a game. "Every single game," he replied emphatically.

As he took the field at the bottom of the first, he saw something new, something he wouldn't ever forget. In the front row of the right field seats, a young boy no more than eight or nine years old, wearing an away Yankees replica jersey with the name Fuller and the No.14.

He had previously only seen Stephanie wearing his jersey, the home pinstripes. For the first time there in Texas, a young fan had his jersey on.

Texas went down in order, as did the Yankees in the top of

the second. But while New York batted in the second, Miles grabbed a ball, signed his name and number, and wrote, "Thanks for the representation." As he took the field for the home half of the second, he first sprinted to right field, right for the kid, leaped high above the wall, reaching completely out, ball in his right hand. He extended the ball right in front of the youngster, perfectly placing it in his glove. The kid lit up. "Mom, he can fly!"

Miles gave him a thumbs-up and reported to centerfield. He made a lifelong fan that day. And he made quite an impression on him and the rest of the sold-out Texas crowd, going 3-4 with two doubles and a single in a 6-2 victory.

He also made quite an impression that night on *Single in The City* writer Meghan Andrews, who watched the game with her friends in Greenwich Village, eager to begin her assignment, her feature on the newest Yankee.

CHAPTER TWENTY-NINE

"I see you with all my heart; do not let me stray from your commands."

Psalm 119:10

September 4, 1993

On a Saturday afternoon thirty-one years ago at Yankee Stadium, New York starting pitcher Jim Abbott did the unthinkable and threw a no-hitter against the Cleveland Indians. Abbott, from Flint, Michigan, was born without a right hand.

A star at the University of Michigan, Abbott was drafted in the first round by the California Angels shortly after helping the United States win gold at the 1988 Summer Olympics in Seoul. The 1987 Golden Spikes Award winner was a member of the Yankees in 1993 and 1994, but the 1994 season was halted on

August 12 due to a players' strike, preventing the East-leading Yankees from a shot at their first World Series title since 1978.

The 2024 Yankees were enjoying a hot streak, chasing down Toronto and Baltimore. New York completed a sweep of the fading Rangers, 11-3, on Wednesday afternoon. Greg Fuller watched his son go 4-5, adding two stolen bases, leading the momentum behind his nickname, Grand Theft Awesome, to escalate.

Greg and his son were able to visit for ninety minutes before the game, both amazed at how his special delivery to the youngster from the night before finished in the top spot on ESPN SportsCenter's Top 10 list. Crazy to consider what a camera can catch.

A little over three weeks ago, Miles could walk freely outside of a stadium or in a city, and no one was the wiser.

Now, he was recognized. More importantly, the Yankees were winning. Baseball was fun, and those who had seen him playing youth baseball in Newnan and Sharpsburg were excited to brag about him to others and accept him as "The One." The kid they saw playing on the dirt nearly twenty years ago was indeed a Major Leaguer.

The Yankees packed for Chicago to play on the northside in another baseball cathedral, Wrigley Field. Thursday was an off day, and Miles never left the hotel. His Uncle Phil had made it to Chicago by early Thursday afternoon. The two enjoyed dinner at the hotel with New York teammate Jason Harbison. Harbison, twenty-seven, was married and rarely left the hotel, completely devoted to his wife, Tara, who worked full-time herself.

Miles and Jason shared many of the same beliefs. Miles respected what he knew of Tara. Miles was on a league minimal salary, a free agent at the end of the season. Jason was a proven big leaguer, making over five million dollars a season. The fact that Jason's wife worked was inspiring to Miles.

Jason, although not as comfortable speaking about his faith in comparison to Miles and Brad Litkenhous, was also a Christian. And when asked, he was more than happy to discuss his closeness with Christ. No one had to prompt Fuller or Litkenhous. They talked for hours on the road, praying frequently to the God they loved. As his faith deepened, Litkenhous asked his Lord and Savior for more responsibilities.

Miles prayed in the locker room before each game. The two decided it was time to publicly display their devotion to God, so, from now on, they would kneel and say a brief prayer when they took the field.

Heisman Trophy winner and former NFL player Tim Tebow received unfair treatment from the media when, as a player, he demonstrated his faith. The left-wing media criticized his Christianity, labeling him a distraction, saying he was bad for team morale and his love of Christ was not good for the locker room.

But the incident involving Buffalo Bills safety Damar Hamlin on January 2, 2023, seemed to calm down some of the criticism of participating in public prayers. Players gathered on that night to pray, and others followed with prayer for Hamlin to beat his cardiac arrest event.

Yankee star Aaron Judge, out for the season, also was seen kneeling before games.

In Chicago, Miles spoke to Phil about possible options for him next year. Miles' acceleration to stardom with the Yankees, his speed, defense, and now hitting, was going to make him a valuable commodity for some team next season. The outstanding twenty-one-year-old Jasson Dominguez was likely the Yankees centerfielder of the future, playing right field now so Miles could hold down center. Miles would be thirty next year. He was likely to get only one significant multi-year contract. But he was excelling on the big stage. Phil reminded him of the popular saying about New York, "If you can make it here, you can make it anywhere!"

Miles' old Stanford roommate, Blake Zhu, and his company were representing Miles. "We take calls from teams frequently," confirmed Blake. "But we are still telling them that you are staying focused on the season."

Miles previously told him, "I am betting on myself. I'm betting on my play, my productivity."

His outstanding productivity continued the next afternoon as the new Yankee went 4-4, all singles, taking two to left field and two hits to right. He swiped three more bases.

The more experience Miles got, the more dangerous he became. He picked up that two Chicago pitchers were tipping their slider deliveries. They weren't staying back on the rubber or breaking their hands properly. A slider needs to be down. The pitchers were lifting their right leg in the stretch, and at that time, their hands should be breaking from the glove.

When the hand remains too long in the glove, the arm is forced to hurry to catch up to get into a throwing frame. Both were having mechanical issues, and Miles was alert enough to pick up on it.

New York won the Friday opener 8-4. The press wanted to hear from Fuller, who was perfect at the plate. "Miles, another four hits, and three more stolen bases. Is it confidence that is making such a difference?" asked a Chicago writer.

"I am certainly not timorous, but I also don't go to the plate overconfident. I am not trying to do too much. I have been criticized all my life for not being able to hit the ball out of the park. I am yet to understand why those critics stick to that talking point. Often, my singles end up being doubles."

"You are yet to be caught attempting to steal. Can you offer any insight into that success?" asked another Chicago scribe.

"I believe that although God gifted me speed, I have some certain mental advantages. At Stanford, I could decipher when a professor wanted to inculcate a point, the devotion to a subject, perhaps not to indoctrinate us, but a concatenate chain of events would develop, and I always saw that coming. Fortunately, my mind is as quick as my body, so I relied on legerity. I knew what the professor wanted us to believe. I was right there, a step ahead. I feel like that helps me on the base paths. Not at the plate but on the base paths. I study the pitcher, and I try to remain a step ahead of him. That's the most honest, veridical answer I can give you."

With that, Miles left the area, only to return a few seconds later. He walked over to the New York beat writer with whom he previously had an inappropriate response after the writer had approached him with some sincere advice.

Miles told him, "I want to apologize for the way I treated you. It was wrong, and I should not have shut you down and told you I would not communicate with you. I am sorry for that contretemps between us. You didn't deserve that."

"Thank you, Miles. I can move forward and leave that behind us. You had a great game today. Congratulations. That statement about your professors wanting to inculcate points, I understand. What I don't understand, what none of us understand, is how a guy that was out of baseball, struggled in the minors when he was there, is dominating major league baseball? You haven't even been thrown out attempting to steal."

Miles was nodding his head in a positive way as to agree when the writer mentioned his success on the base paths. "Don't sell the mental nisus short. I am extremely focused on stealing bases. I take so much heat about my inability to hit homers. So, the fact that I am on base, I can use my gift to turn a single into a double, and to me, that's just like an extra-base hit.

That must be my nightly goal. I must get on base; I must steal bags."

With that, Miles shook his hand. As a Christian, Miles understood when he was wrong and needed to set things straight, he needed to ask for forgiveness. How could he expect Christ to forgive him of his sins if he couldn't apologize to those he had wronged?

The reporter accepted Miles' apology because he agreed that for the Lord to forgive him, he also needed to forgive those who had mistreated him.

After Miles concluded postgame interviews, he prepared to leave on the bus but spotted a friend, Amanda Fieder, who was a diehard Cubs fan from Montgomery, Alabama. The two became friends when Miles played in Biloxi, and they volunteered at a diabetes clinic. Fieder, a Type 1 diabetic, devoted her life to making others more aware of the disease and how, although it was a setback, one still can live a fulfilling life and overcome it.

Fieder introduced Miles to her three friends. He signed autographs, and they all posed for pictures.

"Congratulations, Miles. It is unreal seeing you in centerfield when I think back to those Biloxi days," she told him.

"I am right there with you. Imagine me playing the most romantic position in baseball. If I am dreaming, don't wake me up."

"Is it okay that I am hoping you play for the Cubs next year?"

"I am willing to play for anyone who wants me," Miles said.

On Saturday, Cole pitched and performed to a national television audience and threw one hundred twelve pitches, shutting out the Cubs 4-0.

LeMahieu, playing first base when every Cubs fan preferred to see former Cub Anthony Rizzo, delivered the big blow to the Windy City, a three-run homer in the top of the seventh, putting the game out of reach at 4-0. Cole wasn't about to relinquish the lead.

Miles went hitless with one walk. He didn't exactly get dressed up for a postgame interview, opting to instead wear the No.17 Ohio State football jersey of Carnell Tate, a sophomore wide receiver. That also didn't go over well with fans of all the other Big Ten schools, more like the Big 30, especially in Chicago, closely located to Northwestern and Illinois.

There were plenty of Notre Dame alumni in the Chicago area as well, and there was no love for the Buckeyes with the fans of the Fighting Irish, even though the head coach of the Irish, Marcus Freeman, was a former Buckeyes player.

The Cubs avoided a sweep the next afternoon, but the Yankees had done what needed to be done. In the words of Miles' cousin, Jeff "Hack" Goodwin, *Just win every series.*

The Yankees were going home for three against the Royals and four against the Red Sox, feeling a little more confident with each game. They were on the verge of something truly historic, and each player could feel the buzz, the bombinate in the locker room, that electricity in the air. You can't see it, but you know it's there.

CHAPTER THIRTY

"If you see someone without a smile today, give 'em yours."

Dolly Parton

The Royals lost many important games to the Yankees in the late 70s, including the American League Championship Series of 1976, 1977, and 1978. Kansas City finally got some revenge in the 1980 ALCS, sweeping the Yankees in three before coming up short against the Philadelphia Phillies in the World Series.

The 2024 Royals could only play spoiler; a challenge made more difficult at the trade deadline when New York killer Hernando Fernandez was dealt to the best team in baseball, the Atlanta Braves.

Bobby Witt Jr., Hunter Renfroe, and first baseman/catcher Jeff Estes were the threats in the lineup, but the pitching staff was not deep.

Estes and Witt Jr. both homered in the series, and Michael Massey hit for the cycle in the opener, but the Yankees rolled over Kansas City 7-4, 8-2, 8-4. The Royals weren't able to play spoiler, and to the credit of the home team, the Yankees didn't leave any stone unturned. They knew they needed to bring it each game.

Cole got the ball for the opener of the four-game series against the Red Sox. He was stellar in his previous outing in Chicago. He was almost as good against Boston. The Red Sox scored once in the first and looked poised to put up a crooked number in the third. With two out runners on second and third, Trevor Story drove a ball high and far to the deepest part of the park. Miles got a strong read, extended his glove over the centerfield wall, and robbed the Red Sox shortstop of a three-run homer. "He did it again. He's Grand Theft Awesome in more ways than one," said legendary Yankee radio announcer, John Sterling.

Then Miles turned to the outfield seats and tossed the ball to a young girl with a Jason Giambi jersey on. She was now a life-long fan and had something to talk about at her next show and tell.

Jasson Dominguez put the Yankees on top for good with a two-run homer in the bottom of the fourth, scoring Anthony Volpe in front of him. With New York up 2-1, Miles took the field in the top of the fifth inning.

Miles had about forty-five seconds before the game was to resume. He spotted his newest fan and told her to catch the ball he had in his hand. It wasn't signed, but the seven-year-old girl from Staten Island didn't care. They each threw it back and forth three times. Cell phone after cell phone caught the exchange, and moments later it was up on YouTube for the world to see.

Sterling and analyst, Suzyn Waldman, did their best to share with the New York listeners what they had just seen. "What a moment for that sweet little girl. What a wonderful example of what an individual can do for another. Truly inspiring," said Waldman.

Sterling added, "He's all aces. There's no doubt about it. Miles Fuller is all aces. The city has fallen in love with the guy, and he is finding new ways to help this team win every night," stated Sterling.

Suzyn added, "And to think, he was an eyelash away from being out of baseball, out of the game. What a shame that would have been."

"You are so right, Suzyn! So right," proclaimed Sterling.

The Yankees went on to win 7-2, catching Toronto for first place in the division. Yes, New York was benefiting from a disastrous run by the Blue Jays and Orioles. But outside of Atlanta, no team was playing better, pitching better, fielding better, or hitting better than the Yankees.

New York had three more games with Boston. Clarke Schmidt was the Friday night starter. Schmidt labored but still came up only one out from six full innings. Schmidt got the victory 6-5.

Reliever Scott Brand was the player of the game, getting seven outs. Clay Holmes did the rest. They were the Alabama gang in the bullpen. Brand was from Lineville, and Holmes was from Slocumb, just outside of Dothan.

Miles, hitting ninth, doubled in the sixth, for his only hit. Kevin Downes made the best of a start, this time at third, delivering three hits.

"It will be hard to keep Kevin out of the lineup tomorrow," said Randolph.

The Yankees' one-run win, coupled with Toronto's loss at home to the Cardinals, gave the Yankees the lead on their own for the first time this season.

"We said it a while back. Let's win each game. Let's set out to win each game," Randolph reminded the media.

Miles got to the park on Saturday, thinking about his cousin, Jeff "Hack" Goodwin. This was a four-game series. Hack believed in winning all series, but to win a four-game series, three, not two, wins were necessary.

Jason Harbison preferred the nightlife. Baseball nightlife that is. He loved taking the mound on a crisp September night. His assignment was to keep the good guys in first place. A national TV audience on Fox tuned in at 7:15 p.m., and Harbison was money, going seven strong. It was his top performance of the season, striking out six, and scattering five hits.

Harbison tipped his hat to the crowd as he left with the game headed to the seventh-inning stretch. The Yankees held a 1-0 lead.

Anthony Volpe began the home half of the seventh off with a walk. After two outs without any advancement, Miles came to the plate. Facing one of the nicest guys in the league, Garrett Whitlock, Miles took a deep breath in the box. Whitlock was an easy guy to pull for. He had battled injury after injury, but 2024 was the return of the Whitlock all baseball fans loved.

His fastball is deceptive. It dies away from right-handed hitters. Whitlock was enjoying good control of it on this night. Whitlock's fastball needs to remain varied. When it does, it shows he's got a dominant command.

Whitlock made only one mistake in the contest; his 2-1 offering to Fuller was pitched middle in. Fuller was waiting on it, frankly, needing a mistake. Fuller drove it in between the gap in right and center, plating the speedy Volpe, doubling the New York advantage to 2-0.

Harbison was hoping to pitch the eighth inning but was

lifted for crafty reliever Jonathan Loáisiga. The twenty-nine-year-old Nicaraguan-born Loáisiga got the final six outs of the contest, preserving a 2-1 Yankees win. It took Loáisiga thirty-two pitches, but by getting six outs, he allowed Holmes a chance to work in the Sunday contest fresh, potentially the final contest of a four-game sweep.

In 1978, the Yankees traveled to Boston on September 7, trailing the East-leading Red Sox by four games. At the close of play on September 10th, the Yankees had swept the four-game series at Fenway, outscoring Boston a total of 42-9, and catching the Red Sox at the top of the East standings. The four blowout wins became known as the "Boston Massacre," named after the 1770 incident with British soldiers.

The 2024 Yankees manager Willie Randolph had eight hits in that 1978 series, hitting safely in all four games, headlined by a double and two singles in the opener, lifting his average to .272 on the season.

The former Yankees second baseman approached Miles on Sunday at his locker, "Hey, kid. It's been a while since you had a day off. I'm going to sit you today because we are going to need you next week. Miles, I know you like hitting ninth, and I'm going to keep you there for now. For now, Miles," said the Yankees manager.

Those three hits by Randolph in the opener of the "Boston Massacre" lifted his average to a before-mentioned .272. His twenty-nine-year-old rookie centerfielder was now batting .372, a full 100 points higher. Miles did not have enough bats to be eligible for the batting title, but he was well clear of the .339 of current leader Corey Seager of Texas.

No Fuller in the Sunday contest versus the Red Sox. No problem. New York jumped out of the gate with four in the bottom of the first, including a three-run monster to left by Austin Wells. The Yankees would go on to win 9-4. Holmes wasn't needed late to secure the win, and with New York traveling out west to Seattle, the Yankees were off on Monday.

By the time the game arrived on Tuesday at Seattle, Randolph would have all his high-leverage bullpen guys available, all rested. Tommy Kahnle, Scott Brand, Jonathan Loáisiga, and Clay Holmes. Best of all, Yankees ace Gerrit Cole was due to pitch the opener. Things couldn't be looking better for the first-place Yankees. A great deal of wonderful things can happen to a baseball team during five weeks of the summer. This version of the Yankees had gone from being on life support to being alone in the lead in the American League East. Randolph was eager to see what the team could do this next week, the sixth week since his new centerfielder had arrived from AAA Scranton.

CHAPTER THIRTY-ONE

"If you hear a voice within you say, 'You cannot paint,' then by all means paint, and that voice will be silenced."

Vincent Van Gogh

The Yankees couldn't wait to hit the field running in Seattle. Miles was pleased to discover a couple of his old Stanford teammates would be in attendance in Seattle for the weekend series in Oakland. They may not still be "The Princes of Palo Alto," but it's always refreshing to see a friendly face in the stands.

Gerrit Cole did all he could for the Yankees in 2023, and he was filling that role again in 2024. He made one mistake all night, a two-run homer in the bottom of the third to Seattle phenom Julio Rodriguez. Cole gave the Yankees 7 1/3 innings, surrendering only four hits, while striking out nine.

Miles Fuller went 2-4 at the plate, and New York easily won

6-2. Yankees reliever, Tommy Kahnle, cleaned things up in the eighth inning, and the well-rested Clay Holmes worked a 1-2-3 ninth.

The following night was a little different. The New York lineup read Centerfielder Miles Fuller, hitting second. Most players would cherish that slot. Miles still wanted to hit eighth or ninth. Anthony Volpe started the contest with a double to right, scoring when Miles took a 2-0 fastball to left for another double.

Anthony Rizzo scored Fuller with a single, and the Yankees led by two runs going into the home half of the first.

New York starter, Clarke Schmidt, had a strong showing, holding a 3-0 lead when he departed with two outs in the sixth inning. The well-rested New York bullpen would need to retire ten batters.

Kahnle was first out, his changeup never looking better, stranding a runner at second. With New York still up 3-0 at the seventh inning stretch, all eyes turned to scoreboard-watching. The fading Orioles and Blue Jays continued to spiral downward, with the New York lead growing daily.

Scott Brand, Jonathan Loáisiga, and Ian Hamilton combined to get the last nine outs with Seattle only able to scratch across a single run in the 4-1 New York win.

The Yankees pulled off the sweep the following afternoon, hitting three home runs. A night after being held to only a double in the first, Miles went hitless when placed in the number two slot in the lineup. However, the Yankees didn't miss him that afternoon as New York prevailed, 7-3.

For the first time since his call-up, Fuller had only one hit over eight at-bats. Was it the pressure of hitting second? Would Randolph regret it?

Randolph met with Miles before the team departed for Oakland. "Let's go back to hitting you ninth. Of the Oakland pitching staff, three of the starters were with us. We are familiar with them. Let's see how you do. We may put you back at the top, but for now, let's hit you ninth. I think you won't mind."

"Not at all. But whatever I can do to help us win. If we sweep, we will clinch the division. That would wrap up an incredible six weeks for the Yankees," said the Yankees centerfielder.

"And it would wrap up an incredible six weeks for you. We all know what you've meant to our success these last six weeks this summer," noted Randolph.

Oakland would send out those three former Yankees in each game of the series. The lefty JP Sears would be the first former Yankee to take the mound on Friday night. Sears was from Sumter, South Carolina, just like long-time New York pitcher Jordan Montgomery and New York legend Bobby Richardson. Sears attended Wilson Hall, a private school in Sumter. Wilson Hall was a frequent opponent of Orangeburg Preparatory School in Orangeburg, South Carolina, where Miles attended elementary school and the beginning of middle school. Orangeburg Preparatory is also where former governor of South Carolina and 2024 Republican presidential candidate Nikki Haley graduated.

Miles had met Haley twice. First, at Stanford while Haley was attending a function at the Hoover Institution. Then, one year later, Miles was still at Stanford but congratulated Haley on a keynote speech she gave at an Orangeburg Preparatory graduation he attended in support of a good friend.

Sears pitched very well against New York, outside of two home runs hit by Jorge Lopez and Oswald Cabrera. He left after seven, down 3-1.

Fuller thrived at the bottom of the lineup, registering three hits, all singles, and stealing two bases. Volpe brought him home in the ninth, giving the Yankees some cushion, 4-1. Holmes gave up a single run in the ninth, but New York won 4-2, moving two games within the division title.

Stephanie flew in for the Saturday night and Sunday afternoon games. She took the one hour and thirty-five-minute train ride from Oakland to Palo Alto to have a late lunch and visit with Jordan and Hillary, college friends who still lived close to campus. She didn't reveal much to them about Miles, but she also couldn't conceal her smile when they asked about him.

"Does he have any single friends on the team? I can go younger, too," joked Jordan, looking at Stephanie.

"Surprisingly, most of the team seem happily married. Believe it or not, they are gentlemen. The team is loaded with Southerners," explained Stephanie.

"I'm not sure about the whole no facial hair rule," said Hillary.

"It wasn't an issue for Miles. He was always clean-shaven here and in the minors with the Brewers. If the players have a problem with it, they can grow a beard in the offseason. But my personal feeling is that they look professional. They are the face of the organization," said Stephanie.

Her visit with Jordan and Hillary went long. On her ride back, influenced by seeing her friends from college, Stephanie reminisced about a time in her life before getting to know Miles.

Stephanie Wilson sat at a table with two friends at The Oasis on El Camino Real Road in Menlo Park on the eve of her final day as a junior at Stanford University. This beer garden, a favorite for sixty years of Stanford alumni, permanently closed its doors in 2018 after failing to reach a lease agreement with the owner of the building. Often referred to as "The O," the bar and restaurant became a fixture for members of the Homebrew Computer Club, a famous Silicon Valley group that included

Steve Wozniak of Apple. Stephanie spent many a night there, none more fateful than on this occasion, the very night in 2013 when her future husband, Travis Ziegler, walked into her life.

Ziegler, 26, came in and joined a friend at the bar. It took him less than a minute to spot his future bride. Ziegler bought Stephanie and her friends two rounds of drinks, and then twenty minutes afterward, the six-foot-two-inch blonde-haired attorney asked if he could join them. After ten to twelve minutes, Ziegler excused himself, handing Stephanie his business card as he left.

"You should call him," suggested her friend Jordan.

"Why? I don't call guys."

Her other friend, Claire, cleared things up, "Because he's really good-looking."

It took Stephanie a week, but she caved in. She called him. It would be the biggest mistake of her life.

Her marriage was doomed from the beginning. Travis couldn't help himself. He refused to give up his single life despite being married. He also was verbally abusive, a pugnacious personality that only came out after Stephanie said, "I do."

At the present time, as Stephanie reflected on her days at Stanford, she would have loved to have a chance to do that night over, choosing another Stanford favorite, Miyake, a healthy sushi restaurant, instead of The Oasis.

Stephanie loved her time at Stanford, but it is understandable how she chose to think fondly of her first three years but to eschew memories of her senior session, spent exclusively with her now ex-husband.

Travis was an arriviste, a self-seeker, and she was only an object for him. One can't go back in time, but one can learn from mistakes. Stephanie was determined not to let her time with Travis define her. That wasn't always an easy assignment.

Her first three years at Stanford were innocuous. She became friendly with an elderly couple in their late 70s, and she would often house-sit for them. The Campbells had no kids yet lived in a gigantic 6.7-million-dollar mansion with a guest cottage overlooking a rivage.

Stephanie was an early morning riser and avid reader. The deck just outside the cottage offered a caliginous early morning view of the bay. To her, the misty, dim setting, the blanket of fog, was peaceful.

Her favorite area of the property was a sitooterie 300 yards from the mansion. Stephanie spent hundreds of hours reading and relaxing in the outside building. It made her feel like she was in a gazebo in the 1920s, with a party ongoing in the courtyard. Hemingway or Fitzgerald could have knocked out an additional ten novels from this setting.

Stephanie shared the upscale property with Jordan but honored the Campbells' wishes of keeping company to a minimum. Jordan and Stephanie spent several weekends in the sitooterie, making calimocho cocktails, consisting of fifty percent red wine and fifty percent cola-based soft drinks.

As she ended her thoughts down memory lane, she spotted Miles up to bat on her mobile phone and could not conceal her effulgent smile. Her face lit up at the view of her boyfriend hitting for the Yankees.

She was a girl who had previously and purposely skipped over baseball games. She was now learning to love the game. And she had become Miles Fuller's biggest fan.

By the time she arrived at Oakland-Alameda County Coliseum, New York trailed 2-0 in the fourth inning, failing so far to figure out former Yankee right-hander Luis Medina. The twenty-five-year-old Dominican had only been touched for one hit in four innings of work.

Medina gave up his second hit to Fuller in the fifth, to the right field corner. Fuller turned on the jets and reached third with a triple. Volpe's RBI groundout brought in Fuller, cutting the deficit in half. As Miles watched from home plate, walking back to the visiting dugout, he smiled at his beautiful, tall girlfriend, who made the game just in time to see his triple.

New York starter Brad Litkenhous worked seven strong, leaving down 2-1. Medina also was out of the game after seven, which was good news for the Yankees.

Fuller walked in the eighth and came home on a two-run homer to left by DJ LeMahieu. With Cole pitching the finale on Sunday, Randolph asked Brand to go two innings for a shot at a rare save.

It took Brand forty-four pitches, but he stranded one in the eighth and two in the ninth, moving the Yankees within one game of the East Division Championship.

"I'm just glad they took out Luis after seven. He was hard to figure out. He's a very good pitcher. The A's are set up to succeed, I can tell you that," admitted Miles to a reporter from the *New York Post*.

Much of that success would not occur in Oakland as the Athletics were destined to join the Raiders in Las Vegas soon. The Sunday series finale pitted Yankees ace Gerrit Cole against lefty Ken Waldichuk of the Athletics.

Waldichuk, Medina, Sears, and Cooper Bowman were sent to Oakland just before the trade deadline on August 1, 2022, for heralded Oakland starter Frankie Montas and dependable reliever Lou Trivino.

Montas went just 1-3 in eight starts with the Yankees, compiling an ERA of 6.35. He then missed the entire 2023 season.

Trivino was a remarkable asset to the 2022 Yankees' playoff push to the ALCS. The reliever made twenty-five appearances for the Yankees following the trade deadline, registering a sparkling ERA of 1.66 while striking out twenty-two in one out, short of twenty-two innings of work. Trivino also missed the entire 2023 season, requiring Tommy John surgery on May 2.

The frustration over the trade will continue to grow for Yankees fans as time goes by. But this day, Cole was all New York expected him to be.

The Yankees' ace went eight impressive innings, striking out eleven and limiting Oakland to just one run on two hits. Fuller's two-out RBI double scored two in the bottom of the second, giving the good guys the lead 2-0. It would be all they would need, thanks to Cole's superb performance. But they would get plenty more.

When Waldichuk left after five, New York was up 3-0. Volpe doubled to start the seventh, with Rizzo later homering, increasing the lead to 6-0. When a baseball team clinches a division (or a postseason series), to do it in a relaxing manner is refreshing. A team wants to be in the field when the final out is retired. Then, the locker room celebration, often in the company of champagne, is not to be missed. It's not the finish line, but each hurdle climbed and each obstacle passed gets the team one step closer to their ultimate goal.

Considering where this team stood six weeks ago, where they are now is amazing. They rode the back of a twenty-nine-year-old who was a substitute teacher this time a season ago. General Manager Jason Giambi needed a catalyst, and he found it in a very unlikely way. It was Giambi who watched from the stands as Fuller knocked around Yankees' pitching in that spring contest in March 2023 held at Steinbrenner Field in Tampa. Miles had a bad spring tryout, collecting only nine hits. But he saved four of those while briefly with Atlanta that day against the Yankees.

Miles Fuller always believed in himself. Now, at twenty-nine, the Stanford alumnus and career Minor Leaguer turned unemployed ball player would soon be enjoying his first taste of post-season baseball.

Fuller contributed two hits in the final road game of the season as New York downed Oakland 8-1 to sweep the series and clinch the division.

It was fitting that Giambi, a native of West Covina, California, was the first to greet Miles as the rookie came in to celebrate the division title. Giambi felt right at home in Oakland, having won the AL MVP as an Athletic in 2000. He played for the Yankees from 2002-2008, returning to Oakland in 2009, missing the Yankees World Series title of 2009 by a single season. The Yankees declined their team option on him for 2009. Giambi eventually retired at the age of forty-three after playing for the Cleveland Indians in 2013-2014.

Initially opposed by the veterans, Miles took a turn playing the role of disc jockey during the locker room celebration. However, his decision to play "Waiting" by Tom Petty and "Your Love" by The Outfield was met with approval. As the team continued to drink and celebrate, the newest Yankee played a tune in his own honor, "Centerfield" by John Fogerty.

Tomorrow was the final off day of the regular season for the 2024 Yankees. The Yankees would need a day to recover. But on this day, the 266th day of the year, the 38th Sunday of 2024, and officially the final day of summer, the Yankees' hard work and success of the previous six weeks had given the team every feeling that the fast-approaching fall would be a fall to remember!

CHAPTER THIRTY-TWO

"Kindness is universal. Sometimes, being kind allows others to see the goodness in humanity through you. Always be kinder than necessary."

Germany Kent

"I'm ready for the pretty leaves and that cool, crisp breeze," shouted Yankees second baseman and shortstop Jorge Lopez as he entered the Yankees' clubhouse on Tuesday, September 24. The Yankees were preparing for a week of home games to close out the 2024 regular season.

Lopez and Kevin Downes would be counted on a great deal over these last six games as Randolph attempted to get guys to rest. New York had locked up a bye for the first round of the playoffs, likely to meet the Twins in the divisional series. New York was solidly in the number two seed slot, trailing only the best team in the American League, the Houston Astros - the still-hated Houston Astros.

The National League belonged to the Braves and the Dodgers. Atlanta had the best record in baseball, so the World Series participant from the senior circuit would have to go by way of Atlanta. The Braves were loaded, with no weakness in the lineup.

Miles Fuller still thought about some of the guys he had the pleasure to get to know from the Braves and his brief time with Atlanta in the spring of 2023. From time to time, he also would see Atlanta pitchers John Perkerson and Matt Trucks, as both lived in Newnan. The City of Homes, as Newnan was called, was not a long drive from Truist Park and was a lovely place to live. There was also a level of respect between professional players, no matter where you were from. You knew when you saw one at a batting cage or gym, even if you couldn't name him. The skill, the ability, gave it away. Seeing Trucks throw nearly 100 mph in the offseason also gave it away.

The Braves' pitching staff was deep and was healthier than the previous two seasons. Max Fried was back, Trucks was having the best season of his career, and local product Bryan Lundquist had been added by trade from San Francisco. The best of them all was ace Spencer Strider, the likely N.L. Cy Young Award winner. Had it not been for Strider's twenty-two wins, Max Fried might get the award. Fried had nineteen wins with at least one more start, potentially two left in the regular season. Braves manager Chip Walker had many options at his disposal.

The Yankees went back to Fuller, hitting second in the Tuesday opener against the slumping Orioles. The results brought back mixed reviews. He had one double in five plate appearances.

Clarke Schmidt was the starter and loser for the Yankees, a team that looked like they could use another day to recover. Final score: Orioles 7, Yankees 2.

Like New York, the Orioles were desperate for victories, having collapsed in August and September. Willie Randolph wanted to rest the players, but for the integrity of the game, he also had to be fair, feeling almost obligated to play his best players for other contending playoff teams.

The Yankees' top talent, Aaron Judge, had been lost in August, and, at that time, most had written off the Yankees' chances. Jasson Dominguez, who looked so promising for his brief time up in the Bronx in 2023 had to put forth a valiant attempt to get back to the club after suffering his UCL injury in September of 2023. New York lost one of its bright spots, even if it turned out to be a flicker, in what was a depressing and dreary season for those who love the pinstripes.

The Orioles were fortunate to be playing meaningful games despite the tailspin the club had suffered since the All-Star break. The Yankees are typically not viewed as underdogs, but the 2023 and 2024 versions of the Yankees were not your great-grandfather's 1920s Yankees. The 2024 season was proving to be just as dismal as the previous until a six-foot-six alumnus of Stanford showed up, doing all he could to lighten the blow of losing the six-foot-seven franchise player the team had lost.

Success comes with certain casualties. In addition to being recognized by friends and other players, Miles Fuller had now lost his anonymity. His play dictated that. Once up and playing, his production cost him his freedom to walk through the city unnoticed.

His dream of seeing *Les Misérables* was never going to come to fruition, not on Broadway, not on a date with Stephanie. There may indeed be a "Castle on a Cloud," but he was not going to hear it in New York.

Being the nice guy he was, he signed every autograph that

was requested. He may not have been a "Prince of Palo Alto" anymore, but Yankees Universe had fallen in love with him. Cameras caught him playing catch in the outfield in numerous parks, with both young boys and girls, endearing him to hundreds of thousands despite him not being a media favorite. His love of Christ and his willingness to speak about it publicly and on camera resonated with evangelical Christians everywhere. They, if any group in America, could relate to the media's hate and constant divisive reporting.

Not being on social media, outside of that one Facebook account, helped the centerfielder drown out the noise. Miles was in the Bronx to help the Yankees reach the playoffs and, hopefully, a World Series. He was no gadabout, choosing to keep his private life private, eschewing social media.

It was a great stage to play on for a guy with no contract next season. It was his chance to make an impression on all other clubs, an opportunity to land a huge contract, a stark reversal of his current league minimum salary. He was showcasing his abilities, and as the saying goes, "If you can make it here, you can make it anywhere." If Miles Fuller could produce in the postseason, he was no doubt headed for the life of a parvenu, having already established some celebrity status.

The Yankees were ready to play on Wednesday, supporting starting pitcher Jason Harbison with eleven hits and seven runs. Miles went 3-5 and swiped two more bags. He was asked by one of his not-so-favorite reporters, "What are you thinking about as you are attempting to steal a base?" Miles answered, "I'm singing the lyrics from the song 'Breaking Away' by Balance. 'There's no doubt about my leaving, you know I'll be breaking away.'"

The next day, the reporter posted online that Miles couldn't wait to break away from the Yankees. That led to a sit-down meeting with Giambi and Randolph. He eventually was able to clear the air, and the YES network was kind enough to interview him before the Thursday game with the Orioles. Then the network, in a brilliant moment of epiphany and insight, went to a commercial, playing "Breaking Away" by Balance. When they returned from the commercial, fans could hear "Misunderstanding" by Genesis.

Miles took his frustration out on the Orioles with two doubles and a single. He turned his single into a triple, stealing second and third. The only down part of his day was a forward-diving attempt at a blooper that fell safely to the ground just in front of his glove.

In the spirit of Miles' cousin, Jeff "Hack" Goodwin, the Yankees won the series with a decisive 6-1 victory. Stephanie was at the ballpark, looking great in his No.14 jersey, hair in a ponytail through the back of her dark blue Yankees cap. When allowed into the players' area, she went over to his locker and said to Miles, "How about we fly to Augusta, play Augusta National in the morning, then catch a flight back here for the game?"

He knew she was joking and being sarcastic, but he appreciated the thought. He countered, "How about a week after the season, we get your dad and perhaps Bill Ham in Auburn to play with us?"

She was curious, "Why do we have to wait a week to play once the season is over?"

Miles responded, "If we don't win the World Series, I won't be able to get out of bed for a week."

"Then I guess you better win the World Series."

He responded, "You know, what you said on my recruiting visit was so true."

She sighed, "I try to forget that day since you barely had your driver's license. What did I say?"

"That all of the girls want the Stanford baseball boys."

Stephanie admitted as she reached out to pull him towards her, "Yes, but how many of us get to keep one?"

Pittsburgh came in on Friday to close out the regular season. The Pirates had young talent, getting better by the year, a real threat for the future if they keep the team together.

The Yankees started a couple of Scranton AAA call-ups for the Friday and Saturday games. With the Yankees not slated to begin the playoffs until the following Saturday, ace Gerrit Cole would pitch the final game of the regular season but be limited to seventy or seventy-five pitches.

Miles was given the Friday game off, a contest in which Pittsburgh prevailed 10-5. The Yankees couldn't have looked more uninterested or less focused.

Randolph spoke to the team following the embarrassing loss. "Let's finish the season strong these next two days. That out there tonight, that was not who we are. Let's take some momentum into the postseason," said the beloved Yankees skipper.

The Yankees responded to his appeal the following afternoon. Miles went hitless with a walk, but the Yankees were victorious 5-1.

Stephanie and Miles ordered dinner in on Sunday night, asking Jason and Tara Harbison to join them for a doubleheader, a Hitchcock doubleheader.

Saturday day games always afforded the players more weekend time with their loved ones. The group had to have Carmine's Italian food and paid handsomely to have it delivered. The hotel provided a suite with three televisions, so they viewed *To Catch a Thief* and then *Rear Window* on the middle set, saw Stanford lose another football game on the left side, and watched Ohio State pull out a victory on set three.

Harbison was scheduled to pitch three innings the next afternoon against the Pirates. Harbison gave up two bombs, both to Oneil Cruz, the Pirates' young star named after former New York great Paul O'Neill. O'Neill was a five-time World Series champion, four with the Yankees (1996, 1998, 1999, 2000). He was in the broadcast booth, working on the game for the YES network, seeing his namesake excel right in front of him. There was little to no excellence exhibited by the Yankees on this day. The Pirates took the series with a regular season-ending 7-1 win.

New York was now off until the following Saturday when they would begin a best-of-five American League Division Series. The Yankees had secured the number two seed. Houston was the top seed in the American League.

Miles was asked to do an exclusive interview on Monday by the reporter he respected the most from the *New York Post*. Stephanie joined him, and they met Doug Gilliam in a banquet room at a nearby hotel for the following exchange:

Doug: Your ascension to stardom. Can you define it? It is a real-life underdog story on display in front of millions of eyes.

Miles: I'm honored each time I represent the Yankees. I am just giving all I can because I have to. This could be my only chance at a World Series ring.

Doug: The last time you played for Stanford, explain the devastation of that loss.

Miles: I simply didn't want to take the uniform off. One day you were in this exciting frisson. It's such a thrill. The electricity is palpable. But that glowing feeling in the postseason, full of unrestrained enthusiasm, can be reduced instantly to a flickering lambent of soft radiance.

Doug: You struggled in college during the postseason.

Miles: It was a disaster. I didn't contribute. I let my team down every year.

Doug: How did that make you feel?

Miles: I was humbled. It makes you want to get a hug from your mom. It stays with me, akin to a hiker on a traipse, out aimlessly, never reaching their desired destination.

Doug: What are your plans today? You don't have a game until Saturday.

Miles: Stephanie and I are going to fly over to Harrisonville, Pennsylvania. That is where George Selkirk is buried. I want to pay my respects. I have Mr. Selkirk to thank for the warning track. Safety was significant to him. In many ways, ninety years later, my life is paralleling his. He came up in late July and was a difference-maker. I'm trying to duplicate his accomplishment. I feel his presence in the field.

Doug: The fans love you. They see you playing catch with kids in the stands, signing all those autographs, giving back with your time. Yet the media seems very frustrated with you. Do you want to comment?

Miles: I feel like most of the media have been unfair to me. But I also know they know I'm conservative politically.

Doug: If the Yankees win the World Series, will you visit the White House?

Miles: Although we have been advised not to discuss politics, I would not if invited by President Biden. I might get in trouble for saying that.

Doug: You don't respect him?

Miles: I respect the office. I appreciate his service. But the country needs to be honest. If he were a football coach, he would punt on second down. He attempted to shake hands with invisible people. He took commands from the Easter bunny at the annual White House Easter egg hunt. What happened in Afghanistan was a disaster. His response to Israel being attacked, his no comment on lives lost in Maui...I could go on and on. I fear for him; he seems stravaig, wandering about aimlessly.

Doug: Thanks for the time. Good luck in the postseason.

Miles: I appreciate the sentiment. I need it. I want to help deliver a title to the Yankees Universe.

Doug: One final question. How do you feel about AOC?

Miles: I think very little of her. I have heard she bought season tickets to watch the Electoral College play football. And I probably will get in trouble for saying that, too.

As the interview concluded, the three engaged in small talk. Gilliam requested Miles to speak to him off the record, asking Miles to explain why the hitter believed he was having so much success at baseball's highest level. Miles sincerely shared with him, "I will be honest with you, Doug. It is so much easier to trust big-league pitchers. They throw strikes and exhibit excellent command. In college, at times, I didn't want to dig in because of how erratic the pitching tended to be. A walk for me was an extra-base hit, as I was allowed to utilize my speed to steal bases. There are no free passes at this level."

CHAPTER THIRTY-THREE

"Teach us to number our days and recognize how few they are; help us to spend them as we should."

Psalm 90:12

George Selkirk died in Fort Lauderdale, Florida, on January 19, 1987, fifteen days after his 79th birthday. Selkirk, a five-time World Series Champion, was born in 1908 in Huntsville, Ontario, Canada, and was selected in 1983 in the initial Canadian Baseball Hall of Fame class. Selkirk served in the United States Navy after retiring from baseball and was later a manager in the Yankees farm system and was the general manager of the then Washington Senators (now Texas Rangers). His professional career began in 1927, but he failed to make the major league until 1934. He appeared in 846 major league games, batting .290 and hitting 108 home runs. Later in life, his family moved to Rochester, New York, and he attended Rochester Technical School.

Selkirk's connection with Miles Fuller was undeniable. Both were nearly thirty when they first made the majors, both with the Yankees. They were both outfielders who were called up due to injuries. Both contributed instantly to the success of their teams. Selkirk was responsible for the warning track, a fact that speaks to the current Yankees' centerfielder.

Selkirk was buried in the Siloam United Methodist Cemetery in Harrisonville, Pennsylvania. With New York waiting for a weekend opponent to begin the 2024 playoffs, Miles and Stephanie decided to take her dad's Cessna Citation Excel to Harrisonville, named after the ninth United States President, William Henry Harrison, to pay their respects to Selkirk. They, with the two pilots, landed at the Altoona-Blair County Airport shortly after 1:00 p.m. on Monday. The airport was fifteen miles south of Altoona and approximately a thirty-minute Uber ride to the cemetery.

As they arrived at 9541 Pleasant Ridge Road, the two were moved by the very private setting, the graves, the church, and the cemetery located just in front of the woods. They felt like they were watching a movie set. Stephanie, who had grabbed a box from under her seat, reached for her boyfriend's hand as the two began searching for the marker.

"I don't want to give the impression that I'm a chthonic individual. I'm not obsessed with death. But I do like the idea of paying respects to him, just as I did to Mr. Munson in Ohio," Miles told her.

After a couple of minutes, the two located the grave of the six-time All-Star, who unfortunately lost all five of his World Series rings when his Fort Lauderdale condo was robbed in the 1960s. Selkirk is buried next to his wife, Norma Fox Selkirk, three years his elder, a registered nurse. Stephanie first saw it. "Okay, Miles. I wasn't expecting this. She was born in 1905 and he was born in 1908. She's between two and three years older than him. Tell me you don't think God is sending us a message because I know He is."

"I know He is, too. On his stone, under his death date, it simply reads 'N.Y. Yankee.' I love that," noted Miles.

"I love the 'Reg. Nurse' under Norma's," said Stephanie.

"She gave back to her community. The connection I have with him is unreal. Each time I go back on the warning track and approach the wall, I say something like 'George, help me,' or 'George be with me,' or 'One more time, George.'"

He continued, "My three favorite baseball players are Lou Gehrig, Mariano Rivera, and Mike Mussina. Mr. Selkirk was roommates on the road with Gehrig. They would wrestle together while they were on the road. That's how Mr. Gehrig realized something was wrong, that he discovered he had ALS while wrestling with George."

"I just love that she's three years older than him. I have no words for that other than it mirrors us," said Stephanie.

Miles left a baseball at Selkirk's marker. "George, thank you for your service to our country and for all that you have done for the game of baseball. You understood safety before anyone else. I feel you with me in the field. I hope I make you proud. I'm honored to wear the jersey you put on. Go Yankees!"

Before leaving, Miles told Stephanie how both Selkirk and his wife came from humble beginnings and how his family eventually moved to Rochester, New York. That fact didn't escape Miles. Selkirk hit 108 home runs. Miles was no power hitter. However, his first home run hit in Washington landed in the hands of Rochester native Steven Segerlin, the Auburn graduate. It's a small world, after all.

Stephanie then surprised Miles. "Give me a minute alone here," she requested.

Miles nodded and took thirty steps back. She reached for a small jewelry box, of which Miles could only see the aureate exterior, which served as a preview of what was inside. Stephanie took out a baseball bracelet from the jewelry box and placed it next to the baseball Miles had left. She thanked George for his service to the country and thanked Norma for her service to the community.

"When I came here today, I didn't know what to expect. But being here has been emotional and eye-opening. I'm going to marry Miles, and he loves you, George. He always asks you to be with him in the outfield, on the warning track. I'm asking you to be with me, to help me in this relationship. Miles is a Christ-driven man, and I love him more than I thought possible. So, I'm asking that both of you help us. If possible, show me a sign someday that you are with us."

Just as she wrapped up her request, the winds became the heaviest of the day. The trees in the nearby woods were oscillating back and forth. It was the sign that she had requested. An immediate response. Norma and George were with her. Norma and George were with them.

CHAPTER THIRTY-FOUR

"There's a feeling today among coaches that players believe the game, whatever sport, didn't start until those players began playing."

A.J. Jones
Six Weeks This Summer

The Minnesota Twins and the New York Yankees were scheduled to start the best-of-five A.L. Division Series on Saturday night at Yankee Stadium in the Bronx. The good Lord had other ideas. The rain started falling a little after 10:00 a.m. and was still coming down at the scheduled 8:05 p.m. first pitch time. The game had long been called off before then, officially a rainout at 3:30 p.m. Eastern Time.

Game 1 will now go on Sunday at 7:10 p.m. The forced postponement took away the scheduled travel day on Monday. Game 2 will start on Monday at 4:10 p.m. ET. By the time Gerrit

Cole threw his opening pitch, a 96-mph fastball, it had been a little more than seven days since the Yankees had played an inning on a diamond. Yankees manager Willie Randolph had two primary concerns: Would the Yankees be sluggish after such a long layoff? And was the Pirates series that closed the regular season an auger of things to come?

Because the Twins had already played a series, they were expected to be sharp. The Yankees, on the other side, were more rested, with pitchers lined up. Both teams would have to overcome the loss of the Monday travel day. Perhaps this Yankees team could repeat the success of the 1996 World Championship team. The Yankees and the Braves lost the Monday travel day. Due to a prior rain out, Game 2 was moved to Monday night at Yankee Stadium.

The Braves triumphed to go up 2-0 in the series, but the Yankees never lost again, sweeping the Tuesday, Wednesday, and Thursday games in Atlanta.

Cole faced Carlos Correa with one on in the first, and Correa, hated by the New York crowd for his time in Houston, welcomed the Yankees back to the playoffs (after missing the playoffs in 2023) with a two-run homer to left field.

Panic didn't set in until the completion of the sixth inning; New York now trailing 3-0, the Yankees down to the final nine outs. Cole got two more outs in the seventh, lifted after 106 gutsy pitches.

Reliever Scott Brand brought the Yankees back to the plate, still down 3-0. Fuller started the home half of the seventh with a ball that had eyes right up the middle. Grand Theft Awesome stole second with Anthony Volpe walking.

New York had two on with no outs. If not injured, this would have been the time for Aaron Judge to hit in the lineup. No Yankee fan needed to be reminded of that. Fuller wanted the Yankees to bunt to put two runners in scoring position with a solid chance to put up a crooked number. Instead, New York put up no number, another goose egg, after a strike-out and a double play. Brand came back for the eighth, holding the Twins down, the good guys still trailing 3-0.

It didn't matter. The Yankees never reached base again; the last eight guys retired in order, shut out at home in the opener 3-0.

Stephanie called Miles once he was back in his room, unable to attend in person as she was needed in Montana at an event for her dad's foundation.

"Look, the good news is that was just one game. But what the heck happened, Miles? I kept refreshing my phone, and the score never changed, only the inning."

"We were flat, Baby. I can't tell you why. I thought we were ready, but they held us to three hits. I got one hit, but I never felt comfortable," admitted Miles.

"I'm sorry I can't be there with you. Do you have anyone?"

"Not tonight. But the rain out will allow Dad to be here tomorrow, and Uncle Phil will be in Minnesota on Tuesday and hopefully on Wednesday."

She knew what he was saying. "Meaning you hope there's a game four on Wednesday."

"Exactly!"

She sighed. "You guys have to win tomorrow."

He responded, "We will."

Greg Fuller arrived at Yankee Stadium twenty minutes before the beginning of Game 2. It was a cloudy Monday afternoon, with temperatures remaining at 60. A big smile came to his face when he noticed his only child, Miles, playing catch with a young boy no more than the age of ten.

He knew his son understood the importance of moments. He knows how to give back, to be thankful for the gift, and to use it in any way he can. That ten-year-old would never forget that and would for sure be hassling Mom and Dad for the purchase of the No.14 jersey. Speaking of the No.14, they were starting to pop up more and more in the stands. And for September, it was the number seven ranked jersey in MLB sales. Not bad for a player with less than two months of MLB experience.

Greg Fuller didn't have to wait long to see his son shine in Game 2, doubling down the left-field line, giving the Yankees their first lead of the series, 2-0, in the home half of the second.

Yankees starter Clarke Schmidt settled in nicely, not feeling any pressure in what most would say was a must-win situation for New York. And they were right. The Yankees couldn't afford to go to Minnesota down two games in a best-of-five.

Jasson Dominguez extended the lead to 4-0 in the fourth with his first postseason home run, a moon shot to center. The quick turnaround, a day game after a night game, had helped. The Yankees weren't forced to sit around and think too much about the dismal opening game performance. Coach Willie Randolph had to be careful with his usage of the bullpen, with no day off the next day due to the Game 1 rainout.

Schmidt went six strong, leading 4-2. Brand wasn't an option for the seventh. Kahnle got the Yankees to the eighth, but there was no longer a cushion. Minnesota had cut the Yankees' lead to one. There was no more room for error.

The Yankees' bats had gone silent again. Going into the eighth, there was no panic in the stands. Randolph went to closer Clay Holmes to begin the eighth. The native of Slocumb, Alabama, who was committed to play at Auburn University before deciding to go pro, retired all six hitters he faced. There was no one in the New York clubhouse Miles respected more than Holmes. Clay's father was a pastor. Often, Clay and Miles also would share encouraging scripture with each other.

Miles gave a fist pump, his first of the series when Dominguez caught the final out. Miles then met Dominguez between right and center with a handshake, and the two jogged in together. It was an interesting moment for Miles, jogging in with the Yankees centerfielder of the future. Miles was a free agent at the end of the season, and it was expected that Judge would be moved to right, with Dominguez firmly placed in center.

Miles couldn't worry about that right now. He was focused on winning the series, and he knew his play these last two months had impressed many around the league. He was going to be wearing a jersey next season. Maybe just not pinstripes.

New York fans knew that the Yankees had at least two more games this season. Fans of the Houston Astros couldn't say the same thing. The Yankees had free entertainment on their flight to Minneapolis. The Blue Jays and Astros were playing Game 2 of their series, and the Blue Jays were in command, up 8-2 after seven innings, already leading the series 1-0.

This was big for the Yankees because they were a nightmarish matchup for Toronto, while Houston recently had dominated New York in several postseason meetings.

No off day. No problem for the Yankees' Game 3 starter Brad Litkenhous. In the biggest start of his career, Litkenhous sailed through seven innings, even retiring a hitter in the eighth for his longest outing of the season.

Litkenhous gave up a single run in the bottom of the fourth that tied the contest at the time, 1-1. New York took the lead for good in the fifth when that same guy, Miles Fuller, doubled in Austin Wells from second. The TV broadcaster punctuated the go-ahead hit with, "Momma, there goes that man again!"

Fuller was becoming a real problem for Minnesota. It was almost the same chorus, different verse, in the eighth when Miles singled in Wells from third, changing the scoreboard to 3-1, good guys.

Randolph extended a leash to Litkenhous, who was only removed after a single to Byron Buxton with one out in the aforementioned eighth inning. Randolph went out to get the tired starter, and before he even got to the mound, the rest of the Yankees in the dugout were out in front of the dugout, just off the mound, in a line to salute the great pitching effort.

Randolph, with Holmes down, now had to find five outs from his bullpen, up 3-1, with another game tomorrow. The Twins had the tying run at the plate. The Yankees' skipper had faith in Scott Brand, who had pitched in the Game 1 loss. The native of Lineville, Alabama, faced two hitters, striking out both.

The Yankees failed to mount anything in the ninth. Reliever Jonathan Loáisiga emerged from the bullpen to get the final three outs. It wasn't easy. With two down and two on, Yankee hater Correa came to the plate as the winning run. One swing of the bat from the dangerous Correa would turn the pendulum of the series completely in favor of Minnesota and give the Twins a chance to finish off the Yankees the next night in Minnesota.

Loáisiga didn't back down from Correa. The Minnesota hitter swung through his 1-2 offering, giving the Yankees a 2-1 series edge, the pendulum remaining with the good guys.

The night belonged to Litkenhous. "I can't tell you what a relief this is. I just wanted to contribute. On the plane yesterday, instead of spreading out in the rows, several of us gathered in a circle. We shared what was on our hearts, how thankful we were to be in this position, how far we had come, and then we all prayed. As Miles Fuller said, we could feel the presence of the Lord with us. I can't explain to you how encouraged I felt then and how relaxed I am today. We are in a good position. We hope to wrap this up tomorrow night, but if not, we have the security of knowing Minnesota has to come to our house for the deciding fifth game," explained the winning pitcher.

It was uncertain whether or not the Yankees could finish off the Twins in four. What was completed was the other A.L. Division Series as Toronto had closed out number one seed Houston in four on Wednesday afternoon in Toronto. The Yankees players celebrated as they witnessed the Blue Jays' shocking achievement, led by former Astro George Springer, who homered twice. The Yankees were now the top seed remaining in the American League and would have a home-field advantage against Toronto if they could get by the Twins.

The Minnesota crowd was rowdy and was doing its best to push the Twins past New York. With Atlanta and Los Angeles already securing sweeps in the National League Series, the Twins-Yankees showdown was the final series left undecided.

The best way to put a loud crowd back in the seats is to strike early. That's exactly what DJ LeMahieu did, blasting a two-run homer in the first in support of Yankees starter Jason Harbison. Nighttime was the right time for Harbison, and he was staked to a 4-0 lead before he threw his first pitch.

The lead grew to 6-0 when Anthony Volpe homered in the second, and the Yankees were well on their way to a win. Harbison would pitch 6 1/3 innings, limiting Minnesota to one run on five hits.

Brand got two outs for the Yankees in the seventh, and New York was up 6-1 after seven. Miles changed the scoreboard to 7-1 with a single in the ninth, safely hitting in all four games.

Jose Alvarez pitched the final two innings, giving up a run but securing the series-ending 7-2 win. The victory, coupled with Toronto ousting Houston, meant Alvarez and the Yankees would face his older brother, Oscar Alvarez, and Toronto in the ALCS beginning on Saturday, with Oscar Alvarez likely to start Game 1 on the mound for Toronto.

The Yankees celebrated their divisional series win over the Twins, but it was dialed down as this was a tired team. There was champagne and beer, and yes, "Your Love" and "The Waiting" were played. As Miles left for a private room to call

Stephanie, a new song made an appearance in the rotation, "Anti-Hero" by Taylor Swift.

"Miles, you guys did it. You are four wins from playing in the World Series!"

"I know. My phone is blowing up," stated the outfielder.

"Go celebrate with the guys. I will be there on Friday night. Congratulations! I love you!"

CHAPTER THIRTY-FIVE

"Good teams become great ones when the members trust each other enough to surrender the Me for the We."

Phil Jackson

The Yankees were back in New York preparing for Game 1 of the ALCS to begin the next day, Friday, at 8:05 p.m.

The Dodgers and Atlanta were to open their series in Atlanta on this night to determine who would represent the National League in the World Series. The Braves were on a mission to exorcise the demons of the last two postseasons but were headed towards a dynasty. The dynasty topic wouldn't be changing soon when considering the likes of Acuña Jr., Albies, Olson, and Riley, who were locked up to long-term contracts. The Braves' youngsters contributed once called up to the big show. That has not been the case for the Yankees, except for

Anthony Volpe and Jasson Dominguez, before Dominguez was lost in September of 2023, needing Tommy John surgery.

On the eve of the ALCS, Miles, and Stephanie had dinner at the same hotel that had housed the Yankees centerfielder since he arrived from Scranton. There were a couple of exceptions, but for the most part, it was hotel to stadium and stadium to hotel.

Miles tried to use Thursday night to return as many messages as possible. The problem with having 400 messages is that when you return a text, another one comes seconds later. Stephanie was done returning emails and was ready for her boyfriend to pay her some attention. But he felt the need to return a few more and then make calls that were critical to him. He called his parents, his Uncle Phil, Kenny Morris, Greg Hamilton, and Mike Furbush. He got in touch with all of them except Mike Furbush, who was at the Braves game. No surprise there. He then told Stephanie that he wanted to place one more call and that he had to do it before 8:00 p.m.

"Why is that?" she asked.

"I met this guy on a plane last summer, and he was very interested in my career. We exchanged numbers and started sending each other supportive messages and "Seinfeld" TV show quotes. Well, it turns out that he's the president of the University of Memphis. And he's got this rule about not taking phone calls after 8:00 p.m. or so and cuts off messages a little after that."

"You meet people in strange places," noted Stephanie.

Miles laughed, "And it is a good thing for you. Anyway, he was kind enough last summer to send the university plane to pick me up in Newnan for a Thursday night game between Navy and Memphis. And I thought maybe, just maybe, I could return the favor and ask him if he would like tickets to one of the ALCS games."

She then asked, "Is he a golfer?"

He responded, "He is most definitely a golfer."

"What's his name?"

"Dr. Bill Hardgrave, formerly the Provost at Auburn."

"Since he plays golf, I will just have Dad invite him to play Augusta National with us."

"That would be perfect," confirmed Miles.

"Okay, now that we have fulfilled our outside communication requirements, I want a make-out session with my boyfriend."

"Who is he?"

"Some guy that has a baseball game tomorrow."

"Was he a Prince of Palo Alto?"

She lay on top of him to kiss him, "Yes. And now he's a Bronx Bomber!"

"Wait. I know him. He's the one who has the sexy girlfriend. She's a bit older and looks amazing in the pinstripes jersey."

"Yes, that's her," agreed Stephanie.

By the time Gerrit Cole threw the first pitch of the American League Championship Series, the National League Series was tied at a game each, the Game 2 matinee having just been won by the Dodgers 4-3. Cole was facing Toronto ace Kevin Gausman. In 2023, MLB decided to alter some of the great traditions of the sport, including adding a pitch clock and a time requirement for hitters to be in the box. The players requested additional time for the playoffs but were denied. Cole and Gausman didn't need a clock. Neither gave up a hit in the first five innings. At this rate, the game would be over before the Braves and Dodgers got in the air and headed to the West Coast for Game 3.

Bo Bichette of the Blue Jays destroys left-handed pitchers. Cole was not left-handed, and Bichette was held hitless by the best arm in the American League. Cole went eight innings, only giving up a seventh-inning single run when Vlad Guerrero Jr. singled in Jon Norton. The Yankees scored twice in the sixth, Dominguez and Oswald Cabrera boosting the cause, both doubling.

New York added a bases-loaded walk to Kevin Downes in the home half of the seventh to make it 3-1. Clay Holmes worked the ninth, stranding a runner at second, giving the Yankees the all-important opener.

The Yankees celebrated the Game 1 win by having a late dinner at their clubhouse, the spread at Yankee Stadium being better than anywhere else. Family members were allowed to join, which was good for team morale.

The biggest question for Game 2 was who would take the mound for Toronto. They had acquired two elite pitchers off the waiver wire in Stormy Weathers of the White Sox and Brandon Hughes of the Nationals. Both had won their starts against the Astros in the previous round of the playoffs.

Randolph had the luxury of a fresh bullpen to back up starter Clarke Schmidt, and the team had a day off to follow.

The Blue Jays eventually settled on Hughes, a sixteen-game winner. Hughes put down the first five Yankees in order, but bad luck struck with two out in the bottom of the second when a line drive back to the mound, off the bat of Austin Wells, nailed him in the ankle. Hughes was fortunate that it wasn't broken, but his outing, his day, and his series were over.

"You hate to see a thing like that," Randolph would later say.

The Blue Jays' bullpen, when needed most, couldn't bring their best stuff. Four relievers got nineteen outs but gave up seven runs, and New York won 7-2.

Schmidt went six innings, and to prevent Toronto from seeing any other arms, Randolph asked Ian Hamilton to get the final nine outs. He did exactly that, yielding only one run.

New York held a 2-0 lead in the series. The team felt so good on the flight. It felt like one of those rare occasions when you don't want the flight to end as you reach your destination too quickly. Everyone was enjoying the company around them, the accomplishment of the moment. It was a festive time.

Phil Fuller joined his nephew Miles and girlfriend Stephanie in Toronto on Sunday, an off day. The three had a late lunch, and then Miles departed for a team meeting. Phil and Stephanie decided to play tennis at the hotel and then share a bottle of 2020 Quilceda Creek Palenget Vineyard Cabernet Sauvignon. The Palengat had recently been rated 100 points by *Wine Advocate,* the first for the Palenget, and joining previous 100 points awarded 2020 Quilceda Creek offerings of Columbia Valley, 'Tchelistcheff,' and 'Galitzine,' all cabernet sauvignons. The three then planned to watch the Braves and the Dodgers in a banquet room with Jorge Lopez, Brad Litkenhous, Scott Brand, and Kevin Downes.

Phil Fuller was an elite tennis player as a youth, growing up in a house in Lanett, Alabama, across from the public tennis courts. Stephanie, who played on her high school team, knew none of this. Phil rarely played these days, but the magic never left him. She might as well have been playing Jimmy Connors, another tennis phenom from the public courts. Phil trounced her 6-2, 6-1.

"Haven't you ever heard of taking it easy on a girl?" she teased.

"Hey! I play to win," as he poured her a glass of wine.

"Why, thank you. I love how close you are with Miles."

Phil responded, "Well, before you came around, I would say that his parents and I were his three favorite people."

She was curious, "And now?"

He laughed, "Let's just say that one of the original three is no longer on the medal stand."

"I like that. I can't believe how happy I am, especially compared to life before him. We have a blast doing nothing," she said.

"And I think that sets you up for a long-lasting future."

"I hope so. I respect how he didn't waste time on others after the breakup with his other girlfriend. He wasn't going to waste his time or God's time until he was ready."

Phil confirmed, "That's exactly right. And there is no interference headed your way. That first girlfriend is not coming back."

She smiled, "He doesn't talk about it. He doesn't talk about her."

Phil explained, "They were good for each other in high school. But Brooke changed. She lost her way. She made bad decisions, and it cost her life."

Phil poured more wine and leaned in. "Let me say this. He's never been as happy as he is now."

With that, all one could hear was the clinking sound of their two glasses. "Let's drink to that," said Stephanie.

Phil agreed, "And to be thankful that 2020 was a warm summer and a cool fall. The grapes were fully developed, producing wonderful aromatics and flavors!"

@

In Auburn, Alabama, Forrest Ham was scrolling through e-mails on his phone on Monday morning. He didn't get excited about much, but when he read the e-mail from Miles, he asked his wife, Kate, if their fourteen-year-old daughter, Jennings, was up.

"Not yet. Why?" Kate answered.

Forrest showed her the e-mail: *"I will be glad to do a sit-down interview with Jennings for her school TV station if we face the Braves in the World Series. I can arrange for it to happen with our Public Relations team. The Braves have a great media contact, Beth Marshall. However, here's the dilemma. I will not be able to do it on Sunday before Game 2. It would have to be on the Sunday before Game 7. If there is no Game 7, I will be glad to come to Auburn. I've become a big fan of 7 Brew Coffee, and I got an e-mail alert that Auburn got one last year. One thing worth mentioning is that I will be at church on the morning of what would be scheduled for Game 7. I would love an interview in the Lord's house. – Miles*

If Toronto was going to make it a series, they were going to have to make a statement in Game 3. The loss of Hughes was a severe blow in Game 2. Bichette and Guerrero Jr. were doing their part, but the Blue Jays needed additional offense. They hoped to get it from veteran catcher Danny Arp, inserted into the lineup for the first time.

Stormy Weathers got the crucial call for the Blue Jays. He would be faced by Brad Litkenhous, and it would be hard for Litkenhous to repeat the results of his last performance, but he liked the challenge.

"I know they need this game. I expect them to be aggressive. They are going to come out with guns blazing. If this were a basketball game, it would be like facing Nolan Richardson and his forty minutes of hell," said the Yankee starter to the media before the contest.

Weathers got off to a great beginning, with three shutout innings, but it cost him fifty-seven pitches. He got Fuller to fly out to George Springer in center to begin the third.

The Blue Jays played smart baseball in the home half of the third. Former Newnan High baseball coach Kenny Morris would probably have been smiling if he had tuned in. After Jon Norton walked, Arp sacrificed him to second, and Jody Sandifer singled in Norton to put the Blue Jays up 1-0.

Fuller doubled with one out in the fifth when Weathers hung his changeup, the pitch getting too much of the plate. Volpe doubled Fuller home, tying the contest at 1-1. Weathers then served up a hanging fastball to DJ LeMahieu that plated Volpe.

LeMahieu's single was the final hit allowed by Weathers. He would go six innings, striking out seven, throwing a valiant 112 pitches.

Litkenhous also went six, aided by a defensive gem from Jasson Dominguez in right. His running grab of a short blooper in right preserved the 2-1 New York lead.

Jonathan Loáisiga set the Blue Jays down in order in the seventh. New York was six outs away from a commanding 3-0 series lead.

Miles 'Grand Theft Awesome' Fuller singled with one out in the top of the eighth. Fuller then swiped second but eventually was stranded by Toronto pitcher Oscar Alvarez, the diminutive older brother of Yankees reliever Jose Alvarez. Jose then took the mound for the Yankees. With the go-ahead runner on second with two out and the home crowd in a frenzy, Jose got Sandifer on strikes to strand the runners at second and third.

It was a crushing blow for the Blue Jays. Oscar Alvarez, who had started most of the season for Toronto, returned for the ninth, giving the home crowd hope as he struck out the side in the top of the ninth.

Toronto needed a run to extend the game, and they would have to do it against New York closer Clay Holmes. The Yankees pitcher was a quality player for the Pittsburgh Pirates, but once acquired by New York, his career flourished. He even added pitches to his arsenal.

Holmes put the Yankees within a game of the World Series, retiring Toronto in order. The Yankees were in complete control and would have a chance to wrap the series up the next afternoon.

Randolph was pleased. "This was a great win. Toronto played very well, all the way to the end. We expect the same thing from the Blue Jays tomorrow. It won't be easy to sweep them."

The Yankees coach informed the team that dinner would be

provided to them at the hotel. "We are on a business trip. The day game is tomorrow. Dinner, then to your room. I want to celebrate the pennant in the locker room tomorrow evening and on the plane tomorrow night," instructed Randolph.

The families were also invited, so Phil and Stephanie joined the team at the hotel for a festive Game 3 postgame dinner. Then, it was time for bed for Miles. He did stick around downstairs as Stephanie and Phil drank a glass of 2020 'Galitzine' Cabernet Sauvignon, graded 100 points by *owenbargreen.com*.

He called his parents' home in Newnan. His father was not back from a flight that had left Chicago but was due to land shortly. He reviewed the game with Celeste for about twenty minutes. She told him she was watching every pitch and had not missed a pitch of the Dodgers-Braves series, a series led by Atlanta, three games to one.

"I know how good the Braves are, but with one more win, that means the World Series would be here, and I can see you play in person," said the wife of the pilot who was afraid to fly.

The New York players all abided by Randolph's wishes. The acceptance of getting to bed showed their discipline and how serious they were about finishing this series while hoping the Dodgers could stretch out the battle for the National League pennant.

Toronto was going back to ace Kevin Gausman to give them their best shot, although he was pitching on short rest. Gausman set down the Yankees without trouble in the first, but it cost him twenty-two significant pitches. At this rate, it would be a short afternoon for one of the top pitchers in the American League.

The Yankees decided to go with Ian Hamilton. Jason Harbison was just not the same in the day starts. Harbison was a nocturnal ace. Hamilton would only be able to go two or three innings, so Harbison was going to be needed. Randolph had the Cole card in his pocket to use for Game 5, so he wouldn't hesitate to pitch five or six guys on this day.

Hamilton induced double-play groundouts in each of the first two innings. New York grabbed a 1-0 lead in the top of the third. Fuller led off the third with a double, scoring on a sacrifice two hitters later. It was the perfect "get them on, get them over, get them in" scenario.

Hamilton got help from Fuller in the bottom of the third when the Yankees' rookie gunned down Norton trying to tag from second with one out. Never, ever make the second out at third!

Hamilton retired the first hitter he faced in the fourth, but that was it. He had hit the wall. What a weapon he was, twice in the series, for the Yankees.

Tommy Kahnle was the next pitcher up for the Yankees, and his changeup was on, retiring five hitters while only giving up a fifth-inning single to Sandifer.

New York led 1-0, needing twelve outs to win the pennant. The 1-0 lead increased to 3-0 in the top of the sixth as Dominguez singled in two, chasing Gausman, who gave it his all on short rest.

Randolph went to Holmes next, an eye-opening decision. But it made sense, considering Toronto had the top of the order up. Springer singled and added a steal of second to his stat sheet but was left on third as the inning ended. The Yankees were nine outs from the pennant.

Fuller singled in the top of the seventh, taking a breaking ball from Brandon Veasey right up the middle with no one out. But the Yankees never advanced him, still leading 3-0.

Jose Alvarez didn't need to strand anyone in the seventh. He faced three Blue Jays and got them all out. The Yankees would only get one more hit, a Fuller single. The Yankees' rookie remained hot at the plate, even if he couldn't provide power.

"The rap on him, Miles Fuller, has been he can't hit the long ball. If I'm a general manager, after seeing what we've seen, I want him on my team. I think he has embraced the criticism;

he's the top hitter in the postseason. If you are hitting .400 and stealing bases, does it matter that you don't hit home runs?" asked the television analyst.

Randolph turned to Scott Brand to work the penultimate eighth frame, with Loáisiga in the bullpen if needed. Holmes had been burned earlier in the contest.

Brand was in the soup in the eighth with two on, none out. Randolph got Harbison up to join Loáisiga. The Yankees Universe relaxed a little when Volpe and Lopez pulled off a nifty double play. Brand was at twenty-seven pitches when Bichette brought the crowd to its feet with a two-run homer. Randolph pulled Brand and went to Harbison. It was a strange role for him, his first relief appearance of the season. His best pitch, the four-seamer, was surprisingly substituted for a sweeper and a cutter, and it worked brilliantly.

Of the out retired in the eighth and the three in the ninth, all were groundouts on cutters and sweepers. Harbison got all four batters he faced, closing out the series on a ground ball out to first, Harbison's first career save.

Miles went down to the ground in celebration and relief. His lifelong dream of playing in the World Series would soon be realized, and likely in his backyard, with Greg and Celeste seeing him play in person.

The Yankees were respectful to the Blue Jays and the home crowd, saving the massive celebrations for the clubhouse, where the Yankees would commemorate the American League championship with a trophy, accompanied by singing and dancing and plenty of champagne. Randolph praised his team and had a little bit to say about all of them. The pennant would not have been possible without the dominant pitching of Gerrit Cole, which was just expected, but the team got a huge lift from Brad Litkenhous, Scott Brand, Ian Hamilton, and Clay Holmes. Jasson Dominguez was named MVP. Dominguez had timely hits, like his double in the opener, and shone on the defensive side. Miles out-hit everyone but was thrilled for Dominguez, who missed ten months due to his Tommy John surgery.

Fuller then said before anyone talked to the media, "We have to play Taylor Swift, Tom Petty, the Outfield, John Fogerty, Herman's Hermits, and a new one, "Winning" by Santana." And so all six songs played, and champagne and beer showered all over the visiting clubhouse and all over each other.

Family and friends, knowing that they may be drenched during the celebration, were allowed to enter for the sixth and final song, "Winning," and Phil and Stephanie chose to join Miles. A clubhouse attendant brought them over two champagne bottles that they poured on Miles and Harbison and then on themselves.

It was a glorious time to be a Yankee. New York had just put to bed five straight losses in the AL Championship Series and was likely headed to Atlanta, although the Braves needed one more win.

Stephanie, there in front of Miles, soaking wet from being drenched with champagne, had never looked more attractive to Miles. She didn't need the pinstripes home jersey; something was mysteriously appealing to him about her in his New York road jersey, his No.14 prominently displayed.

Stephanie held Miles' heart, and only one other girl had ever done that. In the end, that first girl didn't deserve him. Miles liked exactly where he was, exactly who she was. She loved his sincerity, sensitivity, and his love of Christ. She had gone all the way out west to find a boyfriend. He was from her state of Georgia. Stephanie had what she now referred to as a "practice marriage." The husband she wanted forever was the one who went to kneel to the Lord in prayer just after the final out was recorded, the sweet boy standing in front of her right now, the one all the Yankee Universe had fallen in love with. She didn't have a crystal ball, yet she sure felt like something was telling her she was into something good!

CHAPTER THIRTY-SIX

"It's what you learn after you think you know it all that really counts."

John Wooden

The Dodgers refused to go quietly into the night. Not only did Los Angeles take Game 5 at home, but two days later, they won Game 6 in Atlanta.

Greg and Celeste had mixed emotions. The Yankees were going to be tremendous underdogs to either Atlanta or Los Angeles, but the latter would be easier to defeat. However, with her refusal to fly, the only chance Celeste had at watching her baby boy in person was for Atlanta to win Game 7.

Braves manager Chip Walker, with the deepest pitching staff in the game, called on Matt Trucks to lead his team to the National League Pennant. Trucks just happened to live in Newnan. He pulled hard for Miles in the spring of 2023 and was disappointed for the career minor leaguer when the Braves cut him loose, not even offering a chance in the minors.

Despite being the grandson of the great Virgil "Fire" Trucks, Matt was not sold on being a baseball player as a kid. He enjoyed fishing and golf. Matt and his grandfather once played together in a charity golf tournament. Virgil was distracted for a bit, and Matt found himself alone at a table with Braves legend Phil Niekro. The Hall of Famer feared Matt would want to discuss baseball and did not warm up to him immediately. The two started talking about fishing, and Niekro became a different person, giving the impression he had known the youngster all his life.

"Knucksie" won 318 games, number 300 coming as a Yankee. Niekro won sixteen games for the Yankees in 1984, making his fifth All-Star team. His 300th win came on October 6, 1985, when he shut out the Blue Jays in Toronto. He was forty-six years old when he became the oldest pitcher in MLB history to record a shutout, and his record stood for twenty-five years until Jamie Moyer, at the age of 47, recorded a shutout in 2010. Niekro holds the record for most seasons played in the majors, twenty-four, without reaching a World Series.

Trucks was determined to get the Braves back to the Fall Classic going 6 2/3 innings, with the Dodgers only able to register one run against the flame thrower. Atlanta was on cruise control after a four-run fifth inning that gave the home team a 6-1 advantage. Ryan Foster and David Hodo did the rest of the work on the mound, and Atlanta advanced to another World Series with a 9-3 victory.

The World Series would begin in two days, on Saturday, with the Braves listed as enormous favorites in Las Vegas. The Yankees watched the final game from the airport on Thursday night, deciding to take off for Atlanta in the fifth inning. It was a gamble to leave early, but Randolph wanted as much time to get his players acclimated to the city and the settings so that they felt composed and prepared for the moment at hand. He understood that many on this team were from the Deep South and would want and need extra time with family and friends. Miles would see his parents briefly on Friday, but the team spent most of the eve of Game 1 at the hotel resting, studying film, and reading scouting reports. Miles treated those scouting reports as if they were scripture from the Bible. He needed to know and understand each tendency of every Atlanta player on the roster.

All the Yankees were exhausted. They had been under a microscope for months. The coverage of the team and the requests from all media outlets would soon increase. Each player needed ample rest. Miles was asleep by 8:00 p.m. This time, the next night, he would be performing on the biggest stage in sports.

CHAPTER THIRTY-SEVEN

"And whatever you do, whether in word or deed,
do it all in the name of the Lord Jesus, giving
thanks to God the Father through Him."

Colossians 3:17

October 20, 1996

Atlanta Braves rookie centerfielder Andruw Jones, only nineteen years of age, homered twice in Game 1 of the 1996 World Series at Yankee Stadium as the defending champions cruised to an opening game 12-1 win.

Jones homered in his first two at-bats, becoming only the second player in World Series history, joining Gene Tenace of Oakland, to accomplish that remarkable feat. He became the youngest ever to homer in a World Series win. His second-inning full-count home run, off Yankee starter Andy Pettitte, broke the mark previously held by Yankee great Mickey Mantle.

Jones, whose jersey was retired by the Braves in a ceremony held September 9, 2023, at Truist Park, played for the Braves from 1996-2007. Jones played for five MLB teams, closing his career in pinstripes with New York in 2011-2012.

The Braves outscored the Yankees 16-1 over the first two games of the 1996 Fall Classic, but after evening the series at 2-2, Pettitte got revenge with a 1-0 shutout in Game 5, the final contest being at Turner Field. The Yankees survived a ninth-inning rally from Atlanta, winning Game 6 with a score of 3-2 and winning the series 4-2.

The 1996 World Series title was the first for the Yankees since 1978. The 2024 World Series was less than two hours from commencing. The Yankees last won the World Series in 2009, which, to baseball fans of the most successful franchise in sports, seemed like an eternity.

But New York baseball fans had reasons to be optimistic. With their decisive win over Toronto in the American League Championship series, the Yankees had halted the streak of losing five straight ALCS, the only team to do that. Winning the series in a sweep also had allowed New York to be rested, with ace Gerrit Cole good to go in the opener.

All media requirements had been met. It was time to focus on the task at hand: the World Series. Yankees manager Willie Randolph had asked his team to be dressed in the clubhouse ninety minutes before the 7:35 p.m. Saturday first pitch time.

Randolph entered the locker room at 6:03 p.m. He looked around the room. "Before we warm up, before you stretch, before you do anything related to the field, I want to tell you how proud of every one of you I am. In early August, the writers and talking heads had already buried you, yet here you are. I'm not going to offer you much advice; just keep playing for each other and give it your best. You don't want to think about this series twenty years from now and have regrets."

"Now, I want you to do something for me. I want you to take at least ten minutes, fifteen if needed. I don't want anyone to say a word. I want you to just sit here and reflect on how you got here. It's an honor to be here tonight. I'm honored to be here with you. I want you to think about the ups and downs of the season. Then, I want you to reflect on who got you to this stage. Who made you what you are today? I want you to play for them tonight. Was it your parents, an older sibling, or a caring coach? Who was it? It might have been all the above. Just sit back and appreciate the moment; be thankful for it, for each other, and for those who played a major role in getting you here."

Miles felt like he was a perspicacious person. He could see through people and pick up on their emotions. He had general insight and knowledge of most situations. But he was surprised at how emotionally moved he was by Randolph's instructions. Although he was looking down, he could recognize the sound of tears from a few of his brothers. They, no doubt, were thinking of a lost parent, grandparent, other relative, or coach. To make this national stage and not to be able to share it with the primary person responsible for getting one there, if it was a deceased parent or sibling, had to be devastating. It was an astonishing sight to see; the players sat in a state of ataraxy, in extreme calmness with no distractions.

Miles thought of his youth coach, Mike Furbush, his high school coach, Kenny Morris, and a local coach named Gregg Hamilton, who had been a tremendous influence on him and had successfully battled cancer for years. His mind then took him to the staff at Stanford University and the great "Nine" Mark Marquess. He closed his eyes, and he could feel the support of his Uncle Phil, Phil Fuller. Then he thought of his parents, Greg and Celeste Fuller. He wanted to give them a World Series ring. He then was grateful for the role Stephanie had played in his life. Finally, and most importantly, he thanked God for the ability to play the game, knowing all things are possible through Christ.

He then thought about a verse in chapter 19 of the book of Matthew in the Bible, "With men it is impossible, but not with God, for with God all things are possible."

He stood up, feeling inspired and thankful, and walked over to Brad Litkenhous and said, "Indeed. A mighty fortress is our God."

The pitcher answered back, "There's no doubt about it."

After a patriotic pre-game, the lineups were introduced, a Braves video pumped up the crowd, and then the Truist Park crowd sang along with the great Elton John to the National Anthem.

The best team in baseball, the loaded Atlanta Braves, called on Max Fried to take the mound since Matt Trucks and Spencer Strider were both unavailable due to the length of the National League Championship Series.

As the Yankees batted in the first, sound had feel. It was exactly why Miles didn't want to bat at the top of the lineup and preferred batting at the bottom. If your favorite football team has one of the best defenses, you love it when the other team gets the ball first, and your defense can establish the tone early and set up the offense with field position.

The Yankees got a first-inning walk, but Fried disposed of them in fourteen pitches. Miles took his first step to center, and, as he suspected, he couldn't feel his feet. It was a cool night in Atlanta, 54 degrees at the first pitch, winds blowing 7-8 mph to right field.

As the game went to the bottom of the first, the main lights were dimmed, as customary, in the stadium. Fans turned on their mobile phones. The atmosphere intimidated some teams. With only the mobile phone lights and interior stadium lights, the park had a rutilant setting, with red light glittering in honor of the Braves.

If Cole was nervous, he didn't show it, striking out two and inducing a groundout in his seventeen-pitch first inning. The Yankees got a two-out walk from Anthony Volpe in the second, bringing up Miles, hitting in the eighth slot in the opener. As he was introduced, Miles got a standing ovation from many of the Atlanta faithful. The Braves crowd is a knowledgeable one, and those in attendance knew his story, knew he was one of their own, from practically just down the road.

Fried opened with a slider away. Fuller was expecting a sinking fastball and was fortunate that it missed the plate. Fried typically got a great deal of swinging misses from his high fastball, so Miles decided to wait for a slider, where the first pitch hit the glove. Fried next pitched two high fastballs; one mistakenly called for a strike, but Volpe was off with the pitch and swiped second rather comfortably.

Miles knew a base hit would mean an RBI and an early Yankees lead in a game New York needed with Cole on the mound. Miles remained locked in, waiting for the slider. Fried granted his wish with the 2-1, a hanging slider that stayed up. Miles didn't do much with it; he didn't have to, shooting it over the hole between second and short, easily scoring Volpe.

Cole kept the Braves hitless through the first four innings. Michael Harris broke up the no-hit bid with a double in the fifth but was stranded at second. The Yankees tallied three runs in the top of the sixth, off Fried and two relievers. The big shot came from Volpe, who tripled in Austin Wells. The seventh hitter in the lineup, tripling in the sixth hitter, increased the New York advantage to 3-0. Volpe then came home on a Fuller RBI sacrifice fly to left field, making it 4-0.

Cole threw seven shutout innings, lifted after just ninety-eight pitches. The Yankees had the best bullpen in baseball, but, in fairness to them, they had not faced many live bats in the last week.

Tommy Kahnle got the first two in the bottom of the eighth, but then Ronald Acuña Jr. hit a blast to center that, people say, still hasn't landed. The Yankees went down 1-2-3 in the ninth, and Randolph, hoping to save Holmes for Game 2, called on Jonathan Loáisiga to retire the hitters in the ninth. He did, although Austin Riley took him out of the park with a one-out homer. The Yankees won the opener 4-2.

"We needed this win," admitted Randolph to the *Atlanta Journal-Constitution*. "We had more rest and our best pitcher going." The philomath Fuller explained, "Atlanta had a taxing series with the Dodgers. We took advantage of that. We would love to go home with a 2-0 lead, but we also expect Atlanta will be hard to beat tomorrow night. The Braves likely feel propitious about their chances of success tomorrow night. The weather will be warmer, and the crowd more active. This will be a tough environment to navigate tomorrow night. I'm really glad we got this one tonight. Gerrit Cole was phenomenal."

CHAPTER THIRTY-EIGHT

"Prayers carry our loved ones into the next life armed with our good wishes and hopes that we'll see them again."

Anonymous

Former major league pitcher Jim Bagby Sr. is buried at Westview Cemetery in Fulton County, a little over thirty minutes from Truist Park. He was the first pitcher to hit a home run in the World Series and one of the last pitchers to win thirty games in a season when he went 31-12 in 1920 for the Cleveland Indians. Bagby Sr. died in Marietta, Georgia, about eighteen minutes from Truist Park, at the young age of 54. His thirty-first win of 1920 clinched the American League pennant for the Indians. Only three other pitchers have won thirty or more games in a season since Bagby. They are Dizzy Dean, Lefty Grove, and Denny McLain.

On October 10, 1920, the thirty-one-year-old homered in the

historic Game 5 of the 1920 World Series. Teammate Elmer Smith became the first player in World Series history to hit a grand slam with his first-inning blast. In addition to the heroics from Bagby, Smith, and Cleveland, teammate Bill Wambsganss turned in the first unassisted triple play in World Series history, getting three outs on his own against Brooklyn in the fifth inning. The Indians went on to win the World Series, and the franchise has won only one more, the 1948 triumph over the Boston Braves in six.

Bagby's son, Jim Bagby Jr., played in the major leagues for four teams, winning ninety-seven games against ninety-six losses. Bagby Jr. also died in Marietta in 1988 at the age of seventy-one. He was cremated.

Miles loved adventure. After attending a church service at the team hotel, his Uncle Phil took him, Brad Litkenhous, and Jose Lopez to visit the grave of Bagby Sr. to pay respects.

A prior work commitment kept Stephanie in Montreal for the first three games of the series, but she was scheduled to join Miles, his father, and his uncle in New York for Game 4. Celeste was enjoying seeing her son in person. Following the Game 1 win, she was even able to sleep in her bed at home. She would revel in the same fate for Game 2.

Miles, his uncle, and two teammates were back at the team hotel by 2:00. He visited his parents alone for fifty minutes.

"Are you nervous about tonight?" asked his mother.

"I am extremely nervous. This is such a huge night for us. If we could steal this game, we would feel very confident about our chances."

Randolph had decided on Clarke Schmidt for his Game 2 starter. This Yankees team was loaded with players with deep southern roots. Schmidt played high school ball in Acworth, Georgia, a little more than thirty minutes from the park where he would pitch the bottom of the first. Schmidt had a solid 2023 despite a rough August start against the Braves in Atlanta.

Game 2 got off to another rough start for the New York pitcher. Matt Olson, another local product, hammered a two-run blast to right to quickly put the home team up 2-0.

The Braves didn't stop there. The best team in baseball scored at least one run in each of the first five innings, leading 7-0 after five. Schmidt lasted five, getting little help from his teammates; only four of the runs were earned.

As the live television broadcast returned from the commercial, the network briefly showed the score. Then, as the score faded on the screen, there was a seven-year-old girl, grinning from ear to ear, holding a baseball and showing it off to everyone in her section.

The inning began, and the announcer noted, "As soon as an out is recorded, we will show you why that adorable young girl is having one of the greatest times of her life. You don't want to miss this."

Two pitches later, there was a ground ball out to first. The playback from in-between the innings began to play. The announcer started speaking, "World Series Game 2 here in Atlanta, and the Braves are in complete control. Fortunately, some people in this world see the big picture. They put others first. Undoubtedly, one of these is speedy Yankees centerfielder Miles Fuller. Here he is playing catch with that young lady in the second row who is decked out in her Atlanta Ronald Acuña Jr. jersey. With extended commercial time, this exchange went on for about ninety seconds. Before his final toss, he stopped to sign the baseball. Just look at the smile on her face, and those around her, and all the camera phones. That's the best thing you are going to see tonight, probably all week."

The other announcer replied, "Miles Fuller has done this before. But this is different. This is the World Series. The entire nation is watching. His team is getting hammered tonight, by no fault of his own, but he understands the positive influence he can have on someone. Some people may criticize this, considering how bad the Yankees are losing. But, as a former player, I find this behavior commendable and inspiring. He's made that kid's night, and this is baseball, our country's favorite pastime. She is never going to forget this. Fuller can't hit home runs. You hear it all the time. But in between innings, he just hit a monster of a homer."

The next batter was up, and the play-by-play broadcaster noted, "The count is 2-1. Fuller has become, to some, a polarizing figure, especially with the New York media. His interviews have become must-see television. You must tune in just to hear him speak. He says words I have never heard of, and when I try to look them up, I can't spell them, so I rarely find out what they mean."

The other broadcaster replied, "Who does love him are Yankees fans and Evangelical Christians."

Then the camera focused on the young girl, her chestnut brown hair being blown by the wind, slightly in front of her face, as she held the signed ball in front of the camera. Below the signature of Miles was the scripture John 1:12. This was a verse that former Yankee great Bobby Richardson, the only player from a losing team named as World Series MVP, often included below his signature: *"All who receive Christ, through faith, become children of God."*

At the time, Miles was unaware of the close-up shot highlighting the scripture. But later, as his phone blew up, he understood it was perfect symmetry. His primary desire was to lead others to Christ, and there was no telling how many people were now looking up John 1:12 and talking about that beautiful game of catch.

The Yankees had few opportunities against Spencer Strider. Strider yielded only two hits, both singles, to Miles. Braves relievers Ryan Foster and David Hodo each worked a scoreless inning, and the Braves destroyed New York, 8-0, to even the series at one game each.

The Yankees finished with just those two singles from Fuller. Randolph was quick to praise Strider in the press room. "My guys were saying they couldn't see the ball. It's hard to hit what you can't see."

Fuller, while giving credit to Strider, was optimistic about getting the series back to New York. "We feel good about splitting two here. This is a tough, tough place to play. We must figure out a way to hit their pitching in Game 3. You must take things one game at a time, but we like our Game 5 starter an awful lot," said the Yankees centerfielder.

Because he was disappointed in the loss, Miles had little to say to his parents in the fifteen minutes he had before getting on the bus to depart for the airport. Mike Furbush and Gregg Hamilton both dropped by briefly, in neutral colors, to sincerely wish him well in New York.

"I think this series is going deep, so let's just plan to see you back here in Atlanta a little down the road," predicted Furbush, his youth baseball coach and die-hard Braves fan.

CHAPTER THIRTY-NINE

"Obstacles don't have to stop you. If you run into a wall, don't turn around and give up. Figure out how to climb it, go through it, or work around it."

Michael Jordan

There are so many former New York Yankee greats that it's hard to pick a favorite. Ask a man or woman in their 40s or 50s and they would likely tell you Don Mattingly. Ask that person's father, and he would likely say, Mickey Mantle. Ask that person's kid, and you may very well get Derek Jeter.

Mantle has passed on from this earth, but the Yankees brought in both Jeter and Mattingly to throw the first pitch before Game 3 at Yankee Stadium. Jeter, known more commonly as "The Captain," won five World Series with the Yankees (1996, 1998, 1999, 2000, 2009), was the A.L. Rookie of the Year (1996), a five-time Gold Glove winner, and unbelievably a fourteen-time American League All-Star. He received 396 of a potential 397 votes when elected to the Hall of Fame, the second highest number of votes in history, trailing only the unanimous selection of teammate, Mariano Rivera. Jeter was the chief executive officer of the Miami Marlins from 2017-2022.

Jason Harbison got the ball in Game 3, opposed by Braves starter, Bryan Lundquist, out of Lassiter High School in Georgia. The Yankees crowd brought the energy just as they had done the entire postseason, in anticipation of seeing the same success. Harbison gave up a leadoff double to Acuña Jr., and then the Braves, on the road, played smart baseball. They played small ball, with Lawrence Hamberlin providing an RBI groundout to first.

Lundquist, a flame thrower, who went 16-6 in the regular season, held a 1-0 lead, giving up only a double to D.J. LeMahieu through four complete innings as the Braves continued to lead, 1-0. Yankee killer, Hernando Fernandez, then provided more than enough cushion, first with a three-run blast in the fifth, then a two-run shot in the seventh. His second homer of the game gave the Braves a 9-0 advantage. The first shot was off Harbison, the latter against Yankee reliever, Jose Alvarez. Alvarez attempted to throw a cutter away, but it had too much break in it, allowing Fernandez to get underneath it, carrying it out to row 16 of the right field seats.

Fuller kept his streak of hitting safely in all postseason games with a two-out double in the home half of the final inning. But he was stranded at second, and Atlanta led the series two games to one and had stolen back home field advantage with its decisive 9-0 win.

Randolph was trying to remain confident after the Game 3

debacle. The Yankees had a combined five hits in the last two games. "We have good hitters. Good hitters work through slumps. When a hitter is struggling, and we have several who are, I think you must be careful not to give them too much inspiration."

Despite the resounding loss, Miles stayed at his locker, answering questions. "I want to apologize to our fans. They came here with a great deal of expectations. I can understand their frustration. We got beaten soundly. You must give the Braves credit. Brad Litkenhous gets the ball tomorrow night, and I think he will be at his best," said the Yankee centerfielder.

When he had finished his media requirements, Miles was told that the skipper wanted to see him. He knocked on the door of Randolph's office. Randolph got up and closed the door and then said, "Miles, I understand you like hitting at the bottom of the lineup. I fully get how it helps you get into the flow of a game. But I need you at the top. You are the only one of us hitting. Gerrit won't need much from us in Game 5. Your hitting at the top might give you an extra at-bat tomorrow. It might be the difference in the outcome," explained the manager.

"I will do whatever I can to help us win," said the free agent.

Litkenhous got the ball for the Yankees in the pivotal Game 4. There's a huge difference in being tied at 2-2, compared to down three games to one.

As Miles was kneeling in prayer in center, Litkenhous, one of his Bible study partners, was doing the same. The two had prayed together in the locker room beforehand, with Game 3 starter Jason Harbison joining them. Litkenhous worked through trouble in the first, stranding Acuña Jr. and David Brewer. The former had walked; the latter singled. But it cost the Yankee starter thirty-one pitches.

The Yankees were facing Matt Trucks, the man responsible for getting Atlanta past the Dodgers. His 132-pitch effort was sensational but required that the NLCS MVP get more rest.

Miles, known to take a pitch, surprised Trucks and every other baseball guru by swinging at the first pitch, a 95-mph fastball which he swatted gently to center. Another base hit for the newest Yankee superstar.

With LeMahieu up, would Randolph put the twenty-nine-year-old rookie in motion? LeMahieu, a former batting champion in both the American and National Leagues, was a great batter to go old school and play hit and run. On a 2-1 curve pitch, Grand Theft Awesome swiped second and took third when Hernando Fernandez, always under the suspicion of enhancing his play and strength with drugs, threw high to the bag at second.

"Must have been the steroids," joked Fuller to third base coach Jorge Posada.

LeMahieu gave the Yankees a 1-0 lead with a deep fly to left, Miles sprinted home, and the Yankees crowd erupted in approval.

The score was still 1-0 in the home half of the second when Miles came back to the plate, none on with two outs. The hottest hitter on the planet saw three straight sliders fall under the zone. Trucks never forced Miles to change his eye level. Miles noticed that, just like the three previous offerings, Trucks was hurrying his arm on the 3-0 pitch. It was another slider down, and Miles got underneath it, lofting it safely to right. LeMahieu then grounded out to third to end the inning.

Trucks faced eleven hitters through three innings. Fuller was 2-2, the rest of New York, 0-8, with one sacrifice. Trucks had already struck out five.

Trucks wasn't the first in his family to play in a World Series. His grandfather, Virgil Oliver "Fire" Trucks, won a World Series ring in 1945 as a member of the Detroit Tigers. The elder Trucks won Game 2 against the Cubs with a complete game effort, allowing only one run, as Detroit leveled the series. The Tigers would win the series in seven, taking the deciding game 9-3 at Wrigley Field in Chicago.

Trucks was born in 1917 in Birmingham, Alabama, and passed away at the age of ninety-five in Calera, Alabama. Yankees fans remember him from that iconic 1960 World Series, the series that New York outscored Pittsburgh 55-27, but lost in seven. Trucks got his second World Series ring as an assistant coach on the Pittsburgh team that defeated the Yankees. Trucks also closed out his seventeen-year career with the Yankees in 1958. The hard-throwing right-hander threw two no-hitters in his career, a career shortened by two years due to his service in the Navy during World War II.

Seventy-nine years after Trucks won his only World Series as a player, his grandson, Matt, was cruising through the Yankees lineup. When Miles came up in the sixth inning, two were out and none were on. He had retired the last eight hitters, seven on strikeouts, giving him twelve Ks in the game.

The television broadcaster summed things up best when he said, "Trucks, the Braves pitcher, refuses to allow the other seven players behind him on the field a chance to play."

The chess game between Fuller and Trucks continued in the sixth, New York clinging to that perilous 1-0 lead. Any hitter who won't admit that at least half of what they do at the plate is guessing is probably lying, save for the greats like Henry Aaron, Tony Gwynn, and the greatest hitter of them all, Ted Williams. Miles had won the previous two games of chess against Trucks. The crafty Atlanta veteran was determined to keep the Yankee speedster off the base paths.

Twenty seconds later, Fuller was circling the base paths with his second career home run, a solid shot to center, easily escaping the admiring Acuña Jr. by twelve to fifteen feet.

Litkenhous had done all he could, going six and a third, throwing 109 pitches. He left the contest to a standing ovation with Austin Riley standing on second base. Litkenhous was mobbed by his appreciative teammates.

Randolph needed eight outs from his outstanding bullpen. He first went to Jonathan Loáisiga, who got the two outs but yielded a double and an RBI to Lawrence Hamberlin, cutting the New York lead in half, 2-1.

Loáisiga returned to the rubber in the eighth. After retiring the leadoff hitter, David Brewer reached on an infield single. It was Acuña's turn at the plate, and Randolph went to his closer, still needing five outs. With the fastball the route to go, Acuña Jr. drove a hanging changeup far to deep center. The wind, blowing about 3 mph out to center, helped carry the ball over the wall. Miles went back to the wall, trying to find Rawlings printed across the center, feeling like he had a shot. "Come on, George, give me some help," he begged of the late George Selkirk.

Miles leaped up as high as he could, and got a passing glance of something, reaching out almost three feet over the wall. The Yankees centerfielder had done it again! This time, he had robbed the best player in the series of a potential game-winning home run. Acuña Jr. had scorched it to straightaway center, which helped Miles with the timing. Miles came down, ball in glove, and relayed it to Lopez, who then doubled off Brewer, keeping the good guys in the lead, 2-1.

The television broadcast showcased the catch by replaying it in five different camera angles. It was at this time that Whitney Adams from Newport Beach was sitting at a bar in Malibu and saw something she couldn't believe. She told her date, "I think I know that guy. Or at least I knew him for a night."

"Excuse me?"

"Years ago, on a trip to Stanford, I met him, and he told me his goal was to be the centerfielder for the Braves."

"Well, he got the right position but the wrong team," the guy said.

Whitney then Googled 'Yankees centerfielder.' Search results returned Aaron Judge. She then Googled 'Yankees centerfielder tonight,' and the name Miles Fuller appeared.

"I can't believe this. That's him! I remember that I laughed when he told me about his dream of playing in the MLB. Well, I am not laughing now. I guess I am going to have to watch the rest of the series," Whitney said.

Due to the various replays of the incredible catch by Fuller, the network chose not to take a commercial break and remained with the game action at Yankees Stadium.

After a 1-2-3 home half of the eighth against Braves reliever John Perkerson, Holmes returned to the mound, three outs from tying the series at two games. He had no Acuña Jr. to face but was far from out of the woods. With two out, Marcell Ozuna walked, bringing up the dangerous lefty hitting Matt Olson. Holmes was laboring, extended for over thirty-five pitches. Olson was spotting the short porch in right. Holmes had Olson at one ball, one strike, when the lefty hitter dropped down on the bat, extending a full swing on a changeup Holmes intended to sink, left to right.

The Yankees' closer left the ball too far in, and Olson drove it to right. Miles watched from centerfield as the ball landed on the second deck. Olson didn't need the short porch. Jimmy Olsen would have laughed because Superman himself couldn't have snared it out of the air. The Braves bench erupted in celebration, with nine of its players waiting for Olson around the on-deck circle. Atlanta led the game 3-2 and was just three outs from taking a commanding 3-1 series lead.

The sound of cheers could be heard resonating throughout the Southeast, at homes, country clubs, bars, and anywhere else the game was shown. The team that so many referred to as "America's Team" was on the verge of stealing Game 4.

Perkerson had done his job and was removed in favor of typical Atlanta closer David Hodo of Alexander City, Alabama. Hodo was known to throw three pitches: fastball, changeup, and slider.

The Yankees were hopeful, but the home team had three hits in eight innings, and they all belonged to a player who wasn't even active on a roster this time one year earlier. A player with two career home runs, one earlier in the night. A player due up second in the ninth. Kevin Downes came off the bench, grounding out to Riley at third. The New York crowd then came to their feet as one. Grand Theft Awesome came to the plate to face Hodo, the game still in doubt.

The announcer on television said something very poignant, "Tonight has been a classic, a truly remarkable game. And this guy at the plate should give hope to us all. He has made a believer of every minor leaguer. He's telling them with his play, 'If I can do it, you can do it.'"

Fuller exhibited excellent strike zone discipline the entire postseason. His team needed him the most at this time. If he could work a walk, that would be as good as a double. Fuller got ahead of Hodo 2-1, reminding himself to utilize fast hands with fewer moving parts. He kept his hands back and didn't try to pull the 2-1 fastball, depositing it down the left field line for a double.

"Outstanding loft in your swing," Posada yelled down to second from his third base bag. "Now, come see me!" The comment from Posada prompted Braves third baseman Riley to call timeout. Would the Yankees dare to try to steal third on Fernandez, the most controversial player in baseball, hated at all parks outside of Atlanta?

Hodo stepped off, using his one disengagement. Hodo and Royals reliever Will Smith were the two fastest working pitchers in the game of baseball, but Fuller was requiring Hodo's most significant mental concentration and testing his patience as well.

Fuller didn't go on the 1-0 pitch, and LeMahieu popped out to Riley at third. Jasson Dominguez was now up, needing a single to tie the game. The Yankees youngster went to the plate expecting to see a sinking fastball, waiting for a sinking fastball, but all he got was three straight sliders, missing the last, giving the Braves a 3-2 win.

It was a significantly painful loss for the Yankees, their backs fully up against the wall. They had wasted a gem of an effort from Litkenhous, Fuller's rob of a homer, and his unlikely homer. The locker room was completely silent following the Game 4 loss, a far cry from the Game 4 series-clinching win in Toronto that ended the ALCS, when the team drank and sang together the late Tom Petty's "The Waiting" and other New York favorites.

The media wanted to seek out Miles. He was asked about New York wasting such a glorious opportunity to tie the series. "We know exactly where we stand. When you face something head-on, something like this, you can't back up or move to a side. We have no choice but to face the challenge, and we are determined to prevail," said the Yankees rookie.

A blogger saluted his performance. "Miles, you've been the best player in this series. The Yankees Universe is all about you. Can you describe how that feels?"

"The support is enormous, and I am so humbled. I've been able to ensorcell even the most pedestrian baseball fans with these captivating performances. I never expected this," said the ball player.

Another reporter asked if he could explain his success. "I've prayed a great deal, turning things over to Christ. I've been assiduous, dedicating myself to detail, and that has helped in preparation."

Miles was then asked to share his thoughts on Yankee killer

Hernando Fernandez. "I would pay dearly to see a docusoap on him. That would be must-see T.V. Let's follow him around over a long period and see what he's up to. If he is clean, he's remarkable. The test came back clean, so I guess he's remarkable," sarcastically said the New York outfielder, well on his way to gathering more hits in a single postseason than any player in Major League history.

Another media member requested that he elaborate. "I don't have much to add. I guess I will say this. He must be a heck of a musician."

The same media member responded, "Why is that?"

"Because when he hits a long ball, I feel like I'm at a symphony. The game is fast-paced until he circles the bases in such slow time, he must feel he's performing an adagio," said the Stanford summa cum laude graduate.

Before he left the press room, Miles had more things to say. "You guys were fair to me tonight, far from the antagonistic media I generally deal with. They are difficult. But I am encouraged by the mutual respect we showed each other in this room tonight. I hope all of you enjoy your evening, and let's get a different result tomorrow night."

A Braves beat writer named Jeremy walked over to Miles. "I know this is not the best time to approach you. That was a tough defeat. But I am in a bit of a bind and could use your help."

"My help? How can I help?" Miles cautiously asked.

"I'm from Atlanta, and so is my girlfriend. Her parents live in Cobb County and, like you, are deeply religious. Last week, I asked them for permission to marry Kathryn. They said yes, under one condition - if I would introduce them to you."

"Like for a picture or autograph?" asked Miles.

"Sure. They see the world the same way you do," said Jeremy.

"And how do you see it?"

"A little differently than you guys. They will be at Game 6 on Saturday, assuming we have a Game 6," added Jeremy.

"There will be a Game 6. I promise you this series still has life," assured Miles. "I will be in the locker room early on Saturday in Atlanta. I will ask a clubhouse attendant to get me when you arrive with them. But you must do one thing for me."

"What would that be?" asked the surprised journalist.

"I want you to grab a Bible and read Genesis. All of it, between now and then. Hand the clubhouse attendant a sheet of paper with two answers. The first question is - how many years did it take Noah to construct the Ark. Secondly, I want you to name each of Noah's sons. You will discover that way before the end, but I want you to read the entire book of Genesis," instructed Miles.

"Okay, I can do that."

"I look forward to meeting them in Atlanta."

With that, the Yankees centerfielder exited the room. One blogger who generally covers the Yankees said aloud, "Well, I don't know who was wearing his jersey tonight, but I liked him."

A print member responded. "Don't be fooled by him. He was being sarcastic. He's pompous. He's arrogant. He's an absolute jerk."

A *New York Post* writer then said, "I think you are being a bit harsh. You don't like him because he is an intellectual."

The one who accused Fuller of being arrogant retaliated, "He is brilliant. But he hasn't changed. He's so intelligent it scares me. The problem is he wants each one of us to know it and acknowledge it. I just pray he signs in another city next year. Let him be a headache for someone in Illinois or California."

CHAPTER FORTY

"Therefore, do not worry about tomorrow, for tomorrow will worry about itself. Each day has enough trouble of its own."

Matthew 6:34

Before Game 5, Miles sat alone by his locker for twenty-three minutes. He could hear his phone blowing up. Most of the incoming messages were encouraging, congratulating him on his incredible play and determined effort.

There was one message he wanted to read again. The night prior, Stephanie's text read, "Terrible weather in Canada. I never got out, stranded at the airport. I will be there tomorrow to see you win! One game at a time. I love you!"

The Braves were feeling good about their chances. Matt Trucks, who was coming off a phenomenal effort, explained their perspective when he stated, "We are in the pole position.

We want to wrap it up tomorrow. But, at worst, they will have to beat us twice at our place. We like our chances. How could we not?" When asked about his dominance outside of Fuller, he said, "That guy is in a zone like we've never faced. I attacked him, and he proved his prowess. He's an intelligent hitter; he won't expand the strike zone. The other guys seemed to be pressing, forcing the issue, probably going after pitches they should have laid off. I also was able to work ahead in the count, force them to guess some," explained the Braves starter.

Major League Baseball constructed a great idea a few months before the start of the 2024 season. Since Game 5 was on a Thursday, and a travel day followed, it would be a meaningful time to celebrate the game and call it "a national day to celebrate baseball." Game 5 start time would move up to 4:45 Eastern Time instead of the 7:35 start time for all other games. This schedule adjustment would allow kids to watch the contest with friends or family. Pacific and Mountain time zone school systems were encouraged to allow classes to be dismissed by 1:30 p.m. so they, too, could participate in the celebration. The idea was to allow the kids of America to enjoy a day of baseball without having to stay up late. If the series didn't conclude after Game 5, the momentum of increased viewership would carry to Game 6, which would be played on a Saturday night without the worry of getting up early for school on Sunday. Teams were for it because if the series was going six, the teams would fly to the destination of Game 6 after Game 5, arriving three hours earlier.

The earlier Game 5 start time prevented Miles from seeing Stephanie before he had to leave for the stadium. He was able to see his father, Uncle Phil, and Blake Zhu, who had flown in the day before. Blake, who was the same age as Stephane, left her ticket at the Will Call window.

Randolph told his team little in the locker room. "Let's don't panic or push today. One batter at a time and have some fun." The team felt encouraged that he didn't need to tell them anything about "Not in Our House" or fire them up. They were aware of the monumental task at hand. No one needed to tell them that, with a loss, there was no tomorrow. He continued, "Bobby Murcer was the only Yankee to be teammates with Mickey Mantle, Whitey Ford, Thurmon Munson, Elston Howard, Roger Maris, Reggie Jackson, Don Mattingly, Ron Guidry, and even myself. He also was one of the bravest men to walk this earth, inspiring others with his cancer fight that he eventually lost. How would you like to be in similar company someday? What if someone says you were the only Yankee to ever play with Gerrit Cole, Aaron Judge, Clay Holmes, Jasson Dominguez, Miles Fuller, and Anthony Volpe?"

The team assembled in a circle, much like a basketball team does after the starting lineups are announced. Dominguez spoke for all, "Let's do this!" The huddle then broke up, and Miles walked over to a nearby mirror. It's a strange feeling for a free agent once his team faces elimination—to look at himself, look at his jersey, and wonder if this is the final time he will ever wear it.

The possibility of facing elimination was staring the center-fielder right back in the face. Fuller had done all he could up to this point at the plate and in the field. He was 8-13, hitting .615 with a home run, and Grand Theft Awesome had stolen a homer, one that would likely go overlooked due to the heroics provided by Atlanta native Matt Olson just one inning later.

If New York needed a win, they had their guy on the mound. Cole was good in the opener but probably needed to be better this late afternoon. With the majority of the nation's children watching at 4:47 p.m., Cole threw the first pitch, a 95 mph outside fastball that Acuña missed. One pitch later, Acuña flew out to Miles in centerfield. The Braves would go down in order in the first.

The home crowd rose as one to support Fuller as he approached the plate. Facing Max Fried, Miles took two pitches down. With Miles looking down, Fernandez moved his glove down on delivery. The pitch was a high 92 mph fastball that Fernandez had to adjust to. Fernandez was moving his glove around as a distraction.

With Miles still looking down, he took a back door curve for strike two and then struck out for the first time in the series on the next pitch, another high fastball.

The Yankees failed to generate anything offensively in the first three innings. Fried was perfect through three. Cole had given up two hits but no runs through three innings.

That changed in the fourth when Fernandez drove a high fastball into the right field seats, plating Olson and putting Atlanta ahead, 2-0. The Yankees had eighteen outs to change their fate, or they would not need to worry about packing for Atlanta.

The Braves led 2-0 in the bottom of the fifth as Fuller came up with Austin Wells on third. Looking down, Fuller wanted a slider away, and Fried complied, with Fuller placing it safely in center, scoring Wells, and cutting the deficit in half. This was another base hit to add to his MLB postseason record.

Dominguez came up two hitters later. The New York youngster spoiled several good pitches, waiting for Fried to make a mistake. Dominguez brought the crowd back to its feet with a blast to left field, putting the Yankees up 3-2.

The Yankees needed nine outs for survival. Cole got the first two in the seventh, but after a double from Fernandez, he was lifted for veteran New York reliever Scott Brand. The Yankee reliever not only did his job in the seventh but also in the eighth.

New York, including Miles, failed to mount anything against the Atlanta bullpen of Ryan Foster, John Perkerson, and crafty veteran Lane Anderson. It was the latter who induced Fuller to ground out to Olsen at first.

The Yankees led 3-2 and needed three outs to extend their season. Brand went back out for the ninth. Having never faced the left-handed power-hitting Fernandez in the postseason, Brand had Wells set up his glove a little off the plate. Brand didn't have a two-seamer, so he didn't have a reliable pitch that would sink to a lefty. But his slider could be used to attack the aggressive Fernandez.

Brand got ahead 0-1 with that slider away, then forced Fernandez to change his eye level, going high with a fastball. It missed, but Brand went right back to it, and Fernandez took it for a strike. Brand then closed out Fernandez with a slider off the plate that the opposing catcher chased.

Brand had done his job, retiring all five batters he faced. The entire team gathered at the mound as Randolph approached him, making the call for Clay Holmes. Then, one Alabama-born Yankee in Brand handed the ball to another in Holmes. Brand got a roaring ovation from the charged-up New York crowd, which now included Stephanie, who had just raced down the steps to join Blake, Greg, and Phil.

Holmes came set and threw seven four-seam fastballs to retire the final two hitters of the contest. The Yankees had escaped with a 3-2 win and cut the Atlanta lead to 3-2 in the series. The entire New York crowd breathed a sigh of relief, knowing the dream would remain for at least another forty-eight to fifty-two hours.

"No time like the present to come in and get the save for us," Greg told Stephanie as he hugged her.

Miles came running in from center, hugged Jorge Lopez, and congratulated Clay Holmes. He then waved to his dad and uncle and spotted his lovely girlfriend for the first time. They gave each other an acknowledgment of approval from a distance. The Yankees were down, but they were not out.

The reporter from the *New York Post* was the first to stop Miles. "You guys were close to being eliminated. How hard is it to play under that type of pressure?"

"Excruciating, to be honest. But that's the situation we have put ourselves in. And give Atlanta credit. There's a reason why they are the best team in baseball. It's been an honor to compete against them. I also want to thank the kids from all over the country who took time today to watch us and celebrate this game we all love. I want to especially say hello to those who love the Yankees, all the kids in New York, New Jersey, and Connecticut, and hello to those watching where I grew up, in Newnan, Georgia, and South Carolina."

Randolph gave his team forty-five extra minutes with their families. Miles first said goodbye to his Uncle Phil and his father because they were headed to the airport, booked on a late-night flight.

"Mom says great job and she will see you tomorrow," related Greg to his son.

"Congratulations, kid. See you on Saturday," said his Uncle Phil.

Then, the three Stanford graduates gathered in a circle - Miles, his girlfriend, and his first college roommate, Blake. They sang "Come Join the Band," the original fight song for the university. Miles sang his favorite part by himself:

After the game
When Stanford red won the day
Praising her name
Down to the field, we'll force our way
And on the green

Then, the other two took over the rest:

Each man who joins the serpentine
With might and main sings the refrain
Forever and Forever Stanford red.

Stanford graduates don't think they are better than you. They know they are better than you. This behavior would have been a problem in the locker room a month ago. Miles was no favorite of the media then, but considering all that he had done for his team and the fan base, this time, the media were more understanding.

"How will you celebrate, with what beverage?" asked a blogger.

"I am not much of a drinker, maybe a bottled water," said Miles.

"How about you guys?" the blogger asked Blake and Stephanie.

Blake pointed to Stephanie to answer first. "I am going to see if I can get them to fix me a Hyson. I had one here before."

The blogger looked lost. Miles helped him out. "It's a green tea from China."

Blake said, "I've had a beer, and I'm going to have a few more."

He walked away and gave Miles and Stephanie a few minutes alone.

"I thought it was over," he told her.

"I was keeping up with it, the best I could, with my cell phone."

"When did you get here?' he asked her.

"The top of the ninth inning," she said.

"Good grief! That qualifies you for the save," he said.

"Your dad told me the same thing."

After laughing, he reached out, hugged her, and told her, "Thank you for supporting me."

She responded, "I don't mind that Brooke was your first love. That is not even important. I just want to be your last love, your final love. That would be perfect. This is the most fun I have ever had. It's you, us, our love of God, the baseball, all of it. See you in Atlanta!"

CHAPTER FORTY-ONE

"God is working in you, giving you the desire and the power to do what pleases Him."

Philippians 2:13

Miles was back in Atlanta and, after forty-five minutes, got a notification from his father. He was safe on the ground at Hartsfield-Jackson Atlanta International Airport.

He would wake to all the local Atlanta channels on Friday morning, talking Braves, Braves, Braves, the Saturday night game, and more Braves. He may have been home, but he was in enemy territory.

His Uncle Phil slept in until almost 10:00 a.m. Then he hit the ground running. He was well-connected and had scored four extra seats last week for potential sixth and seventh games in Atlanta. Phil would sit with Greg, Celeste, and Stephanie in the family seating area. Miles had acquired two tickets for Blake and a friend of his from Los Angeles.

Phil would have to think about what to do with the other seats. They were in the front row of the outfield, center-right, no doubt.

He gave two to golfing buddies, both alumni of Ohio State. He knew Miles would approve of that. Phil then went to visit a friend of his who had a child with a long-term illness at Children's Healthcare of Atlanta. He inquired if the friend and his wife might be able to take a break from the hospital and attend the game. While they were deeply touched, they didn't want to leave their child's bedside, even for a night.

Before Phil left the hospital, he got in line at the coffee shop in the lobby to get a latte and started talking to two young women. Both were in their 20s with long blonde hair. One was an employee of the hospital and was older, probably closer to her late 20s. They were talking about yesterday's baseball contest in New York when they got in line behind him. Phil told them, "I know it's hard to believe, but I was at the game last night."

The younger blonde quickly asked, "How?"

"This is probably harder to believe, but one of the Yankees is my nephew."

The older of the two, "You must be kidding with us. No way."

The younger blonde asked, "Which one?"

Phil went for his phone and opened it to his camera roll, "This one, No.14. He is my nephew."

He then showed them pictures of Miles at the plate, on the big screen, in the dugout, and then together in the Yankees' clubhouse and locker room after the game.

The older of the two, who turned out to be Emily, responded, "You weren't kidding!"

"No, not at all," said Phil.

Emily then shared something with him, "Annie here has talked for a week about how cute Miles is. So, we aren't going to allow this opportunity to learn more about him get away."

Annie, only twenty-one years old, said, "So, does the nephew have a girlfriend? Wikipedia doesn't say anything about a wife," she declared as she laughed.

Phil released a loud laugh. "He's not married, but he does have a girlfriend. Only the second one he's ever had."

They talked for about fifteen more minutes, and then Emily noted that she needed to get back to work. They said goodbye to Phil. He headed for the exit, and they walked down the other side of the hallway. He stopped and turned back, "Hey, which one of you would be the most responsible?"

Emily asked, "Why?"

Phil then reached into his pocket and took out four tickets.

He looked at both and handed four tickets, two for each game, to Annie. "These are yours for both of you to use on two conditions."

"What's that?" Annie excitedly asked.

"First of all, since these are on the front row in center, I want lots of pictures of No.14."

Annie quickly replied, "No problem there. And..."

Phil took a card out of his wallet. If Atlanta wins tomorrow night, I need you to mail me the Game 7 seats. They will be reimbursed. My number also is on the card."

Annie agreed to the conditions. "No problem with that either."

Phil then told them he needed to go. "I have to go give away my Auburn football tickets."

Emily, with her eyes wide open, remarked. "Wait. I can help you there. I graduated from Auburn. We both did."

Phil responded with a quick "War Eagle!"

Emily said, "We will have to talk about that next time."

Miles had no way of knowing it, but that early afternoon

exchange with Annie Wells and her sister Emily was going to potentially lead to changing the trajectory of his life. After all, great things happen to many at Children's Healthcare of Atlanta, offering the best in pediatric care to Georgia's kids and teens so they can get back to just being kids.

CHAPTER FORTY-TWO

"I don't doubt that the Holy Spirit guides your decisions from within when you make them with the intention of pleasing God. The error would be to think that He speaks only within, whereas in reality, He speaks also through scripture, the Church, Christian friends, books, et cetera."

C. S. Lewis

Celeste Fuller could not wait to see her son in person. But first, she and Greg had an assignment to pick up his girlfriend Stephanie at the airport. Then, they would get over to Miles around 5:30 p.m. on Friday and wait for him to be done with team meetings to finish at 6:30 p.m.

Phil Fuller had reserved a private dining room at Chops, located in One Buckhead Plaza off West Paces Ferry Road in Atlanta. Phil was a frequent visitor to the establishment, which served the best prime-aged beef and fresh seafood.

Phil had thoughtfully invited Blake Zhu and his friend, Cam Yuan, to join them. But Blake couldn't wrap up a work obligation promptly. Stephanie hated he couldn't make it. Although she was fond of the Fuller family, Blake's presence helped equal things.

Miles wasn't crazy about being away from the team hotel but only required that he be back early. At times, he enjoyed being on the road by himself. But Stephanie would stay with him on that night and then at Phil's in nearby Sandy Springs on Saturday night.

Celeste, seated next to Miles at dinner, was counting down the hours until she could see Miles play for the Yankees in person. Her unwillingness to fly had robbed her of so much of her son's time with the Yankees, on and off the field. She and Greg would return to Newnan that night but planned on staying two nights for two games with Phil in Sandy Springs on Saturday and Sunday nights.

Dinner was outstanding, with Miles finishing off a salad and a specially cooked New York strip steak. The Yankees had a curfew of 11:00 p.m. He and Stephanie were back at the hotel by 9:30. Greg and Celeste headed back to Newnan one more night in their home before Miles took the field at nearby Truist Park. The circumstance reminded Miles of one of his favorite songs, "One Day More," from his favorite musical, *Les Misérables*.

Phil joined Stephanie for a couple of glasses of wine at the team hotel. Miles was reviewing team notes on his iPad, reading scouting reports on potential Atlanta pitchers, and examining the tendencies of Atlanta hitters.

"This part of the job reminds me of Alfred Lutter III in *The Bad News Bears*. He always had the scouting reports and stats of the opposing team," said Miles.

"What was his name in the movie?" asked Phil.

"Alfred Ogilvie in the film, Alfred Lutter in real life," said Miles.

"Good actor, if I remember correctly," said Phil as he sipped from his glass of Jones Family Wine.

Miles added, "He is a Stanford graduate, class of 1984. Good actor but a better businessman and investor. He's an American entrepreneur, former CTO of Cumulus Media."

Stephanie added, "I loved the original when he tells his coach, 'Outside of Timmy Lupus, I'm probably the worst player in this league.'"

Phil responded, "My favorite was that Tanner kid who yelled and cursed at everyone."

Miles then said, "He seems to be almost everyone's favorite!"

Phil then chimed back to his right-handed hitting nephew, "Well, you are my favorite now!"

Stephanie agreed, "Mine too!"

Miles, not feeling any pressure yet, said, "Well, I can make that unanimous. Me three!"

Celeste phoned Miles to tell him goodnight and asked, "Is there anything we can do for you, Miles? Anything to help the cause? We feel so helpless."

Miles answered back, "I know how you feel. It reminds me of the spelling bee. I was so relieved to make it to the prime-time finals twice. It wasn't easy, but I got there. But once everyone tuned in to the nationally televised finals, I choked."

Now, on speaker phone, Greg corrected him, "Finishing in the top five is not choking!"

"Perhaps not. But tomorrow night, this could be settled if this is the final episode, the climax of events. I'm fine right now, but I'm going to be terrified tomorrow night," said Miles.

His mother was concerned. "Why? You've been remarkable this entire postseason! You can win these two games."

He agreed, "Yes. But I have a history of failing at the end.

The spelling bee, each year when my Stanford team needed me the most, my terrible spring with the Braves in 2023."

Celeste had the answer, "You need to pray about it. Pray for God to help you with the anxiety and stress. Pray that God uses you to impact others, to do something tomorrow night to lead them to Christ. Right now, let's all pray.

With that, Greg and Celeste locked hands at home in Newnan while Phil, Stephanie, and Miles did the same at the team hotel. They all went to the Lord in prayer.

CHAPTER FORTY-THREE

"The evil that men do lives after them; the good is oft interred with their bones."

William Shakespeare, *Julius Caesar*

Miles arrived at Truist Park a little after 3:30 p.m. Tom Petty had it right; the waiting was the hardest part. The media caught him in a No.92 Caden Curry Ohio State jersey. After all, it was not just Halloween Eve but also a college football game day.

He was cleanly shaven, with short light brown hair, much to the approval of the Yankees brass. As he entered the away clubhouse, he was greeted by New York equipment staff and trainers. Like the special teams personnel at a football game, the training staff, clubhouse crew, and equipment staff are the first on the scene.

Miles found his locker in the clubhouse, on the far right, as he entered the room. He put his bag in his locker and took out his phone. There were over a thousand text messages that went unread. Still doing little on social media, his curiosity got the best of him. He checked Facebook to see how many new friend requests had come in. He was astonished to see almost 13,000 seekers of his virtual friendship, almost all unaware of him this time last year.

Randolph decided to go with Game 3 starter Jason Harbison on short rest. If Harbison could get four or five innings, then he would call on Game 2 starter Clarke Schmidt on full rest to potentially get the Yankees to the next day when Game 4 starter Brad Litkenhous would get the ball to start the deciding Game 7.

One question all the media wanted to know was the availability of Cole, the Game 5 hero, and the reason the Yankees were even in Atlanta. Scott Brand was the only Yankees reliever unavailable for this game.

Randolph addressed Cole's status, "I think he's done all he can for us. He, Fuller, and Fernandez have been the best three players in the series."

A reporter asked, "If you get to tomorrow, would Cole be available in relief with two days' rest?"

"We have to get through tonight, but I would think not."

Miles then called Stephanie, who had a way of relaxing and soothing him. Guys at Stanford always wanted to talk to her, to hear her sweet southern voice.

He then called Mark Marquess "Nine" himself, who believed in him, greatly influenced him, and put him in this position to succeed.

He called his parents to check on them. They were on their way from Newnan. "After we win tonight, I want you guys to go home instead of staying in Sandy Springs. I'm going to invite some of the guys to attend church with me tomorrow in Newnan at Central Baptist."

Celeste understood, "Okay. I get it."

Miles then said, "One more thing. I know it will be late when I can get home. But I'm going to speak to Coach Randolph and see if I can stay with you guys tonight. I need you to take Stephanie with you so we can be under one roof."

Celeste came back, "I love the idea of worshipping together. Did you see the story in the *AJC* about you? They mentioned your love of *Les Misérables*, old movies, Stanford, Ohio State, Auburn, and Art & Jake's restaurant in Newnan."

"I have not seen it, but I spoke to them yesterday. I also told them that Courtney at Art & Jake's is a tremendous restaurant manager."

"It was in the article. And it also mentioned your dad and I and your thankfulness for Mark Marquess, Kenny Morris, Greg Hamilton, and Mike Furbush," said Celeste.

"That will be a keeper. I just hope there's something good in the paper about me and the Yankees tomorrow."

A clubhouse attendant came over to see Miles at his locker. He handed him a note. It said one hundred twenty years is a common belief, although that is disputed because people reading the Bible often confuse the 120-year countdown to the flood as the time it took to build the Ark. But Noah had his first son when he was five hundred years old, and the countdown was then at one hundred. His three sons were Japheth, Shem, and Ham.

Miles was impressed with the reading and the research. He told the attendant to tell Jeremy he would be there in three minutes. Miles put on a long-sleeved green polo shirt and walked out the entrance of the locker room, then turned right and went down the hallway. Jeremy waved him over.

"Miles, I would like to introduce you to my girlfriend

Kathryn and her parents, Hannah and Ray."

Miles shook hands. "It is my pleasure to meet all of you."

A true Southerner and about fifty-three or fifty-four, Hannah responded, "Shaking your hand was nice, but I want a hug. Can I get a hug? We are a family that believes in hugs."

"You absolutely can, but what is all of this Braves swag?" as he pointed to their shirts, coats, and hats.

They all laughed. "Well, we've loved the Braves all of our lives," explained Ray, a little older than sixty. He added, "Before you, I would have said Hank Aaron was my favorite ball player. But the way you speak about Christ, the way you take on the media, we told Jeremy we will be glad to have him in the family, but first, we wanted to meet you and thank you for sticking up for us Christians."

Miles responded, "That won't change. It may not always be on the baseball field, but I will always fight for Christ and his followers. My faith demands it. We will be the winning side."

Kathryn then pointed out, "You probably already know this, but tonight, all of our Atlanta fans will be screaming for the Braves and, at the same time, cheering for you."

"I will take any support I can," admitted the ball player.

They took time for pictures, and Ray thanked him and wished him well. "You need to run for President one day," he instructed Miles.

"It's on the radar," Miles told him.

"I think you would be the most intelligent President we have ever had," said Kathryn, age twenty-six, about five feet six, with short blonde hair.

Miles laughed for a couple of seconds. "I appreciate that. It does get on my nerves how the liberal left believes they are so intelligent that they must think for the rest of us. I feel like we know exactly what we are doing, and we know what we need."

Hannah hugged him once more, and he signed Ray's Atlanta cap before he left. It was nearing time for Miles to get focused on the assignment at hand. New York needed a win in enemy territory to set up a winner-take-all all Game 7.

CHAPTER FORTY-FOUR

"When you pass through the waters, I will be with you; when through the rivers, they won't sweep over you. When you walk through the fire, you won't be scorched, and flame won't burn you."

Isaiah 43:2

The television broadcast team welcomed its viewership to Game 6 of the World Series on Halloween Eve. People didn't have to be in disguise; there were men and women of all ages wearing the No.13 jersey of Ronald Acuña Jr. There was no telling how many kids in Georgia and in the Southeast were out trick-or-treating over that next couple of days, dressed as the Braves megastar. Many cities urge residents to trick-or-treat on Saturday if the 31st falls on a Sunday.

Miles had visited with his Uncle Phil seventy minutes before he took the field for warmups and his ceremonial visit to the warning track in center. Phil had told him the day before about meeting the beautiful Wells sisters, one of whom was single. Phil shared with him exactly where they would be sitting. When Miles took the field for sprints, he noticed their seat location and locked it in.

Randolph instructed his team to have fun and to take things one pitch at a time.

Miles was now 9-17 in the series, with an average of .529. He was four hits short of the thirteen mark, the World Series record shared by Bobby Richardson (Yankees) in 1964, the late Lou Brock (Cardinals) in 1968, and Marty Barrett (Red Sox) in 1986.

Braves starter Spencer Strider was ready for the task at hand. The Yankees were going to have to locate his overwhelming fastball.

"His fastball is so good. He can afford to attack the plate," noted Yankee Kevin Downes earlier to a reporter.

Miles was introduced to the crowd and got a polite welcome. After taking a 98-mph fastball right down the middle, the crowd for New York started a "Let's Go, Yankees!" chant that was quickly defeated by the disapproval of the home crowd.

Fuller then fouled off two pitches, took a fastball high, and, on the fifth pitch, grounded out to Olson at first.

Trotting back to the dugout, he met DJ LeMahieu walking to the plate from the on-deck circle. He paused, telling his teammate, "The fastball is lively, lots of movement," Miles warned him.

The Yankees were erased in order. Harbison worked himself in and out of trouble in the home half of the first. New York failed to get a base runner in the second, third, or fourth innings. Strider had struck out seven of the twelve hitters he faced.

Harbison surrendered his only run via an RBI double from Michael Harris in the fourth, lifting Atlanta to a 1-0 lead.

Harbison got through the inning, with Schmidt set to work the fifth.

It was a cold Halloween eve, temperatures now under fifty, winds slightly blowing out to right. As Schmidt warmed up, Yankees' star Gerrit Cole reported to the bullpen, perhaps to offer encouragement or boost morale.

The Yankees, although hitless, only trailed by a run, 1-0, going to the fifth. Strider struck out four more over the next two innings, and Anthony Volpe was the first Yankee hitter to get the ball out of the infield with a soft fly to center that finished off New York in the sixth.

By now, all through the ballpark, those announcing and those watching were talking about Strider and his potential to throw the second perfect game in World Series history. Don Larsen, who played for the Yankees from 1955 to 1959, threw the only perfect game in World Series history in Game 5 of thc 1956 series against the Brooklyn Dodgers. Larsen won two World Series as a Yankee in 1956 and 1958, taking MVP honors in the 1956 classic. It was a remarkable accomplishment for the pitcher, often known for "Long Nights Out on the Town and Short Days on the Mound." Larsen played fifteen years in the majors, dying on New Year's Day of 2020 at the age of 90.

While Strider was determined to join him in immortality, Schmidt, pitching close to home, was well-rested and in command of all his pitches. Schmidt had worked two perfect innings of relief as Miles approached the plate to lead off the seventh in what could potentially be his final at-bat of the series, season, and Yankees career.

Strider was only at eighty-four pitches through six innings. He would only need four pitches to retire Miles, the center-fielder popping out in foul territory at first. Strider then retired the next two on strikeouts.

Schmidt knew there was no room for error, and although he

gave up a two-out double in the seventh inning, he completed his third scoreless inning of relief.

The Yankees were six outs from elimination, still trailing 1-0. Strider was six outs from joining Larsen in baseball lore, to be talked about for generations.

If Strider was nervous in the eighth, he didn't show it. As Yankee Gerrit Cole did some stretches and exercises in the New York bullpen, up at the plate, no Yankee made contact in the top of the eighth.

Randolph opted to stay with Schmidt, and the University of South Carolina product worked around a one-out walk, greatly aided by Fuller, who threw out a runner at the plate who attempted to score. This kept New York within a single run, 1-0.

That single run seemed like a herculean assignment. Strider was at 109 pitches and was due to face the bottom of the lineup. Someone was going to have to reach to get Miles to the plate, with his streak of hitting safely in each postseason game on the line as well.

Randolph went to Downes to pinch-hit. The Yankee hitter from Alice, Texas, was an asset off the bench. He fouled off three 1-2 pitches before making contact, grounding out to Riley at third. Strider needed two outs at 116 pitches, two outs to a championship, and two outs from the second perfect game in World Series history.

The Yankees, on the other hand, needed something magical, staring at an ignominious fate on one of the greatest stages in sports or life.

Austin Wells was next, and after a check-swing called strike, he grounded back to Strider. The Braves pitcher jogged towards first, then threw underhand to Olson.

It was absolute pandemonium at Truist Park. The fate of the Yankees rested in the hands of twenty-three-year-old Anthony Volpe. He was not a superstar like single-season homerun king Aaron Judge, who was lost for the season to injury in August, and the reason the man on deck, Miles Fuller, had been called up to make his major league debut.

Strider was only one out or three strikes from perfection. Volpe stood in; the right-hander laid off a fastball out of the zone. The next pitch got inside, plunking Volpe in between the New and York on his jersey. The speedy Volpe took first base, perfect game gone, no-hitter intact.

Television cameras went to the Braves' bench. Atlanta closer David Hodo was ready to get the call. Not a single Braves fan wanted to see the bullpen door flash open. Fuller took a couple of practice swings, then closed his eyes, turning his head to the right, opening his eyes to look down at Volpe. One had to ask, would Miles give Volpe a pitch or two to help his chances of stealing second?

Then, the Braves decided to stay with Strider, and the crowd erupted in its approval. The twenty-nine-year-old Fuller stood in the box, the entire Yankees Universe needing a player that one couldn't even find a baseball card of before the season started. Only a few cards were now available, with a small percentage of postseason sets distributed by the publishing companies.

The crowd was ready, with everyone on their feet. Strider was ready. Miles Fuller was ready. Boy, was he ready! Strider's 119th delivery of the night would be his final one, reaching the center of the plate at 95 mph, exiting the bat of Fuller at 117.4 mph, and coming to rest deep in the second deck of Truist Park's right field seats.

Braves outfielder Lawrence Hamberlin never moved and didn't even turn back to give it a courtesy look. He didn't have to. Volpe had stopped halfway between first and second; his arms extended high as if he was signaling a touchdown. Fuller had his third home run of his career, his second of the World Series, and his tenth hit in the six games played.

As the Yankees waited for Fuller to circle the basepaths, the T.V. play-by-play announcer declared, "Here on the night before

Halloween, I believe it's safe to say that the Boogeyman has nightmares about him, about Miles Fuller, from just down the road in Newnan, Georgia."

Smoltz, who lived locally, and Miles had attended his camp that day long ago in Fayetteville, added, "In fact, Miles is the monster hiding under every kid's bed in Atlanta, in Georgia, in all of the Southeast."

The play-by-play announcer replied, "At bedtime, there will be thousands of parents and their children inspecting the floor for him. I mean, I have no words."

Another announcer tried to explain the significance of what had just transpired in front of him. "I've been to six world's fairs. I had thought I had seen it all."

No perfect game. No shutout. No complete game. No victory for Strider. The stunned Atlanta crowd loved him no less, cheering their fallen hero as he left the field.

In their centerfield seats, the Wells sisters - Annie and Emily, were speechless. In the players' VIP seats, Greg and Celeste were paralyzed by what had just happened, Uncle Phil holding on to both. Stephanie, trying to take in the moment, put her hands in her lap, head down, and just started crying. It was that overwhelming. Her boyfriend, who didn't even have a contract for the next season at that moment, was the most popular athlete in the world and would soon be trending on every social media platform.

But the game was not over. Randolph didn't immediately celebrate the homer. He grabbed the phone and called down to the bullpen to get Cole throwing. Cole is not available? Nonsense. The Yankees needed three outs to send the series to a seventh final and deciding game.

DJ LeMahieu took two strikes from Hodo, eventually requiring the Braves closer to throw six pitches to retire him as he hoped to give Cole additional time to warm up.

Randolph then bought him a few more minutes by sending

Schmidt, who had been sensational, back to the mound to warm up for the ninth, with no intention of allowing him to face a hitter. Randolph then walked slowly to the mound and pointed for Cole.

The Atlanta crowd, just like the Fullers, were paralyzed and stunned. People could not believe what had just happened. The Atlanta fans couldn't process the events of the top of the ninth.

Cole came out on one day's rest, shutting down the Braves 1-2-3 on seventeen pitches. The 2024 World Series was headed to a seventh game—the best two words in sports. The best two words in the English language.

Not sixty seconds after it was over, Fox producers pulled Fuller to the side to be interviewed.

"You've just hit one of the biggest home runs in history. Can you describe the emotions you are feeling?"

"I can try my best. But first, I want to thank my Lord and Savior, Jesus Christ. I believe with Him, all things and anything is possible. I want to use this platform to thank you for allowing me to remind all watching that there is only one way to get to the Father. John 14:6 tells us Jesus stated, 'I am the way and the truth and the life. No one comes to the Father except through Me.'"

"I thank you for the question, but it needs to be said: what just happened is wonderful and amazing. But God's victory is certain. One day, He will reward the faithful and judge the unfaithful. It was just a game. I implore all who can hear me not to be on Satan's side; that is the losing side," said the Yankees centerfielder.

Another attempt was made by the reporter. Miles responded, "I'm very blessed. I just took a swing and hoped for the best. But make no mistake. Strider was the best player on the field tonight. He was outstanding, and we were very fortunate to get the win. We are beyond fortunate to still be alive in the series."

After the interview, Miles couldn't find Stephanie or his

parents, so he joined his celebrating teammates in the locker room. He was mobbed by his teammates, looking around, making sure only players and coaches were in the room.

"We have to play it, Coach. We have to play "The Waiting" and follow it up with "Your Love" by the Outfield and "Centerfield" by John Fogerty." These were the same three songs Miles played on his cellphone as he sat alone in the locker room a few hours before game time.

"We will talk to the media. But first, we sing, dance, and celebrate. All three songs," okayed the New York Skipper.

The team jumped on tables and put their arms around each other. Plain and simple, they had a ball. For the second straight game, they had risen from the dead. The Yankees had one hit - *one hit* – and yet were one of two teams playing a game that was winner-take-all the very next day.

Forty-five reporters wanted to ask Miles questions. He preferred to see the press at his locker, but this time, he was required to go to the media room.

The very first question was a stunner; it was not concerning the game but was about after the game. The journalist said, "Liberal media are reporting that you had controversial comments after the game, that you were condemning all who weren't Christians, and that your comments weren't inclusive for all, but instead hateful and disrespectful. Is that true?"

"You must be from Berkley or worse? I have no comment other than I will continue praying for them," responded the New York centerfielder.

"Miles, were you aware, or was it your plan to be so controversial?"

The ball player looked around the room. "Were we all just at the same game? This is why Americans don't trust you guys. I truly believe that God put me in this situation today to share His great love and grace and His invitation to all. If that makes me controversial, then so be it. Now, does anyone have a question concerning baseball?"

"How good was Strider?" asked one of the Atlanta stations.

Miles took a deep breath. "He was unhittable. The best I have ever faced. He didn't miss with his pitches. In my first three approaches, I was cognizant of remaining patient, but that was only getting me behind in the count. Then, when he's got two strikes on you, it's hard not to swing outside the zone. We were struggling, and we've been struggling, so we find ourselves guessing and expanding the zone. That's a perilous situation to be in," explained the Game 6 hero.

"Is that why you swung at the first pitch in the ninth?"

"I was hoping Strider was wanting to get ahead of me. Perhaps I also thought I might get a fastball with Volpe on first."

"How good was your look? The exit velocity was impressive," said a New York writer.

"I didn't see it at all. I was guessing the position and was fortunate and blessed to make contact. He provided the power. God was with me. I had help."

Miles then stopped. "I want to say Strider was the story tonight. What he did was historic, and we were all witnessing something that had not happened in seventy-eight years. His effort needs to be celebrated and applauded. I must pay homage to him. He's also a very good person. When I was with the Braves in the spring of 2023, he was very kind and welcoming. I recall him holding different fêtes, always wanting to raise money for charities. He's one of the best."

Another reporter he had never seen spoke. "Miles, what you just accomplished must be a dream come true. You just sent this series to a seventh game. You weren't even on the team until August. How meaningful is it to you to pull that off and execute under all that pressure and keep your team alive?"

Miles waited several seconds to respond. He was a bit choked up. Slowly, he began to speak. "Not bad for a guy who has heard all his life that he can't hit the long ball. No way he's going to make the majors. He plays center, and one must be a run producer in that position. Yes, it's satisfying. College kids could write a disquisition about the unfair treatment I have received regarding my inability to hit home runs. If this were a movie, no one would buy into the diegesis of the story. No way this plot could come to fruition. No, not him. So, yes, tonight is the zenith for me, but only if we win tomorrow night."

There was a follow-up. "And if the Braves win Game 7?"

"They will be deserving champions. They have the best team in baseball. It must be lonely at the top."

The questions stopped as Stephanie made a surprising appearance in the room. "I'm usually a private person when it comes to relationships and friends. But this beautiful person who just came into the room is my girlfriend and fellow Stanford alumnus, Stephanie. And I just want to get a hug from her," said the New York centerfielder.

The two embraced for about twenty-five seconds, with cameras repeatedly clicking.

"How will you two celebrate tonight?" asked a reporter.

"Nothing too elaborate or complex. We have church in the morning. There is a big baseball game tomorrow and no telling what will be required to win, considering what we just went through. But I've got church and an exclusive interview with the cutest, most honest, unfeigned journalist I know. Unlike the national media, she understands the role of a journalist. I would think that you and those you work with would be better, do better. The country deserves it. All the men and women who have served our country, the real heroes, deserve all our best. That goes for Republicans and Democrats. Thank you for your questions. Be safe tonight."

One jerk journalist asked Stephanie why she put up with him. "It's been fun. He's fun and loyal. Unlike you, he's tolerant of others. Maybe you should try it," said the thirty-two-year-old wearing a Yankees cap and a No.14 jersey.

As the couple was leaving, Miles was asked who would be getting the exclusive tomorrow. He replied, "A fourteen-year-old named Jennings Ham. She still has integrity. She hasn't been corrupted by her colleagues yet. I hope she is never nobbled," stated the baseball player.

When Miles was out of the room, one of the national reporters said something about him. "I know the New York guys have had issues with him. He wants us to feel shame. He's an arrogant jerk. I don't give a blank about how intelligent he is. I hope he strikes out five times tomorrow night."

Greg and Celeste didn't wait for him. They didn't need to. He was headed home to Newnan for the night.

Miles would sleep in his bedroom at his parents' house with no baseball contract after tomorrow night. He was the hero of Game 6. People throughout the country would be talking about him tomorrow at church, at lunch, and on golf courses. It would be mentioned over and over, during the biggest moment of his life, on the grandest stage, that he gave thanks to God.

As one preacher told his Houston, Texas, congregation, "I'm no fan of the Yankees. I am a fan of Miles Fuller. What he did live last night on national television made news in heaven."

His heroics of the night had transfixed a country. And there he was, at his parents' home, on the eve of Halloween, on the upcoming biggest night of his life. He had never felt so comfortable so at home, on the road.

CHAPTER FORTY-FIVE

Then he said, "Jesus, remember me when you come into your kingdom." Jesus answered him, "Truly I tell you, today you will be with me in paradise."

Luke 23:42-43

Norma Haynes is a jewel in Newnan, Georgia. A former neighbor of the Fuller family, Norma, in her 80s, yet still more beautiful than any twenty-year-old, is the most patriotic person you will ever meet. She's also known to be the person who can get things done. When another former neighbor came up with an idea, she contacted Norma.

Since the Braves and the Yankees were playing in the World Series, and the neighborhood had a player on the Yankees' roster, all homes in the neighborhood would be asked to put a

Yankees sign in their yard on the morning of the final game if the series went seven games.

As Brad and Jorge entered the Fuller neighborhood to ride with Miles to Central Baptist Church in downtown Newnan, they counted thirty-one "Let's Go, Yankees" yard signs. The gestures were meant to show support for Greg and Celeste.

Three New York Yankees had entered the neighborhood discreetly and without media coverage or fanfare. It was a fortuitous break that the three saw the signs as well. These were neighbors being there for each other. It was a safe bet that twenty-eight or twenty-nine of those households would be screaming for the Braves at 8:00 p.m. But a little after 8:00 a.m., they were being friendly neighbors. Norma pulled for the Braves and the Georgia Bulldogs. And nothing was going to change that.

If Miles was asked to name a few men he respected, most would be preachers or other Christ-driven men. He would probably include Dr. Joel Richardson, a long-time pastor at Central Baptist Church; Dr. George Mathison, former pastor of Auburn United Methodist Church in Auburn, Alabama, and current leader of Christ Methodist Church of Auburn; Miles Fidell, lead pastor of Auburn Community Church in Auburn, Alabama; Dr. Robert Jeffress, senior pastor of First Baptist Church in Dallas, Texas; and the Reverend Darrell C. Scott, the co-founder of the New Spirit Revival Center in Cleveland Heights, Ohio.

On this day, he was grateful to hear Richardson preach since the pastor had retired and had a reduced schedule from when Miles was in middle school and high school.

In a moment of thoughtfulness and solidarity, Miles had reached out to Braves stars John Perkerson and Matt Trucks, who lived locally, to join them. He became friends with both in the spring of 2023. They, in turn, invited David Brewer and Lawrence Hamberlin.

Yankee pitcher Jason Harbison and his wife Tara took the

short drive from the team hotel to join them. Regular attending church members had no idea that a combined eight players who later in the night would be opposing each other would be publicly displaying their love of Christ. It was not planned, not announced. They were all worshipping as one.

The only ovation came when Richardson introduced Perkerson and Trucks, saying, "My understanding is that two of you live very close to here. On behalf of our church family, I would like to invite both of you to visit again very soon."

Richardson lauded Miles Fuller for his on-field post-game interview, citing how he used the platform as a vehicle to share God's word. He then preached from Lamentations, Chapter 3. Having celebrities in the Central service was nothing new. Country music sensation Alan Jackson had deep roots in the church, with family members contributing to the choir for years.

As the service concluded, Richardson posed for a picture with the eight, standing in the middle of them. The players from the two teams shared brief interactions before church members started asking for autographs and pictures.

Stephanie visited with Sarah, the girlfriend of John Perkerson, and with Tasha, the wife of David Brewer, a fine defensive infielder and frequent late-inning glove specialist for the Braves. Miles then had an idea, politely excusing himself from a conversation to seek out Matt Trucks, the grandson of Virgil "Fire" Trucks.

"Hey, I've got a family friend, his wife, and kids coming here in fifteen minutes to interview for his fourteen-year-old daughter's school T.V. station. Great people. I would think they would love it if you appeared as well—one person from each team. I told Jennings, the fourteen-year-old on-air reporter, that if we won last night, I would be here today. How about it? Are you up for a fun sit-down?"

"I don't see why not," said Trucks.

Forrest Ham arrived a few minutes later. He shook hands

with Miles. "She's already got her list of questions," Forrest told Miles.

"Should I be worried?"

"Maybe," said the father, laughing.

Miles then shared his idea. "Matt Trucks is here. I thought it might be good for Jennings and her crew if she talked to him as well. One from each side, show the sportsmanship, good life lessons."

"Okay. Give her a few minutes to prepare for Trucks."

A couple of other kids set up three cameras, and one placed a boom microphone over Miles and Matt, who were seated beside each other. Jennings, a ninth grader with straight dark hair, sat off to the right, notepad in her lap, wearing Atlanta's Austin Riley jersey.

She was given the countdown and, like a pro, looked into the camera. "I'm Jennings Ham, and I would like to thank Central Baptist Church in Newnan, Georgia, for allowing us from Auburn to conduct this interview before Sunday's Game 7 of the World Series. I'm pleased to be joined by New York Yankee Miles Fuller, who is from Newnan and is my family's friend, and Matt Trucks of the Atlanta Braves, who has moved to Newnan."

Both players thanked her for wanting to talk with them.

She started with Matt. "We took a vote at school on Friday, and ninety-two percent of us decided we wanted the Braves to win. How does that make you feel, and do you believe it will happen?"

"I certainly hope so. Please thank your classmates for their support. We've had a great season, we've been the best team in baseball, and we have the home crowd. If I can talk this other guy into going to the movies tonight, I would like our chances," said the pitcher.

"How do you feel about the game, Miles?"

"I enjoyed Game 6, but I know it will be tough tonight. The Braves are outstanding. Matt here is outstanding, and he's a very good person. I want to thank the eight percent who picked us. We will do our best. But it has been an honor to face them."

The young reporter then asked which team they pulled for in college football.

"Roll Tide. The University of Alabama," said Trucks quickly.

Miles responded. "I have three. My parents took me to Auburn games all my life. I love the Ohio State Buckeyes, and although we are struggling, my school is the Stanford Cardinal."

Jennings said to Miles, "War Eagle!"

She asked both, "What kept you going, even when you were at your lowest?"

Miles responded first. "Certainly, my faith in the Lord played the most prominent role. I kept telling my parents, my girlfriend, and anyone who would listen that I didn't believe that I was done with baseball, even last year when I was out of baseball. I was willing to accept God's plan, even if that meant never putting on the uniform again. However, I believed He wanted me to have a platform so I could speak on behalf of Evangelical Christians, and the platform that baseball provided would enable me a chance to lead others to Christ."

Matt followed that thorough explanation with a sincere response. "I think it has to be acknowledged that what Miles has done has been good for all those who believe in Christ. I was blessed with an easier path, but I also know how fortunate I am. Many of my teammates have dealt with serious injuries, and instead of talking about a low point of my career, I would like to single out a guy like my teammate Chris Sale, who has been a tremendous contributor to our cause this season, even though he has overcome years and years of injuries."

Jennings then asked both players who inspired them to be where they are today.

Matt answered first, "My parents had a great plan for me from the beginning. They knew that I had a gift, and that gift was being able to throw the ball very hard and very accurately.

Certainly, having a grandfather who was a big-league pitcher helped my path to the majors."

Miles then said, "First, before I talk about who has inspired me, I want to once again point out that the real hero of last night's game was Spencer Strider. What he was able to do, you just don't see done in baseball. And it's only appropriate that I acknowledge Matt for being here today because tonight is the biggest game of his life. He will be the one that Atlanta gives the ball to, and the fact that he is here on that same day speaks volumes about who he is and the character he always exhibits. As far as inspiration goes, it's impossible for me to identify one. Once again, I am just feeling blessed to enjoy this ride. I feel like I can stand up for Evangelical Christians and give them a voice when we are often criticized. I certainly am excited about my future in baseball, and I would like to add one thing. If I can make it on this level, there are so many others who are playing at a lower level who could be equally as successful."

Jennings then closed by saying, "Matt, thank you for your time. I hope you win tonight. What is your favorite Bible verse?"

Matt went with Philippians 4:13 for his answer.

"How about you, Miles?"

"That's a great question. Thank you for that question. Please keep your integrity. Those in the media could use some. For me, it's Luke Chapter 23. When the good thief, whom Catholics refer to as St. Dismas, hung next to Jesus on the cross and asked the Lord to remember him when He came into his kingdom. Then Jesus said to him, 'Today you will be with Me in Paradise.'"

Jennings was curious. "Why is that your favorite scripture, Miles?"

Miles explained, "If you ever go to a funeral, and the person was a believer in Christ, you will probably hear the pastor say that the person is in a better place. Or, maybe a friend or a family member says they are in a better place. Those are comforting words. But now, close your eyes and imagine Jesus telling you that you will be with Him in Paradise. How can it get better than that?" noted the Yankees centerfielder.

"Oh! I almost forgot. One final question. Do you guys have girlfriends?"

Matt responded, "Believe it or not, I'm single!"

Miles replied, "It's almost unbelievable because he can sing and play the guitar. I do have a girlfriend, Stephanie, from Augusta, Georgia. I am very fortunate she puts up with me because many in the media say I am an arrogant jerk."

Jennings thanked both and signed off with another "Go, Braves!"

Lopez and Litkenhous were waiting over to the side, as were the other three members of the Braves. Only Harbison departed. Miles shook hands with Lawrence Hamberlin, saluted goodbye to Perkerson, Brewer, and Trucks, and the Yankees were on the way.

Hamberlin then asked the other three Braves, "Am I the only one here who believes Miles will be playing for us next year?"

Brewer agreed, "It sure has that feel."

Miles had two more people he needed to see. He had invited Beatrice and Esther to the church service and subsequent interview. The two had noted in a text that they needed to attend services at their home church. Beatrice was singing in the choir, but they would come over to Central Baptist following the service and see Miles after his interview.

Miles introduced them to Stephanie and his New York teammates, Brad and Jorge. They all took pictures together.

"We heard you slept in your bed last night," said Esther.

"It was nice," confirmed Miles.

"Well, you are going to love this, but Esther has bought the house next to me," said Beatrice.

"I do love that. Now, the two of you can be there for each other."

Beatrice and Esther then thanked Stephanie for the way she treated Miles and for loving their favorite former co-worker.

"My Dad says she's a keeper," said Miles.

They all hugged goodbye, but Miles had arranged for one huge surprise. He reached into his pocket and pulled out tickets for the deciding game.

"I hope you will come. I know it's Halloween, and you may have a commitment, but if you can, please come. If not, give them to someone important to you who loves God, someone who will appreciate them."

"We will be there!" said Esther excitedly.

They all hugged again and said goodbye.

As Miles started walking to the car, an African American male who looked to be around fifty-five years old came up to him, holding a baseball. The man was shaking, but not just from the cold. He was taciturn, struggling to collect his composure, and Miles leaned in to understand better his attempt at speaking.

"My...my...my father is in hospice care. My father doesn't have but a couple of days left to live. He's a Braves fan but has kept up with your career, listening to Newnan games on AM radio, your minor league games, and watching you now. He's always believed in you. Will you sign this baseball for him? I don't believe you have a bigger fan," said the man, still shaking, obviously upset over his dad's condition.

Stephanie, standing beside Miles, grabbed his left arm, placing her arm quickly and powerfully around his. It was an attempt to convey to Miles, *yes you will, and ask him the name for the ball.*

Miles instead looked at the man, "Where is your dad now?" The son replied as tears rolled down his face, "He is in the hospice facility about five miles from here."

Miles knew some moments were bigger than baseball. "Excuse me for three minutes. But don't go anywhere," he told the son.

The Yankees centerfielder stepped back, turned around, and phoned Braves reliever John Perkerson, who was just at the worship service at Central Baptist Church.

Perkerson, the most laid-back individual to ever walk on the surface of the earth, answered immediately.

"Hey, John. You have to be close."

Perkerson interrupted him, "If you are stranded and need a ride to the stadium, I'm not going to be a good Samaritan and help the Yankees win this series."

Miles answered back, "I need you to be a good Samaritan but in a different way. A man is here in the church parking lot. His father loves the Braves but is dying. Can you meet me in the hospice parking lot in seven or eight minutes?"

"I'm only two minutes from there now," responded the Braves reliever.

Miles went back and told the man, whose name was Isaac, "I can do better than just sign this ball. Let's go say hello to your father. I've also invited John Perkerson to join us."

Stephanie told Miles how special this was. "This is far more important than winning a ballgame, even one of tonight's magnitude."

Perkerson was waiting for them in the hospice facility parking lot. Stephanie introduced Isaac to the Braves pitcher. They all walked into the hospice center together.

Isaac then led them down the left hallway and went into his dad's room. He briefly spoke to his father, Isaac Sr., then motioned for Miles to come in.

The elder Isaac tried unsuccessfully to sit up and say hello. Miles walked to his bed, "No, please don't get up. Just relax. I understand you are known as Mr. Isaac. I'm Miles. It's a pleasure to meet you."

The father squeezed the ball player's hand. Miles then welcomed Perkerson in to join them. Perkerson greeted Isaac Sr.

Isaac Jr. then told Miles that up until two weeks ago, his father was constantly on the internet, checking his stats and defending Miles regarding the New York press.

"He's very proud that you are from Newnan. He feels like you represent all of us. My dad pulls extremely hard for you. He wants the Braves to win, but he hopes you get five hits."

Then, the father put a thumbs up to agree. Miles had signed the baseball and handed it to Perkerson to do the same.

"Mr. Isaac, John here is one heck of a pitcher. He's also a great friend. I was hoping to be his teammate last year."

The dying man then gained enough strength to say, "I wish he was your teammate now."

"As do I," said Perkerson.

Each player got on a side of the patient's bed, and Isaac Jr. took photographs with his phone. Perkerson then signed his Braves cap for the son.

Miles asked Mr. Isaac if he could say a prayer. Mr. Isaac nodded and smiled. Miles then gently grabbed the hand of Isaac Sr. and went to the Lord in prayer. "Lord, thank you for the life of your son, Isaac. He has fought the good fight here, and we know you will be welcoming him into heaven soon. I thank you for the life he has lived here and for the example he has made for his family. We know you have a plan for him, and we know we will see him again. Thank you, Lord, for all you do for us and the promise of eternal life. Amen."

Mr. Isaac squeezed Miles' hand as Isaac Jr. gave a smile of both gratitude and sadness. As Miles walked out of the room with the others, he silently prayed that God would give this sweet family comfort and peace.

Due to the unexpected visit with Mr. Isaac, Miles and Stephanie raced to the car and sped up I-85 North toward Atlanta and the team hotel. Even though Miles knew that he was cutting his arrival time close, he was reminded that some special moments were more important than baseball. Luckily, Miles made it to the hotel for the team meeting with one minute to spare.

Randolph noted, "Nice of you to decide to join us."

Miles, still feeling great about his Game 6 accomplishments, jokingly asked Randolph, "Hey, Coach, do you need me to take a day off?" Randolph and the rest of the team broke out in laughter. The Yankees were less than six hours from Game 7 of the 2024 World Series. It was a Halloween to remember.

CHAPTER FORTY-SIX

"Autumn embraces change, even as she is falling to pieces."

Angie Weiland-Crosby

All the Yankees were allowed to go back to their rooms for three hours. Randolph urged them to meditate, relax, and even sleep. Miles chose the latter. Stephanie met Phil downstairs, and the two decided to have a glass of wine before they departed for the stadium. Tom Eddy delivered another winner.

The news reported that over 40,000 fans had lined the streets of Atlanta to cheer on the Braves caravan. The Yankees, with a police escort, were scheduled to leave the hotel at 5:35 p.m.

New York media reported that over 300 babies born in the last fourteen hours in New York had been named Miles, and another twenty, mostly girls, had been named Fuller. Similar reports from Atlanta markets had located at least thirty newborns named Miles. Evangelical Christians were watching and speaking out. They were paying attention. They were doing their part to forfend evil. The good guys were fighting back, and the Lord was using Miles as a vehicle to allow their voices to be heard.

With Fox televising the NFL, the final game of a scheduled doubleheader was to begin shortly after 4:00 p.m. The baseball game was moved back to start at 8:20 p.m. So much for that good-feeling story about kids not having to stay up late to see the end of the game.

When the Yankees got to their clubhouse, they were cheered by some but jeered by many others. Miles went to his locker and immediately noticed the ball that he had signed for Emily Wells but had failed to deliver. It read, "Thanks for giving back at the hospital. You are the real hero!"

Miles pulled out his phone and went right back to his place against the wall, listening to those same songs: "The Waiting" by Tom Petty, "Your Love" by the Outfield, "Centerfield" by John Fogerty, and "Anti-Hero" by Taylor Swift. He played each of them twice.

Then, it was time for Randolph to speak to the team. He urged his guys to just have fun. "Play smart. Play for each other. Don't force anything. Believe in yourselves. Take advantage of this opportunity," said the manager.

Miles then walked over to sit on a bench with Game 7 starter Brad Litkenhous. On his way over to him, he passed Yankees young star Jasson Dominguez, who had worked so hard to return from a torn UCL suffered on September 10, 2023. "This is why you are here tonight. I believe in you," he told Dominguez.

As Litkenhous and Miles went over the Braves scouting report again, shortstop Anthony Volpe reviewed it with them. The Yankees were still in t-shirts and warmup gear, some in sweatpants.

It had to be an image appreciated in heaven. Litkenhous and

Fuller had just sat beside each other hours before in Newnan at Central Baptist. They were now discussing strategy and would soon be praying together.

Litkenhous told Miles, "My goal is not to allow Hernando (Fernandez) to beat us. That would be the biggest nightmare of them all."

"I can't see him hurting you," replied Miles.

"Why is that?"

"He's evil, he's dishonest. He is the epitome of a picaresque hero. They may love him here, but deep down, they know the truth," said the centerfielder.

Litkenhous responded, "That may be, but he comes up to the plate with a certain amount of panache, and the crowd eats it up. That confidence and the way he rocks his bat back and forth gets on my nerves."

Miles put him at ease. "Just remember how much better looking you are than him. How much smarter you are. Hernando believes the harder you shake the bottle of water, the better it tastes."

"Yeah, that's right. He's not hurting me or beating us tonight."

Harbison was the most relaxed Yankee. He knew he was done for the series. Clarke Schmit was, as well. And Randolph had said emphatically that Cole was unavailable. No one in the media had pieced together that it took the Yankees three starting pitchers to secure the Game 6 win. The bullpen was loaded, and all hands were available and on deck.

Miles went out to the outfield, specifically to the warning track. While sporting a Christian McCaffrey Stanford football jersey, he did a few sprints and warmed up with Dominguez. After the final toss with the fully recovered Dominguez, Miles reached into his glove, grabbed a signed ball for Emily Wells, and replicated his earlier leap into the stands, placing the ball in her lap. He landed safely on his feet and jogged back to the Yankees dugout, eventually returning to the clubhouse.

The network television broadcast returned from a commercial and zoomed in on Miles walking back to the dugout from the warning track. The television host asked her viewers, "What will we see from Miles Fuller tonight? His ninth-inning home run one night ago is why we are here. I spoke with Atlanta All-Star outfielder Lawrence Hamberlin earlier tonight, and he shared with me a story from last weekend here in Atlanta. His daughter Claudia had told her father, the veteran Atlanta power hitter, that she really wanted to meet Fuller. As it turned out, the three ended up in a hallway outside a training room, and Lawrence asked Miles if the three could take a selfie together. Lawrence then said his daughter was like, 'No, Dad. You just *take* the picture.' I asked the Atlanta outfielder about Miles' reaction. He answered, 'I can say this. I could not respect him more. I will always respect him. He treated my daughter like a contemporary, like a colleague, instead of a kid. It was thoughtful, appreciative, and impressive.'"

The TV host wrapped up the segment, suggesting, "This is a huge night for Hamberlin. He's also a free agent at the end of the season, and considering his age, likely facing retirement. You know he would love to end his career with a ring. What a way to go out, on top."

Just before Newnan's own Alan Jackson sang the National Anthem, Annie Wells sent a text to Phil Fuller, followed by fifty pictures of Miles in the outfield. Annie had brought an envelope and a sheet of paper to write Miles a note. In the text to Phil, she asked him to quickly meet her. He did.

"Hey, thanks," as she hugged him. "Please give this to Miles tonight if the Yankees lose."

"If they lose?" Phil asked.

"Correct. If they lose," confirmed Annie.

Phil then asked, "And if they win?"

Annie strongly stated, "Throw it away. Please throw it away."

CHAPTER FORTY-SEVEN

"By prevailing over all obstacles and distractions, one may unfailingly arrive at his chosen goal or destination."

Christopher Columbus

Miles started listening to music on his phone, grabbing a seat on the floor against the wall. There was about seven feet from the wall to his locker. He backed into that area, almost as if to hide.

He was now one of the most famous people in the world. In the USA alone, a national T.V. audience had watched in prime time his one swing of the bat in the final frame, lifting his team and the Yankees Universe from elimination to the brink of its twenty-eighth World Series Championship.

Evangelical Christians in the United States loved him. Not only for his taking a knee in centerfield, praying to his Lord and

Savior but also for his postgame comments immediately following the Game 6 victory. It was the talk throughout the day in Sunday school classes across America. "Did you see that baseball player from New York after he hit that home run in the ninth inning?" one member would say to another thousands of times on Sunday at churches.

How many times did a pastor from the pulpit speak of it during worship service? How many times had it been mentioned of his selfless act, repeatedly praising Strider for his excellence during the contest? The world could use more of that, individuals who were gracious and respectful of others.

For a few minutes, he looked back at his life. Miles even thought back to his relationship with Brooke. It was over, done with, long before her untimely death, but he would have done anything to have intervened and prevented it. While he was struggling in the minors, her life was out of control. Brooke Yarbrough put her trust in the wrong people, sacrificing her morals and values to be in the "in crowd," to be a part of the popular crowd, the upper echelon of her sorority.

It was ironic that the final night of her life was spent with Grace because she was an individual who had no grace despite her name. Grace made plenty of bad decisions, often lying to her parents about others to make herself look better. It happens all the time. Individuals make mistakes, know they are on the wrong side of issues, yet recruit others to help them ameliorate the embarrassment of their actions.

Grace and Brooke had things in common. They didn't find each other by accident. But instead of accepting responsibility for their bad behavior and for the lies they told concerning others, they remained obdurate. Both became hardened, resistant to softening influences who wanted to get them back on the right track. Good people, just like Ellie, had attempted to bring them back. But both Brooke and Grace were immutable to her sincere efforts, and the two friends lost their lives together.

As Jason Harbison crossed in front of Miles, he snapped his fingers, bringing Miles back to reality. Miles was frustrated with himself for thinking about Brooke on this pivotal night. As tragic as those memories were, he needed to regain his focus on the task at hand.

CHAPTER FORTY-EIGHT

"Reflect upon your present blessings – of which every man has many – not on your past misfortunes, of which all men have some."

Charles Dickens

October 7, 1952

Ebbets Field in Brooklyn was the setting for the seventh and final game of the 1952 World Series. Mickey Mantle, a twenty-year-old youth, stood at the plate facing Joe Black of the Brooklyn Dodgers. The Commerce, Oklahoma, native drilled a 3-1 fastball from Black that cleared an advertised sign for "Fine Schaefer Beer" on the right field wall. It was Mantle's second home run in as many days, and the first two of his record eighteen career World Series home runs.

Mantle played his entire career (1951-1968) for the Yankees, winning seven World Series and hitting 536 home runs.

Inducted into the Hall of Fame in 1974, the legendary Yankee died of liver cancer at the age of sixty-three in Dallas, Texas, in 1995.

His two home runs in Games 6 and 7 of that 1952 World Series did not escape Miles Fuller. Now, seventy-two years later, this Yankees outfielder was a Game 7 homerun away from joining Mantle in that distinguished club, a homer in each of the last two games of his first World Series. Fuller was no Mantle, although he had already hit two dingers in the Fall Classic. Two of his three career homers were in a World Series, which was astonishing for a World Series freshman.

As Fox welcomed a record-setting viewership, analyst John Smoltz summed things up the best when he said, "I don't know what else these two teams can give us. In one corner, you have the Braves, the 2021 champions, the best team in baseball. A more than 5-1 favorite to win this series before Game 1. In the other corner, the most storied team in sports, the twenty-seven-time World Champions, were struggling until the last two months of the season, but they came into this battle tonight with confidence and swagger, mostly generated by a player you couldn't even get a baseball card of two months ago. But Miles Fuller has delivered on the biggest stage, and the great Gerrit Cole, unavailable tonight, was clutch with two wins and a save. Adding to the intensity is that Fuller is from just down the road in Newnan and attended church today in his hometown. It has been reported that he was joined by New York teammates and members of the Braves."

The other announcer then said, "Let's not forget that Fuller, about to leadoff this Halloween contest, is a free agent come tomorrow, and teams around the league are aware of what we've seen this postseason."

Smoltz responded, "That's a great point. Contending teams will be seeking his services. Some great players struggle with the pressure that comes with the postseason. Others thrive. Fuller has certainly thrived on the biggest stage, and contending teams will invest in those who can perform on this stage."

The other announcer said, "You should know about delivering in the postseason. My esteemed partner was 15-4 in the postseason, arguably the best postseason pitcher. We hope you have your popcorn. It's time for the best two words in sports. Game Seven."

With aches and pains all over his body, it was Miles Fuller who approached the plate in his No.14 jersey, now the top-selling jersey in the MLB. With all due respect to Roosevelt, it was Miles Fuller who was now The Man in The Arena.

Miles was pleased not to feel foggy despite not getting much sleep the night before. He thought for sure he would feel sluggish, nervous, or cumbersome. However, he had never performed in such a dramatic setting; all those who play the game dream of being on this stage. For Miles, it wasn't nerves. He felt he was in a familiar situation, yet one he was experiencing for the first time.

"The last time Miles was at the plate, the ball still has yet to land," said Smoltz.

Braves starter Matt Trucks' first delivery was fast, 98 mph, high and inside, basically brushing back the Game 6 homerun hitter. So much for that good sportsmanship feeling of worshiping at church together, then appearing together for an exclusive interview for an aspiring journalist.

Two pitches later, Trucks was ahead, 1-2. Miles was looking for his best fastball, and the Braves starter froze him with a solid sinking changeup. The hottest hitter in the series was down on strikes. The crowd roared. The Yankees went down in order.

Litkenhous knew when he took the mound that he was on a short leash—pitching on less rest than normal, with little room for error, considering the lack of offense from the punchless Yankees.

The Yankee starter was ahead 0-2 to Matt Olson but hung his

curve, and Olson landed it in the right center seats. It was 1-0 Atlanta. *Winner takes all.*

New York catcher Austin Wells tied things in the top of the second with a clutch two-out double and RBI. Tied at 1-1. *Winner takes all.*

Litkenhous retired the next seven Braves he faced, with Fernandez applying the only scare, a deep threat caught by Dominguez on the warning track.

Fuller, 0-2 on the night, led off the top of the fifth with a double down the left field line. New York was unable to get a sacrifice down, and following a walk, Trucks extricated himself out of trouble, inducing a ground ball double play.

Runs were at a premium through five, but the Yankees chased Trucks in the sixth after a leadoff walk. The grandson of the famous former major leaguer would not be getting a victory on this night. At best, it would be a no-decision.

The Braves went to closer David Hodo. Although he had thrown just a few pitches the night before, Hodo was good to go for twenty-five or thirty pitches. Hodo saved several pitches as the Yankees obliged with another 6-4-3 double play. Another zero went up on the board. After five and a half innings, the game remained tied at 1-1. *Winner takes all.*

Randolph made the painful decision to pull Litkenhous after five innings of work. Jonathan Loáisiga stranded two in the sixth. It was still tied at 1-1 after six complete. *Winner takes all.*

Fuller gave the Yankees hope with a one-out single in the seventh, right up the middle, off Hodo. Braves manager Chip Walker had a decision. Stay with Hodo, or go to another member of his talented staff. He chose to go to Bryan Lundquist, a starter and the local product from Lassiter High School.

Lundquist had dreamed all his life of pitching for Atlanta in a Game 7. He wasn't about to fail. With Grand Theft Awesome on first and a threat to steal, Lundquist worked quickly to the plate, all four-seam high-velocity fastballs. Miles took off on the

1-1 pitch, just sliding ahead of a perfect throw from Fernandez. Or so it was initially called. The Braves challenged the call, and it was overturned. Fernandez had thrown Grand Theft Awesome out. Still tied at 1-1. Stretch time. *Winner takes all.*

Loáisiga got the first out in the seventh, but Michael Harris singled to right to end his night. Randolph pulled Loáisiga, bringing in Jose Alvarez, the lefty from Mexico. Alvarez faced Jerred Kelencic and was greeted by a single to right field, with Harris, the potential game-winning run, going to third.

Randolph went to the mound, but not for a change. Alvarez had not yet faced three hitters. This was a strategy visit on where to play the defense, as Atlanta was just ninety feet from the lead.

Orlando Arcia was next and took two fastballs, one called for a strike, although both appeared high. With Alvarez dangerously not changing Arcia's eye level, his next 93 mph delivery was in the same spot, and the hitter got all of it. Arcia drove it high and deep to center. Grand Theft Awesome went back as far as he could go, begging the spirit of George Selkirk to be with him, as he went from the warning track, leaping at the wall, glove extended, and brought back a ball that was definitely a three-run homer.

"That's unbelievable! He's done it again. Grand Theft Awesome just climbed the wall, and he needed all six feet six inches of him," said Yankees broadcaster and former Braves announcer John Sterling.

Fuller's effort was amazing, his play inspiring enough to mirror a fairytale book or movie. And although this catch was another you had to see to believe, it only saved two runs, as Harris tagged and walked in from third, putting Atlanta up 2-1.

There were mixed reactions from the home crowd. Some were relieved that the Braves had the lead. Others were upset that Arcia had been robbed and thought that the scoreboard should read 4-1. Others couldn't believe what they had just seen again from the Yankees centerfielder. Alvarez stranded Kelencic, but the Braves were ahead 2-1 after seven complete. Atlanta was six outs from its second World Series title in three years. Braves 2, Yankees 1. *Winner takes all.*

Walker stayed with Lundquist until he lost Wells with a one-out walk. Next up was John Perkerson, and although he yielded a single, he stranded two New York runners. Braves 2, Yankees 1. *Winner takes all.*

Alvarez was in the soup in the bottom of the eighth, having surrendered a single and a walk. Two were on, and none were out. Loáisiga was already burned, so it would be either closer Clay Holmes or veteran Scott Brand. Both had been great in clutch situations all season.

Randolph gave the ball to Holmes. Following a successful Braves sacrifice, an intentional walk loaded the bases for Atlanta, with only one out, but set up a potential force at all bases.

Holmes faced David Brewer, a defensive sub in the top of the eighth, far more known for his glove. Holmes got Brewer to chase a slider that Brewer didn't do much with, Holmes meeting it at the mound, throwing home to Wells, who in turn threw to first to get Brewer out. The Yankees were still in it. Braves 2, Yankees 1. Atlanta was only three outs away. *Winner takes all!*

Perkerson was removed for Reynaldo Lopez. Anthony Volpe reached on a swinging bunt to third with one out. Orlando Cabrera flew out to center on the second pitch to him. Volpe went back to tag, but the fly ball to center was nowhere deep enough to risk getting thrown out at second.

That did it for Lopez. He had pulled Atlanta to within one out of the crown. Kevin Downes, a quality veteran bat off the Yankees bench, was called on to pinch-hit. Downes had one responsibility: Get on base and extend the game to Miles Fuller on deck. How cruel would it be if the hottest hitter on the planet was left on deck as the 2024 World Series ended?

Downes didn't disappoint, lining a single to left field off the fresh arm of Ryan Foster, Volpe stopping at second. The Yankees had plenty of speed on the bases. Anything in a gap would swing the game around and give the good guys the lead, needing only three outs for their twenty-eighth championship.

Fuller versus Foster. Game on the line. Series on the line. Title on the line. All fans on their feet.

Foster's best pitch was his slider, but he also possessed a very good changeup. He was a dependable veteran, but every Atlanta fan was questioning why Walker burned Hodo so early in the contest.

Stephanie could not bear to watch and was perhaps the only person sitting in her seat. Greg and Celeste were both offering their only child encouragement, knowing he couldn't actually hear them. His Uncle Phil was gazing up at the heavens, seeking divine help, wanting God's intervention.

There stood the man at the plate with no future playing contract, no baseball card for any kid to collect, and the weight of all those who love the pinstripes, the "Yankees Universe," on his shoulders. Great Yankees, such as Mariano Rivera, Bernie Williams, Andy Pettitte, Derek Jeter, and broadcasters David Cone and Paul O'Neill, were all cheering him on and counting on him one more time. The four hundred and fifty thousand dollar winning share for each player from the World Series would more than double what Fuller made in his two months in the league.

The Braves were playing deep, with no doubles, as Foster missed way outside with a 92-mph fastball. Fuller then looked a little in from that spot and decided to guess the next pitch would be a slider just off the plate.

Foster obliged and hit that exact spot. Miles was all over it. He smartly used the Braves' defensive alignment against them, executing the looping single with flawless technical precision and his unique bravura in front of Atlanta right fielder

Lawrence Hamberlin. The Braves' right fielder, new to the team in 2024, probably made the best decision of the entire series by playing the ball off the bounce. While he had no chance to get the speedy Volpe at home, had he dived and missed, and the ball had gotten behind him or away from him, the fleet-footed Downes also would have scored, pushing the Yankees ahead.

Downes was forced to stop at third. All those fans crazy about the pinstripes knew what was coming next. Fuller would be put in motion to either give the Yankees two runners in scoring position, or New York would try to steal a run by sending Miles, then Downes from third. Miles, Grand Theft Awesome Fuller went on the first pitch, with Fernandez not even attempting to throw and Yankees hitter Jorge Lopez never thinking of swinging.

Walker came to the mound for a strategic visit. Jorge Lopez would be followed by LeMahieu, a two-time batting champ on deck. Atlanta needed to get Lopez out. The Yankees had two blazers on the bases. A Lopez single would provide two runs and a somewhat comfortable 4-2 advantage.

Foster pitched Lopez backward, or, in other words, instead of utilizing a first-pitch fastball to get ahead, he threw a beautiful back-door breaking ball for strike one. Miles, standing on second, said to himself, "I'm glad he didn't start me with that."

If hitting is guessing, then Lopez was left to guess, and Foster tossed an inside curve that jammed the Yankee hitter, popping out to Brewer. Yankees – 2, Braves – 2. Going to the bottom of the ninth. *Winner takes all!*

A television broadcaster said what nearly every baseball fan in America was thinking, "It would be a shame if we don't play extra innings. A series like this, one of the best in history, almost deserves an extra innings finish."

Another broadcaster countered, "I can tell you that Braves fans don't want that. I don't know if the hearts of those who love these teams can stand it."

Austin Riley took Holmes' first delivery of the bottom of the ninth off the wall in left. The Yankees were in immediate trouble. Riley was sacrificed to third. The title-winning run was only ninety feet away at third. Randolph decided to intentionally walk the next two hitters, setting up a force at every base.

Lawrence Hamberlin was up, with Hernando Fernandez on deck. Ducks were all over the pond. So many ways to win. The Yankees brought in their outfield. Fuller came in so far that he was less than twenty feet back of the second base bag. Holmes was almost forty pitches in, so Randolph gave the ball to Scott Brand. It took Hamberlin only one pitch to take his shot at being forever loved in Atlanta, and he shot a line drive over second base but right to Miles. Had Miles been playing anywhere else, the ball would have safely been down, and the series would be over. It was something one didn't usually see in baseball. The velocity was so hard as Miles reached out to his left to snag it; the ball nearly took his glove with it. Bobby Richardson, the Yankee great, had to be smiling at that catch.

The Yankees, in a giant mess, were now one out from giving America "free baseball" on this night, a night that had provided plenty of tricks and treats.

Fernandez came to the plate, and Brand threw his first changeup of the evening low. Down 1-0, Brand then missed with a fastball low. There was nowhere to put Fernandez. The Braves were only two balls from another title. Brand threw a 96-mph fastball. It was down. Fernandez saw it but drove it foul. Brand was perilously working down, down, down but not changing Fernandez's eye level. Brand then threw a change down that caught the lower part of the zone but was called a ball. The Yankees bench went ballistic, booing vociferously. Could this incredible series end with a walk-off base on balls?

Brand asked for time, stepped off the mound, and attempted to collect himself. Miles prayed for a strike. The entire planet, including Fernandez, knew what was coming next. Fernandez was up 3-1 on the count, everything down.

Brand now was forced to change the eye level, so he went high with a four-seam 95 mph fastball. Fernandez saw it and hammered it to deep center, the wind providing extra lift. Miles, tracking it, said to himself, "Here we go again, George. I'm going to need some help."

The ball continued to carry, the six-foot-six-inch Yankee outfielder now back to the wall. Fox Television narrated it this way, "Fuller goes back, back, back. We've seen this blockbuster movie before. He's at the wall, he leaps, and extends the glove. It's gone, it's gone! Not this time for Grand Theft Awesome. Hernando Fernandez has hit a grand slam, and Atlanta has won the series in walk-off fashion! It's all treats for Atlanta on this night, probably all night, all year!"

As every New York fan put their heads down, Fuller was replicating the gesture in Atlanta. He leaped over the wall and extended his glove as far as he could but never touched it, the ball escaping by at least two feet. Sometimes, the good guys don't win. As Fuller came down from the wall, he resembled a firefighter coming down a pole. He slid down the wall, sitting on the ground, his head as low as it had ever been; his team defeated 6-2.

Those inside the stadium were delirious. Beer and water landed all around Miles, showering down from the outfield seats. Fernandez was being drowned in water, Gatorade, and anything else any Atlanta player could find.

This thrilling series had taken one more improbable turn. Stephanie sat in tears. Greg and his brother Phil, too stunned to move, watching a nightmare play out in front of them. Celeste, her eyes locked on her son, as Volpe came from the infield and was assisted by Dominguez to help the dejected warrior to his feet. It was an unmerciful ending for Miles, his teammates, and all of those who love the most successful franchise in the history of sports. Although there was no bloodshed, the loss was so heavy that it had a sanguinary feel to it.

If this was his final dance with the Yankees, it was not the beautiful last waltz Miles had envisioned. But he protected the legacy of the pinstripes to the last dying seconds. The pride and the passion for all those who love the pinstripes. He was a hero in defeat, the best player of the entire postseason.

As he got close to the Yankees' dugout, he half-waved with his glove to his parents, who were both crushed for their only child.

Fernandez was now the one being interviewed.

"Hernando, did you know it was gone when you hit it?"

"It certainly felt like it, but with all that guy has done in center this entire series, I wasn't about to start celebrating until I saw his reaction."

There was a follow-up question. "You guys are the team of the 2020s. This win cements that. Can you describe that?"

Fernandez explained, "We've got the best fans in the world. We thrive off them. This is a dynasty, and we aren't done. We are very hungry. The Yankees' franchise is the measuring stick of greatness, and one day, we want to be in the company of the 20s Yankees, 50s Yankees, 60s Yankees, and even the 90s Yankees."

"I think you are well on your way. Congratulations!"

Randolph first wanted to speak with his team. "This season, this run, what a privilege it has been for me to be with you guys. You left it all out on the field. All you can do is your best, and you gave yourselves, your families, your friends, and all who pull for us the best. This sport can be cruel. Some days, all you can do is tip your hat to the opponent. We've got nothing to be ashamed of. They made one more play than us. I love each one of you," said the first-year Yankees manager.

Uncle Phil handed Annie's envelope to a clubhouse attendant, who left it inside his locker. Miles was now with the media, certainly a reversal of fortunes from just the night before.

"Miles, how close were you to that final ball?" he was first asked.

"Honestly, not very close. It kept carrying. I thank you for the question, and while I want to congratulate the Braves, many of whom I got to know in the spring of 2023 with my failed tryout, I want to apologize to our fans for not winning. I love the passion of the Yankees Universe. Your support is immense and mountainous."

A reporter asked, "A great deal has been mentioned about you being a free agent come tomorrow. Would you like a return to the Yankees?"

"I would love that. Representing the Yankees has been the highest honor of my life, and my wish is that others who have been stuck in the minors or even out of baseball, like me, get the opportunity to perform in the big leagues. That being said, I am human, and I would be lying to you if I said I would not be seeking a Brobdingnagian payout. I will be thirty next season, and this is probably the only time I will get an opportunity for a large contract," explained the outfielder.

The media weren't finished with Miles. "Miles, are you aware that you have just been named the MVP of the series? And do you have any regrets about anything that happened during the series?"

"I did not know about being named MVP. I regret the times that my team needed me and I didn't deliver. I regret that kids all over New York have to go to school these next few days severely disappointed. I regret that we let down our fans. Perhaps we would have won tonight if I didn't get caught stealing second base. I regret that the completion of this series didn't offer the satisfying denouement we and our fans were hoping for."

Another reporter continued to push, "Do you regret any remark you said to any member of the media?"

"I think you expect me to say yes. As an organization, we don't discuss politics. Some of you have twisted my words and made it look like I violated that policy. I would just say I am tolerant of other opinions, and I believe you in the media should be, too."

"Since you live so close to here, will you be returning to New York in the morning with the Yankees?"

Miles replied, "No. I'm staying at our team hotel tonight and probably for a couple of more days. I want to see some local friends."

The host jumped in, "Any more questions for Miles?"

A member of *USA Today* asked, "If you could choose the team that meets your demands, the team to play for next year, who would that be?"

"I'm putting that in God's hands. I will say this. Right now, I feel the same way I did after my last game at Stanford. I did not want to take the jersey off because I knew I was never going to put it back on. I don't want to take this jersey off because I am terrified of not representing the organization and standards this uniform represents. Thank you, and as I have said, congratulations to Atlanta. They deserve to be called a dynasty," he said.

October 31, 2024, was the final day of fifteen days in the fall when the Yankees took the field. They had beaten the Twins in the divisional series in four games, 3-1. The Yankees had swept the Blue Jays, the team they chased most of the summer, in four games in the ALCS. And they had fallen short in seven games, contested on seven unforgettable days in the fall, in the World Series.

Stephanie was waiting for Miles in the team family room. His parents had already started to make their way back to Newnan. The streets of Atlanta were chaotic and dangerous, although the majority were celebrating with good intentions. Widespread Panic was playing a special Halloween concert at State Farm Arena in Atlanta, only amplifying the mayhem.

Blake Zhu had messaged Miles that he had made lunch reservations for them and Stephanie the following morning at 11:00 a.m. at the team hotel, then reserved a meeting room to discuss a plan moving forward as he would be running point, representing the interest of his company and that of his former Stanford roommate. Millions of dollars would soon be on the table, and he was confident his friend would have multiple options.

Miles then decided he would turn off his phone for a few days. He needed time to recover from such a draining experience but was thankful for the thoughtfulness of those who cared about him.

The team told the players that there were fifteen minutes before the buses rolled out to the hotel. He asked Stephanie to call his Uncle Phil, see if he was okay, and see if he could join them tomorrow at lunch and later in the meeting. A more trusted consigliere Miles did not have.

Miles then went back to his locker alone. In the distance, he could hear the home team and their friends and families still celebrating.

Miles sat down on a chair in front of his locker and started sobbing. It had been a whirlwind six weeks of summer and fifteen days of fall. Miles then thought of all the people who had impacted his life over his twenty-nine years of existence, and the tears continued to fall like a waterfall down a mountainside.

Yankees general manager Jason Giambi, in a suit and tie, stood at the entrance of the room next to his manager, Willie

Randolph. Jorge Lopez came over to Miles at his locker to comfort the fallen combatant.

Giambi said to Randolph, "Aaron Judge will be back next season, but there's a place for Fuller in pinstripes. When I see a player like that, emotional like that, it shows me how much the game, the series, the season meant to him. I don't know the future, but we will do what we can to sign him."

Randolph responded, "If we had three of him, we would have swept the series."

As Stephanie continued to wait in the family area of the clubhouse, Miles packed up his locker, noticing for the first time a small white envelope in his locker. He opened it, not knowing where it came from.

It read:

Miles,

I am so sorry you lost this game. You deserved to win. But better things are ahead. And although you placed the signed baseball to the wrong one of us tonight, you are the big winner. Tonight, you met your future wife for the first time, and you will only get to say that once. I know you love Les Mis. I believe I will become your favorite all-time Cosette. A Christian can't interfere with God's plans. Thank your Uncle Phil for the ball (you can sign mine in person) and for his assistance with this. Here's my number, and if you lose it, as a backup, your uncle has it. We will talk soon. There is indeed a "Castle on a Cloud."

- Annie

Miles sat back down and read it again. He had a girlfriend who loved him. He should have thrown it away. Instead, he put it in his pocket.

He walked out and saw Stephanie trying to smile despite all the heartbreak. She grabbed his hand, unaware of the camera crew waiting to take photos on the other side of the door. "Let's do this together," said Stephanie.

"What, walk out to the bus?" he asked.

"No, let's walk through this world hand in hand together," she suggested and added, "And it doesn't matter where you play next year; I will join you."

He said nothing as he smiled, checking with his left hand that the note from Annie was secure in his pocket.

Nothing on this earth is guaranteed. There is no promise of tomorrow. But for six weeks this summer and fifteen days in the fall, Miles Fuller was The One. His performance on the baseball field during those periods will be talked about here on earth for centuries.

And along his journey, and more importantly, he even made news in heaven.

"Give thanks to the Lord, call upon His name; make known His deeds among the peoples."

1 Chronicles 16:8

A MESSAGE FROM THE AUTHOR

Miles Fuller is a Christ-driven individual. Miles is not perfect. Like you and I, he is flawed. While he is borderline brilliant, he makes mistakes in this novel, such as speaking about politics at graduation and his close-minded reaction to a reporter he disliked, who, at the time, shared sincere feedback.

What I hope you find most appealing about Miles is his desire to lead others to God's kingdom. His goal in life is to lead others to Christ because, from the time he accepted Jesus as his Savior, he understood that was the command left by Christ.

That is why I wanted to write this book. Once I am gone from this earth, if one individual comes across this publication and takes an interest in Christ, then I will consider this a victory.

If I can offer any advice, I would suggest that you surround yourself with Christian friends. How a non-believer overcomes adversity without the encouragement of a Christian support staff is beyond me.

My warning is to be cautious with those who you select. The

wolf is always at the door. People have an agenda, and they will deceive you in many ways. I have not always been able to detect a liar or manipulator and have been used by evildoers. In the Bible, Sodom, for example, was full of pure evil. That unfortunate behavior still exists here on our earth.

My biggest challenge as a Christian is forgiving those who have sinned against me. However, Jesus, in Matthew 5 from his Sermon on the Mount, instructed us to love our enemies.

Jesus and Stephen shared similar statements as they faced death. They pleaded for God to forgive those who were killing them. Surely, if Jesus and Stephen could do that, I can forgive those who have sinned against me. Surely you can, as well.

There is no one in the Bible whom Miles respected more than Stephen, the first Christian martyr. There are almost twenty mentions of Jesus sitting at the right hand of God in the New Testament. Acts 7:55 states that Stephen saw Jesus standing, not sitting.

Bible scholars continue to dispute exactly what Jesus' standing meant. Miles believes that Jesus stood to welcome Stephen into heaven. Close your eyes for a few seconds and imagine Christ standing for you as you enter heaven. Now, imagine living a life worthy enough to have Christ stand for you as you enter heaven.

My thanks to my wife, Tara Jones, and Wendy McMillan for the encouragement and editing suggestions they provided. Their dedicated and diligent efforts will never be forgotten.

I would also like to thank Tension Books for their belief in this project. I encourage the reader to support other authors and novels from this publisher.

I also want to give a nod to the staff of 7 Brew Coffee in Auburn, Alabama. Headlined by the management duo of Hayden and Michaela, the staff provided inspiring words and contagious laughter, along with the finest coffee, as I completed this book. In doing so, they left an impression on me, erasing the acerbic outlook I had for the next generation and replacing it with hope for the future for those here on this earth.

"No prophecy was ever made by an act of human will, but men moved by the Holy Spirit spoken from God." – 2 Peter 1:21

ACKNOWLEDGMENTS

I would like to acknowledge the encouragement that my mother, Carolyn Jones, and my sister, Karen Griffin, provided from the moment I told them I would attempt this project.

The greatest gift my parents gave Karen and me was our reward of being raised in a Christian conservative home, all but ensuring our eternal lives.

I would also like to acknowledge the "Joy" Sunday School Class of Parkway Baptist Church in Auburn. My thanks to Dub, Mark, Buddy, Hal, Dee Dee, Paige, Jeff, Ken, Robin, and Tara for their interest in this novel.

I have had the privilege of leading a Bible study from my house for 18 years. To Rick, Brad, David, Michael, Joe, and Neil, thank you for worshipping with me and for the accountability you all bring to our meetings.

In my attempt to work on this project, I was delayed twice with painful corneal ulcers in my right eye. My gratitude to the staff of Basden Eye Care in Auburn, Alabama. Most significantly I want to recognize Dr. Brett A. Basden, O.D., and Dr. Daniel J. Eagan, O.D. They quickly diagnosed the threat and treated these ulcers that could have developed into blinding corneal infections. Without them, the story of Miles Fuller goes untold.

In conclusion, be mindful when casting your vote in a local, state, or national election. If you are a Christian, I plead with you to vote your Biblical convictions. It's time to restore the rights of Christians.

I am proud to be a follower of Jesus Christ. Won't you join me? Let's pray he comes back quickly!

ABOUT THE AUTHOR

A.J. Jones is an award-winning newspaper journalist and has been a successful television show host for fourteen years.

His exceptional memory of sports-related events and facts combined with his remarkable ability as a storyteller makes for an enjoyable experience for the reader. A super fan of baseball, and the New York Yankees in particular, Jones provides a textured account of a fictional MLB season.

When he isn't writing, A.J. enjoys listening to 80s music and watching hockey, basketball, football, baseball, horse racing, and all Olympic sports. He and his wife Tara live in Auburn, Alabama, and revel in seeing classic and Oscar-nominated movies.

ENJOY THE FIRST CHAPTER OF THE FOLLOW UP NOVEL TO SIX WEEKS THIS SUMMER: FALL AND RECOVER BY A.J. JONES. COMING FALL 2024.

"Love God; love others; do your best in all you do, even if you fall short!"

Bethany Hamilton

On the morning following the final game loss of the World Series, Miles canceled an early lunch meeting with Blake Zhu and Phil Fuller. The six-foot-six-inch speedster suffered a sleepless night, the first of many that would follow.

Instead, he and Stephanie chose to escape to Destin, Florida, for several days. Who could blame him for wanting to be elsewhere? Coverage of the series was on every channel. Celebrations in Atlanta were ongoing with a huge parade scheduled in two days on Wednesday.

Miles still intended to keep his cell phone off. He didn't need to look at the internet or open a newspaper. He already knew what was in there, and it was nothing he wanted to relive. There was nothing he wanted to read, nothing he wanted to see.

He phoned only his parents and returned one call to Cooper

Allen, the upperclassman Miles unseated when he was a sophomore at Newnan High School. Cooper had requested that Miles meet him next time he was in Newnan. That next time would be later this morning. He asked Stephanie to stop at the first Newnan exit off Interstate 85, where Cooper awaited him with baseballs to sign. Cooper's six-year-old nephew was with him and anxious to meet the World Series Most Valuable Player.

Miles, one night earlier, had become only the second player in history from a losing team to be named World Series MVP. He was preceded by the now eighty-nine-year-old Bobby Richardson, the great New York Yankee who won the award in 1960.

Miles, who could have been labeled a bibliophile in high school and certainly at Stanford, had packed only one book for his trip to the beach. Amazingly, it was Richardson's memoir, titled *Impact Player*, co-written with David Thomas. Richardson, a native of Sumter, South Carolina, was also a devoted Christian. The signed book had been sent to Miles in 2023 by family friends Hilda and Jerry Harrelson, who also lived in Sumter.

The odds of a losing player being named MVP of the World Series were astronomical. The chances that same individual would grab the book of the only other losing player to be named MVP on the morning of the seventh game were next to impossible. Yet, it happened. In between episodes of *The Andy Griffith Show*, the book served as a desired distraction for Miles. *Impact Player* could also describe Miles. Winning a World Series MVP wasn't the only two things these Yankees had in common.

Not much was said over the first fifteen minutes of the drive between Miles and Stephanie. Miles, with sunglasses on and no hat, wore a Stanford white pullover and blue jeans. For the road trip, Stephanie opted for comfort and wore an oversized sweatshirt with faux leather leggings.

Another ten minutes went by with little communication. The two were pleased to reach the outskirts of Atlanta, now away from the heart of the city.

Stephanie decided to attempt to get her boyfriend to laugh. "Good morning, sports fans. We are pumped today to have with us the player who now has more base hits in one postseason than any player in history. Welcome to the show, 2024 World Series MVP Miles Fuller."

Miles looked slowly over to his left with a look like – *Are we really doing this?*

Stephanie responded by dipping her head to her right shoulder as if to signal – *I'm waiting for your response.*

"Okay! Great to be with you today, Stephanie," he reluctantly complied.

"It's my understanding that you are headed to the beach with your significant other. It's understandable you need some rest and relaxation. What are you looking forward to the most?"

Miles answered, "Eating at Louisiana Lagniappe!"

Stephanie came back with, "Sounds interesting, probably Cajun. And do you know what lagniappe means, Miles?"

Miles looked at her in a strange way yet again, "Have you just met me? You are aware I'm a district, regional, and state vocabulary champion and two-time top five finalist of the Scripps National Spelling Bee!"

"That only tells me you know how to spell it, Miles."

"Can I get it in a sentence?" he said, still grudgingly

"No, you can't. That would give it away," she fired back.

"Okay. Lagniappe is something given as a bonus or gift. It is a word English speakers learned from French-speaking folks in Louisiana. It is spelled l-a-g-n-i-a-p-p-e. I don't hear a buzzer, so I must be correct."

"Hey, don't look at me. I just request the word. It's your job to spell it and define it, but I believe you passed this round," said Stephanie.

Miles returned, "Great, let's go to commercial."

Miles then put her BMW radio on SiriusXM Channel 8, more commonly known as 80s on 8. "Rock and Roll Girls" by John Fogerty was playing. His mind immediately went back to that night, his junior year at Stanford. He recalled to himself seeing the girl who turned out to be Whitney and her four friends on the dance floor.

He had not thought of or heard that song played since that night, although the same couldn't be said for Fogerty's No.1 smash, "Centerfield," which had become a recent daily staple for the baseball player.

As Miles and Stephanie pulled into the scheduled meeting place, the first convenience store off of I-85 in Newnan, Miles couldn't help but want to close his eyes and turn the clock back twenty-four hours, his previous visit to his hometown of Newnan. Not only did he grab the Richardson book yesterday morning, but more importantly, he attended worship service at Central Baptist Church with a combined seven other players from the two teams less than twelve hours before Atlanta's walk-off win.

Stephanie and Miles only had to wait a couple of minutes for Cooper to arrive. "I really appreciate this, Miles. I don't even know what to say to you, to be honest with you. You've been on the television for three weeks. We watched all the playoff games, and here you are. I can tell you this: it was unbelievable to see you perform on the biggest stage, and you made us all proud. I've been able to tell so many people that I played high school ball with you," said his former Newnan Cougar teammate.

Miles introduced Stephanie to Cooper. Then Cooper introduced his young nephew, Remi, to them. "It's my great pleasure," said the baseball player who was operating on no sleep. Miles even gave him a hug and a high five.

"They call me Remi, but it is short for my real name, Jeremiah. I am named after a man in the Bible."

"That is awesome. I have read about that great prophet," replied Miles.

"I wouldn't allow him to wear his Atlanta hat. I told him it was too soon, too soon," noted Cooper.

"I appreciate that. I'm afraid I'm going to have to accept seeing them and move on from it."

"How close were you to catching the final ball?" asked a curious Remi.

"I was in the neighborhood, but I got a piece of the wall on the way up, so as I turned to guide my glove to the place I was guessing it would be, since it was still carrying, it was higher than my glove. I tried, but I'm afraid I will think about it every day. Probably every hour for the rest of my life."

Miles was fresh off the most significant loss of his athletic career, absolutely exhausted, yet still saw the big picture. He knew he needed to give back. Miles also knew that all who played the game, on any level, would have loved to have been him for six weeks of unforgettable summer baseball and another magical fifteen days of competition played in the fall.

Below his signature, on each baseball, he inscribed 1 Corinthians 15:57-58.

Miles and Stephanie said goodbye to Cooper and Remi. As they returned to the car, she asked him, "Why did you choose those verses?"

"Because our labor on this earth is not in vain. I want to encourage others to be immovable in their faith. God will reward us with eternity. You and I are secure. We have two potential outcomes. Either He's coming, or we are going."

Made in the USA
Columbia, SC
05 March 2025